Now or Never

A Mapleton Novel

Diana Deehan

Titles By Diana Deehan

Mapleton Series

Make or Break (FREE copy at www.dianadeehan.com)
Fight or Flight
Now or Never
All or Nothing
Love or Leave

This book is dedicated to my long-suffering husband, Will, who reads all my first drafts even though he hates romcoms.

Maybe one day I'll write something you actually want to read, with dragons and wizards and orcs and gruesome battle scenes that leave people crying in the fetal position begging for the mercy of death.

Probly not, tho.

Sorry, love you! Sorry, sorry, love you!

ONE

Exactly one month after moving into the enormous manor she'd inherited in the quiet town of Mapleton, Chelsea Davenport had an epiphany; she was just like the old man from the movie *Up*.

It wasn't easy to accept at first, but the more she thought about it, the more obvious it became. The only difference between the two of them was that instead of refusing to leave a house behind, she was refusing to let go of her childhood dream, even though it was doing nothing but dragging her down.

That dream? Writing and directing her own feature film with her best friend, Jae.

A dream she'd worked toward her whole life.

A dream that would *never* come to fruition.

She had been indulging in that fantasy all the way up until her first tax bill arrived on the twelve-bedroom, sprawling, broken-down Monroe Manor, and she realized she could no longer afford to make ends meet, let alone take on the risk of making a movie.

Still, she believed it was worth the extra expense to live there instead of the crappy apartment she'd had for the last few years. Her number one priority was giving her son, Ben, a stable home and a nice school in a safe community, but she couldn't have it all. Something had to give. And that something was her fledgling career as an indie filmmaker.

It was time to call it quits and move on before the whole thing started dragging them down.

She glanced in the rear-view mirror at Ben and smiled before turning her old car down the gravel driveway of her new home. It was totally worth giving up her dream for Ben. She needed safety, stability, and most of all, a decent and steady paycheque. It was a small price to pay to keep him safe. If she had to, she'd give up everything for Ben, and she'd do it with a smile on her face.

She braked to a crunching stop, then killed the engine. Ben didn't waste a second after the car stopped before bounding out of the back passenger door, and Chelsea was once again incredibly thankful they were now living on a huge piece of private property where she didn't have to worry about her little guy running into traffic or bumping into a drug dealer.

She stepped out of the car and made her way to the trunk where Ben stood bouncing on his toes.

"Mama, open it up!"

"Okay, okay," she said before sliding her key into the rusted keyhole of her twenty-year-old car. She wiggled it just so until the trunk popped open, then grabbed the new-to-Ben two-wheel bicycle they'd picked up at a garage sale that morning. It was dark blue, nearly as rusty as her car, and the plastic seat was ripped, but it was the best she could do, considering they'd gone back-to-school shopping earlier that day and her bank account was bleeding.

Badly.

Ben didn't seem to mind that his bike was ancient, though. As soon as she set the bike on the driveway, he grabbed the handles, pushing the bike side to side and making whooshing noises as if flying down the side of a mountain.

"I'm gonna go so fast!"

Chelsea put on a smile, but inwardly she cringed. He was a sweet, smart boy. But also incredibly clumsy. When he wasn't tripping over his own feet and walking into table legs, he was falling down stairs. Most of the time, he'd just shake it off. But whenever he really hurt himself, his soft, round face would scrunch up in pain, and giant drops of tears would tumble down his chubby little cheeks.

It was the worst.

"Promise you won't bike without your helmet?"

Ben jerked his head up and down. "Promise."

"Good, your helmet is upstairs in your room. You'll have to stop biking when Aunt Jae gets here so we can help her unpack."

Ben tilted his head up, eyes focusing on a fluffy white cloud in the distant blue sky. "Are Aunt Jae and Aunt Natalie sisters?"

Chelsea smiled at his furrowed brow and tousled his hair. Ever since Aunt Natalie had come on the scene, Ben had had a lot more questions about familial relations. Unfortunately, some of those questions led to further questions that she'd rather not have to answer.

"No, you just call her Aunt Jae because she's our best friend."

Ben's eyes brightened. "I want to see her now."

"Me, too, buddy," she said. "Let's grab our stuff and get your helmet."

She took a deep breath and blew it out through her teeth as she grabbed the shopping bags from the car and walked up the stairs into the house with Ben. She'd been thrilled when Jae suggested moving in to the manor. They'd had a blast living together in film school, and Chelsea could certainly use the help to pay the bills. Plus, Jae had very little family, and she loved Ben as if he were her own son.

And the love was certainly mutual.

But there were things that had changed, and Chelsea was putting off talking to Jae about them for as long as possible.

She had just pushed open the door when the sound of tires crunching along gravel pulled her attention to a small U-Haul truck coming up the driveway.

"Aunt Jae!" Ben called.

"Wait on the porch until she stops!" Chelsea said, dropping their bags just inside the door.

The truck came to a stop, and Jae hopped out, gracefully landing on her white sneakers. Her long, shiny, nearly black hair was fluttering in the breeze, just as soft and beautiful as the features of her face. She threw her arms open wide. "Benny! Chels!"

Chelsea and Ben both took off running toward Jae as if it had been a century since they'd seen her last. Not three days.

When they pulled apart, Jae took a step back and let out a low whistle. "This house, Chelsea. Oh my god! How do you *own* this?"

Chelsea followed her line of sight, looking at the multiple balconies, the fancy tiled roof that desperately needed work, and the rickety windows. "The better question is 'How do you afford it?'" Chelsea said, hoping this would segue to the gigantic issue hanging over her head.

Jae rubbed her upper arm and gave her a sympathetic look. "I'm guessing you haven't had luck getting us more roommates?"

"Unfortunately, no. I listed it everywhere, too."

"And the location scout sites?"

"Crickets."

Jae lifted a carefree shoulder and quirked the corner of her mouth in a move that Chelsea had seen hundreds, if not thousands, of times before. She also knew the words that would immediately follow.

"We'll figure it out . . ."

Chelsea smiled and added the usual, ". . . eventually."

A flood of memories followed: their first time directing a short film for class when everything that could go wrong did go wrong; the time they came home from class and found out that Jae's father, who'd been so proud of his daughter, had died suddenly and she needed to go back to South Korea for the funeral. Or the time they were sitting on the side of the tub, hand in hand, surrounded by the smell of vomit as two pink lines began to form.

They always moved forward, together. And they always had their shared goals that acted as a light at the end of whatever dark tunnel they were walking through.

But Chelsea was sick to death of walking through dark tunnels. She needed stability, and that meant letting go and allowing her balloon house to fall off the edge of a cliff so she could save the weird bird, a.k.a. Ben.

"Jae, there's something—"

"Here," Jae said, not hearing her whisper. She passed Chelsea a brown box from the U-Haul truck. "There aren't many. And I've got some light ones that Ben can take." She looked up and scanned the driveway. "Where did he go, anyway?"

Chelsea sighed. "Probably ran up to his room to get his helmet. I bought him a bike."

Jae's perfect dark eyebrows rose from their usually low position over her striking dark eyes. "Bike? As in, two wheels?"

Chelsea nodded.

"Training wheels?"

"Nope."

"Oh God," she said, shoulders slumping and eyes quickly scanning the dozen boxes in the truck. "Let's unpack the booze first. If I have to watch your kid fall and cry, I'm gonna need a drink."

Chelsea smiled slightly, but it dropped. "I have a feeling you're going to be needing a lot of drinks tonight."

Jae gave a funny look but shook it off. "Your sister's coming tonight, right? Natalie?"

Chelsea nodded. "Yeah. She's excited to meet you finally."

Jae stopped, narrowed her eyes. "What's up with you? Why are you sighing so much? Is it Natalie?"

"No," Chelsea said quickly, then sank her teeth into her lower lip and glanced up at her best friend.

"Do you not want me moving in anymore?" Jae asked after a beat of silence. "Because I already got used to the idea of seeing you and Ben every day. And I'm not gonna lie, knowing I'll be toiling away at my soul-sucking job in a *mansion* is the only thing keeping me employed. That and knowing we can work on our film each night."

Chelsea kept chewing her lip, wondering how to say what she'd been wanting to say ever since she got her first property tax bill.

"I guess it will take some adjusting," Jae continued. "Living in a little town. I'll have to get a car eventually and—"

"I can't make our film."

It was as if someone had yelled "Cut!" All the action screeched to a halt as Jae's mouth formed what looked like ten different words before a syllable came out.

"You can't—"

"Got it!" Ben shouted from the porch, stuffing his helmet onto his head and attempting to buckle it up. "Wanna see me ride?"

Jae blinked a few times before forcing her mouth closed and slapping a fake smile on her face. She stabbed Chelsea with a glare before covering it and turning to the porch. "Sure, Benny. Let's see."

Chelsea deflated as Jae gently fastened the strap under Ben's chin. She knew this wasn't over. Jae had simply tabled it for later when Ben would be asleep and wouldn't be able to hear them fight.

They both knew that Chelsea pulling the plug on the screenplay they'd written together wouldn't go over without a knock-down, drag-out fight. They'd rewritten that script countless times, cried over it, dreamed about filming one day. It had consumed the last few years of their lives.

But Chelsea knew she couldn't go on like that. She needed to be practical. And nothing—not even Jae—could change her mind.

She'd set her sights on the light at the end of the tunnel, and she was moving toward it, come hell or high water.

· · · · ● · ● · · · ·

Chelsea tiptoed through Ben's dark room to the rhythmic sound of his deep breathing. He had always been a good sleeper, but now that they were in a new home, and there was a huge distance between his room and the living area, he needed the assurance of his mom sitting in the rocking chair while he slipped off to dreamland.

Chelsea didn't mind sitting with him. In fact, it was her favourite time of the day. Almost meditative. She went into the adjacent room, grabbed two pairs of black yoga pants and the sewing kit off her bed, then went down the stairs.

Halfway to the kitchen, the heavenly smell of chocolate brownies filled the air. She closed her eyes and inhaled. They smelled so good.

She rounded the corner into the kitchen and dropped her pants and sewing kit onto the oak kitchen table, just as Jae was pulling a pan of brownies from the oven.

"You moving in here is the best thing that's happened to me since having Ben."

Jae placed the glass dish on a trivet on the counter, then ripped off her oven mitts and slapped them down in the drawer. She slowly turned, taking her time before making eye contact with a glare. "Don't be so sure."

Chelsea winced. "Jae—"

"Look, I know things are tight—"

"Things *were* tight. Now they're strangling."

A knock on the door sounded through the room, and Chelsea turned on her heel toward it. "Sorry," she said, already walking away from the fight. "That's Natalie."

She knew it would only buy her a few minutes, but she'd take any lifeline offered at this point. She and Jae had dreamed of making their film together for nearly six years. Walking away from it killed her, but it wasn't enough to have a dream and a banger script. The timing had to be right, too.

Chelsea swung the door open to find Natalie standing on the porch, a bottle of red in one hand and white in the other.

"I brought wine!" she said with a dazzling smile.

Chelsea smiled back. "Then, please, come on in."

Natalie pulled her into a brief hug as she walked in and toed off her sneakers. "Love what you've done with the place," she said.

Chelsea laughed. She had done little, other than move in her sparse IKEA furniture and hang her vintage movie poster collection on the walls. Ben's toys, coats, and shoes had taken over everything else.

"It looks better," Natalie said. "Like a home."

They exchanged a smile, then walked to the kitchen.

"Oh my god, what smells so good?" Natalie asked, turning the corner.

"That would be Jae," Chelsea said, gesturing to her bestie, who hadn't yet dropped the scowl. "She's an incredible baker. Jae, this is Natalie."

Jae curled the corner of her mouth up a fraction at Natalie, but it disappeared almost immediately.

Chelsea sighed.

Natalie took in the tension. "Uh, everything okay?"

"No."

Chelsea rolled her eyes at Jae's flat response.

"Well, I brought wine," Natalie said, placing the bottles down and walking to the cupboard as Chelsea locked in with Jae in a stare. "I opened the bottles before I left Ethan's so the wine would have time to breathe." She popped the corks out, then looked up. "Red or white?"

Chelsea broke eye contact and sank into the worn old kitchen chair. "Red, please," she said on a sigh.

"Okay," Natalie asked, pouring the wine and narrowing her eyes at Jae. "Do I have to throw this girl out of your house?"

Chelsea laughed as Jae crossed her arms. "I live here. I pay rent. No one's throwing me anywhere."

"Someone talk," Natalie said, pouring two more glasses and bringing them to the table.

Chelsea took a gulp of wine and a deep breath, then opened up the sewing basket and picked up her yoga pants. "I've been thinking lately that I need to change course with my career."

Jae snorted as she brought the brownies to the table and sat down across from Chelsea. "You mean, give up."

Chelsea unravelled the black thread and slid it through the hole of the needle. "Fine. I've been thinking of giving up. I'm broke as fuck, and my property taxes are more than my rent was. Also, Ben is starting school next week, so now is a good time to focus more on a new career."

Natalie nodded, looking convinced. She took a sip and turned to Jae. "That sounds reasonable. What's your problem?"

"My problem . . ." Jae started, glare returning, "is that Chelsea and I wrote an absolute masterpiece screenplay, and we were going to shoot it when Ben started school. I know, and she knows, that it's good enough to launch our careers. It's been our plan from the first week we met at film school. And now she's giving up."

"I'm giving up because I can't keep living like this," Chelsea said, voice breaking as she held up the fabric in her hands. "I'm sewing back together the seams of Walmart-brand yoga pants that I bought second-hand three years ago because I can't afford anything." The emotion bubbled in her throat. "I'm sick of just scraping by. I need a steady paycheque. Not the writing jobs I've been stuck in since school. I need to get on set and work my way up so I can pay my bills."

Jae slumped into her seat and took a drink. "Next thing you know, you'll be telling me you want to sell it."

Chelsea squeezed her eyes shut. "Actually, I do think we should sell it."

Jae shook her head and stabbed into the brownies. She cut them into generous squares and passed them out. She took two slow bites, glaring at Chelsea before speaking again.

"You'd really let some no-talent hack make *our* movie?"

Chelsea blew out a breath. "We can write another one someday."

Jae's shoulders slumped. "Fine. As much as I hate it, I won't stop you from selling, and I can't make it on my own. Just, please tell me this isn't because of Ja—"

"Don't even say it," Chelsea said, cutting off her friend as her sister sat up in her seat.

"Ja-don't-even-say-it?" Natalie asked, her eyes flitting between Chelsea and Jae. "Is that Ben's dad?"

Chelsea closed her eyes, hoping if she couldn't see, she wouldn't hear, either. But she could feel their stares piercing her eyelids.

"Yes," Jae said. "His career is going well. He landed a big directing job—"

"Okay, enough." Chelsea shovelled some brownie into her mouth and stood up. "I told you I don't want to know anything about that turd," she said around a mouthful of deliciousness.

"So, you never see him?" Natalie asked.

Chelsea shook her head. "Only twice a year. He sees Ben on his birthday and Christmas."

"So, he *does* have a relationship with Ben?"

Jae snorted. "If you can call it that. He doesn't even give her any support."

Chelsea hummed in agreement. She didn't get a cheque until Ben was three, but she understood why. He'd been just as young as she was, and just as broke. But she'd thought they would do it together, and he'd had other plans.

Over the years, he'd sent her some bits of money, here and there, but never enough to pay an actual bill. After a while, Chelsea had given up and gone for it alone. She was a pretty decent writer and editor. If she worked all day and night, she could get by.

She swallowed, walked to the counter, refilled her glass, and took a drink. She could feel Natalie's eyes tracking her.

"So he left you to raise your son alone and went off to pursue his career?" Natalie asked.

Chelsea shot a sarcastic smile and stuffed the rest of the brownie in her face.

"What an asshole. God, I hate assholes."

"Well, that's not *exactly*—"

"Jae . . ." Chelsea warned. "Don't start."

"Tell me," Natalie said, leaning forward.

"When did this become a full-on tea spilling?" Chelsea wondered out loud, but she was ignored.

Jae leaned toward Natalie. "A few months after he left, he came back. Told Chelsea how wrong and stupid he was. Begged for another chance."

Chelsea rolled her eyes. "He wasn't sorry at all. He just felt guilty, the selfish ass."

Jae leaned closer to Natalie. "He's a *hot* selfish ass," she said in a stage whisper, making Natalie's eyebrows rise. "Tall, dark . . . fuckable," Jae added. "I couldn't believe she shot him down."

Natalie scrunched up her nose. "Selfish asses aren't hot, no matter how fuckable."

Jae nodded, but then shrugged. "I'm not convinced he's that much of an ass, to be honest. He acted like an asshole, but he was completely head over testicles in love with Chelsea."

Natalie cocked an eyebrow. "You think she should have taken him back?"

"You guys know I can hear you, right?" Chelsea asked.

Once again, they ignored her.

Jae shrugged. "Not necessarily. But she shouldn't let it control everything she does, years after the fact. Did you know she won't have sex? Like, ever? She's too scared of getting pregnant."

"Ugh, Jae . . ."

Natalie twirled on Chelsea. "What?!"

"Okay, sleeping kid upstairs. No screaming."

"You never . . . like, *ever*?" Natalie's eyes went so wide you could land a plane on her cornea. "He wasn't your last, was he?"

Chelsea sighed. No point in lying now. "Last. First. Only . . ."

Natalie's jaw slowly unhinged until it was nearly on the floor.

Chelsea wanted to crawl into a hole. And she hadn't even admitted the most embarrassing part: that she'd never even been on an actual date before. She shook it off. "Can we please talk about something else now? Anything else?"

They all reached for their wineglasses, took drinks until Natalie finally broke the silence.

"I guess I never had to worry about you and Adam, then, eh?"

A thrill shot through Chelsea's veins at the mention of the man who had asked her out at the baseball tournament. She could still feel his eyes on hers, the energy that radiated off him, the intensity of his cocky smile.

Then she remembered he'd run off after seeing Ben and told herself he was a dick, just like that other dick.

"Adam?" Jae asked, sitting up in her seat. "Who's Adam?"

"Adam is my boyfriend's best friend," Natalie said. "He's ridiculous, and way too good looking, and a total player. When I first met him, he was going out with his old high school English teacher. Ethan said he's only had one girlfriend his whole life." She turned contemplative for a beat. "Although . . ."

Chelsea swallowed another gulp of wine, trying not to make it obvious that her butt was moving closer to the edge of her seat.

"Although . . . what?" Jae asked, her butt also on edge.

Natalie took a breath, blew it out. "I don't want to sound like a gossip, but I know he was interested in you, and I want you to know what he's like."

Interested.

The thought of Adam being interested in her made her want to take her panties off. "Okaayy . . ."

"He had a vasectomy."

Chelsea nearly choked.

"Two years ago."

"What?" Jae scream-asked. "How old is he?"

"Thirty-one."

"Wow," Jae said, leaning back. "He must really not want kids."

Chelsea slumped back in her seat and mentally pulled her panties back up. No wonder he ran away in shock and horror when her sweet little boy came over and called her Mama. At least now she knew, and she could use that information to stop the fantasies about him that would roll through her mind every once in a while.

She shook off the thought. Those fantasies always made her feel like a terrible mother, because in them, she was childless when he asked her out, and she said yes, and they went on a date together, then back to his place where she pretty much let him do whatever he wanted to her.

He looked like a guy who knew what he wanted to do and how to do it.

"You okay?" Natalie asked.

She looked up and realized she had gone silent, lost in her thoughts for the last few minutes. "Yeah," she said, standing, vowing to never think about Adam again and hoping she could actually make that happen. Now that she was living in Mapleton, running into him was an inevitability. She'd just keep her distance.

"Time for the white?" she asked, walking to the counter and reaching for the untouched bottle of wine just as her phone pinged with a new email.

She opened her mail app and recognized the sender immediately.

"Everything okay, Chels?" Jae asked.

Chelsea opened the email, scanned the text, and broke into a smile. "It's a location scout. They want to come here on Tuesday to check out the property." She flipped to her calendar and looked at her day. It was Ben's first day of school. Other than that, she just had her normal, thankless, mindless freelance work to do all day, which was perfect. It gave her a couple days to cut the grass and pull the weeds before they came.

She sent off a reply saying "Absolutely!" and brought the bottle of white wine to the table.

"That's perfect, Chels," Jae said. "Hopefully, they'll like it."

"Man," Natalie said, filling her glass. "In Spain, there was a hotel that was the highlight of our tour, where they filmed a Ryan Gosling movie. Wouldn't it be cool if this was the place people wanted to stay at, where So-and-So filmed *What's It Called*?"

Chelsea and Jae exchanged a knowing smile. They knew what it was really like to have an entire production crew take over a little town for months at a time. It all seemed very glamorous and exciting at first. Hopefully, she wouldn't piss off the entire town she'd just moved to.

But even that was wishful thinking. She knew how the industry worked. There were so many things that factored into a decision like this. Space for trailers, whether the Director of Photography liked the lighting, catering, the logistics of housing the crew, and on and on.

She didn't want to get her hopes up.

"That would be great, but just in case it doesn't happen, I'm gonna get to work on these pants. How's work going, Nat?"

As Natalie filled them in on her new tour job, Chelsea reached for the pants and started threading the needle through the torn fabric. Hopefully, her luck was turning, and this would be the last time she'd have to repair the damn things. Maybe they'd love her property, cut her a big cheque, and she could buy a new pair of second-hand Walmart leggings.

Sigh.

Two

Adam parked his rusty white construction truck across from Brin's Café and hopped out onto the street. Main Street in Mapleton was as busy as always that afternoon. A steady stream of vehicles flowed north toward the beach, no doubt packed with coolers, beach toys, and excited children. Adam smiled and stood at the side of his truck, waiting for an opening.

He knew it wouldn't take long before a local would come by and part the sea for him. Sure enough, a purple Jeep with the roof and doors off came down the street, under the posted limit, with country music blaring and a black BMW convertible impatiently swerving behind it. Adam smiled wide and held out his hand in a wave as the Jeep slowed to a stop and his cousin's hand waved back.

"Oh, come on!" a faint voice shouted from the BMW.

Adam let out a laugh and jogged across the street. "Thanks, Mia!"

"No problem," she said, taking her time easing off the brakes.

"You gotta be fucking kidding me!" the BMW guy yelled.

Adam laughed and ducked into the café as Mia flipped the guy off. He headed for the pickup counter, where he knew Dani would have his order waiting for him, passing a table with two pretty brunettes who gave him a look he knew well. Any other time, he would have stopped and said hi, but he was in too much of a hurry, so he threw up his blinders and ignored their smiling eyes.

To his surprise, his new business partner, Max, was standing at the counter, blocking his way.

Adam checked the time on the wall quickly. His day was absolutely packed. He'd spent the early morning at the bank, finalizing Max's business loan for the pub they were purchasing, and the late morning going over the last details of Float Fest with the event coordinator he'd hired. He had three minutes to get to his dad's office for a meeting that had been sprung on him an hour ago.

But he had to get coffee first.

And the coffee was being blocked by the big, broody Max.

He decided it would be fastest to face his friend head-on, so he slapped Max on the back and put on an overbright voice.

"Maximilian. How are we feeling?"

Max spun toward Adam, his signature scowl in place, anxiety-induced rage bubbling just below the surface of his skin. "Shitty."

Adam rolled his eyes, leaned over the counter, and gave Dani a little wave. She rolled her eyes and got his tray. He didn't really have time to reassure Max for the thousandth time that day that they were making a good choice, but he wasn't one to let a friend implode alone, either.

"Look," he said, glancing to make sure no one was around to hear. "I know it's a lot of money—"

"It's way too fucking much money," Max growled, cutting him off, then scrubbing both hands over his face.

"It's just the right amount, Max."

"Yeah, that's easy for you to say."

Adam went quiet. "Don't be a dick. I offered to fund the—"

Max cut him off with a shake of his head, his scowl slipping. "Sorry. I just . . . If this doesn't work . . ."

"This *will* work. The pub is a gut-job. It's going to be a lot of work and investment, but it'll be the best place in town for a meal and a beer when we're done with it. We've already got a world-class chef on board, and that head brewer, Will Something-or-Other from Churchill, is coming for an interview in a few weeks. We'll get started on the demo after Float Fe—"

"After? No. We need to start now."

Adam shook his head and glanced over the counter at Dani, who was ignoring him. God, she hated him. He cleared his throat and gave her a smile, and she reluctantly came with the tray.

"It's only a couple weeks, Max. Then you'll be a business owner. Master of your own destiny. All your dreams are coming true!" he said, grabbing the tray.

"Feels more like a nightmare."

Adam laughed and patted Max on the back. "I gotta go. I'll see you at the arena, eight o'clock," he called halfway out of the café. "The new guy you told me about is coming for an interview. Don't forget about Float Fest!"

He jogged out the door, saw an opening in the traffic, and dashed through to his truck. Less than one minute later, he walked into the Vale Construction offices to the sound of the chime on the door.

"I'm not late!" he yelled, before someone could accuse him of it, but the room was empty. "Jill?"

The missing receptionist, who'd been working there for longer than he'd been alive, popped out of the break room, wiping her mouth with a napkin.

"Hi, Adam."

"Oh, sorry. Didn't realize it was lunch. Don't stop for me."

Jill shook her silver-streaked head and pushed her green glasses up her nose. "I was just finishing up, dear. Have you eaten? There's pizza in the break room."

"I'll grab some in a minute. Is Dad here?"

Jill glanced at the clock on the monitor in front of her. "Looks like he's late," she said with a smirk.

Adam broke into a grin. "Oh, this is good," he said, putting the coffee tray down and pulling one out. His dad was constantly harassing him for being late.

Jill smiled and took the cup with her name on it. "You're a sweetheart, Adam. Don't give Lawrence a hard time for being late. He's going through some stuff."

The blood drained from Adam's face as he conjured the only memory he had of his father being late. It was twenty years ago after Adam's hockey practice. When his dad pulled up to the front steps of the arena, Adam opened the door, and his father's green eyes were bloodshot from the tears he was fighting back. "Get in, we need to talk" tumbled from his downturned mouth.

A warm hand gently rested on his, pulling him back from the memory of that horrible day when he found out about his mother's diagnosis. He looked up to find Jill, face full of sorrow, looking at him.

"Nothing's wrong, Adam. I promise."

Adam nodded, shaking it off. He'd opened his mouth to ask what kind of stuff his father was going through, when a noise sounded outside and, suddenly, the room went dark.

"What the—"

He turned toward the front door and saw a massive vehicle parked directly in front of the entrance blocking the sunlight. He strode through the door, too shocked to hear the chime, just as his father opened the door to an absolutely huge RV.

"Adam!"

He stared at his father. "Is this an RV?"

"Nothing gets past you, does it?" his father said with a laugh. "Wait . . . look at this."

His dad pressed a button, and a mechanical *whir* sounded as a set of three metal stairs emerged from under the RV and extended toward Adam.

"Come on up!"

"You bought an RV?" Adam asked as he climbed the stairs. His dad sat down in the driver's seat and touched a couple of buttons. He fell into the chair beside him, astonished, until his stepmom, Denise, came out from . . . somewhere.

The thing was fucking massive.

"I finally talked him into it!" she said, bouncing on her heels. She grabbed a pair of scissors and started opening boxes on the floor. Out came a toaster, a coffeemaker, even an iron. She opened the cupboards and started placing the items inside.

"What . . ." Adam stammered, looking for words. "Are you moving in here?"

His dad laughed.

"We're going on vacation, Adam," Denise said.

"I have literally *never* seen you two take a vacation."

"All the more reason to go!"

Adam shook his head, trying to make sense of his father actually taking a break from work. "When?"

Denise called from behind him, "Now!"

"Now?!" Adam slumped in his seat. "Where are you going?"

"Everywhere!" Denise called again, making his dad grin with unfettered glee.

The shock on Adam's face must have been evident, because his dad stopped and turned to him. "You're the one who kept badgering us about taking a break. It's all we've heard since Christmas. Life is meant to be lived, and all that. Can you believe this, Denise?"

Adam gave his dad a hard blink. He *had* been badgering them. He just never thought they'd actually listen.

"Where exactly is everywhere?"

His dad took the wheel and looked over the dashboard as if he were marvelling at a mountain range in the distance, not the weed shop on the corner next to the gas station.

"Straight across Canada. We're headed east first. We'll be gone about six weeks."

"Six . . ." Adam trailed off, wondering how much more his already filled slate could handle. "When I said you guys should go on vacation, I meant, like, a week in Mexico."

His dad grimaced. "You know I don't like hotels."

Adam rolled his eyes. He'd heard his father complain a million times about sleeping on a bed thousands of strangers had slept on. He should have seen this coming.

He was about to list all the shit he already had going on and tell his dad that the business loan for the pub came through, but the sound of Denise happily humming behind him and his father's grin stopped him.

They needed a break. They deserved it.

He took a deep breath. "Okay. What do you need from me?"

His dad turned with a smile. "I thought I had it all covered, but Roger suddenly blew out his knee. I need you to manage my crew while he recovers from surgery. At least four weeks."

Shit. Shit. Shit.

"What's the job?"

His dad's grin widened. "That's the good news. It's Ethan and Natalie's house."

Adam's brows pulled together. "That's not supposed to be until the spring."

"I bumped it up. The Ashtons decided to go all out on a huge addition to their property. Outdoor kitchen, stables, in-ground pool, the works. They're willing to wait until the spring, so I swapped their job for Ethan's."

Adam rolled through a list of all the shit he'd have to get done. It wasn't impossible, as long as he stopped sleeping. But Ethan and Natalie had been so happy going through the blueprints, he knew they'd be thrilled that their house would be built early.

He looked over at his dad, now standing with his stepmom in the kitchen, giggling over some contraption, happier than he'd seen him in a long time.

Okay.

He could do this.

"No problem," he said, injecting his usual arrogance. "I'll take care of everything here. You two have fun."

"Thanks, Adam. Just one other thing."

Good God, what now?

His dad walked to his bag on the bench seat in the eating area and pulled out a small stack of papers. "We need permission to use the driveway at Monroe Manor for the build, so I need you to get Chelsea Davenport to sign this, for the insurance."

Adam winced as he stared at her name on the paper.

"It shouldn't be a problem. She's Natalie's sister, right?"

"Yeah, it's not that, exactly . . ."

His dad's face fell. "Really, Adam? How? She's lived here, what? Ten days?"

Denise snickered.

"No, it's not . . . We didn't . . ." he said, looking out the window and remembering her aquamarine eyes, and her unbelievable lips, and her general curvy squishy-fuckable-ness.

Tier One.

Adam shook it all off. "Just give me the damn papers," he said, snatching them from his father's hands and starting toward the door.

"I haven't told Ethan, yet," his dad said. "Thought you might like to do it."

"I'm going to see him at the arena tonight. I'm sure he'll be happy. You leaving tomorrow?"

Denise came and threw her arms around his neck, squeezing until he leaned into the embrace. "Yes. We'll miss you, Adam. You know we don't like being away from you."

Adam rolled his eyes, though, if there were a gun to his head, he'd have to admit he liked their concern. Actually, it wouldn't require a gun. He freely told the truth because he couldn't tell a lie to save an orphan's life.

"I'll be fine. Ethan's house will be fine. You will be fine. Everything is fine. Just go have fun. I'll see you when you get back."

His dad pulled him into a hug, too. Then Adam walked out the door and to his truck, wondering what it would take to get Ethan to deliver the papers to Chelsea for him, and whether he was willing to be such a coward.

• • • • • ● • • • ·

Adam stepped onto the ice and skated over to where his teammates had gathered by the net. It was their first time on the ice that fall. Usually, they would transition to their rec-league hockey right after baseball ended in the summer. But after the Derek debacle, they needed another teammate, and it seemed Max had come through.

Max leaned against his hockey stick across from Jake, their goaltender, and Connor. With them was the new guy that Max had recommended to join their team. He stood a few inches shorter than Max, but then, so did the rest of them. Max had insisted that Adam *not* interview him, but after what Ethan had gone through with Derek, he felt compelled to protect his inner circle from dickheads.

"Hey," Adam said, joining his team and sizing up the new guy. "You must be Antonio."

The new guy nodded. "Yeah. You must be Adam?"

Adam took his hand firmly, nodded, and narrowed his eyes at Antonio. He didn't look like a dickhead. He looked like an Italian model with perfectly coiffed dark hair and pretty-boy eyes. "I hear you play well."

Antonio nodded and tugged his hand away, as if he were dealing with a psychopath. "I played triple A with Max during my senior year of high school. It's been a while since I've been on the ice, though."

Adam nodded. He didn't really care whether the guy could play. He just wanted to feel him out, make sure he was normal. "What do you do?"

"I'm a physician at Mapleton General and the clinic here in town. Hoping to start my practice soon."

Adam smiled. "I guess it can't hurt to have a doctor on the team."

Antonio lifted an eyebrow and glanced at Max, who rolled his eyes.

"Just one more question before you're in. Are you—"

"Wait," Antonio said, cutting him off with a disbelieving grin. "Is this an interview?"

Max let out a groan as Jake and Connor snickered.

"Yes. Unfortunately, it's necessary. Are you going to sleep with anyone's girlfriend?"

Antonio's dark brows shot up. "What?"

"Are you?" Adam pressed.

Antonio shook his head. "Of course I won't sleep with your girlfriend."

"Not his girlfriend," Max said. "He means everyone else's girlfriends. He's too ridiculous to find a girl that will date him, as you can see."

Adam rolled his eyes. "That's not true. I don't date on principle."

A confused look rolled over Antonio's features. "What principle is that?"

"Here we fucking go with the rankings," Max said, rolling his eyes.

Antonio exchanged a quick glance with Max. "You rank women?" he said with a laugh. "I bet they *love* that. I have three sisters who'd take your balls off hearing that."

"I don't do it to be a dick. It just helps . . . keep things organized. Besides, I'm sure none of your sisters would make the ranking, anyway."

Antonio's good-natured smile dropped like an anchor. "What does that mean?"

Adam gained some respect for Antonio at that moment. He was clearly protective of his family, a trait that Adam admired.

"No, you misunderstand—"

The loud crash of the door in the boards closing drew his attention. Adam turned to find Ethan skating toward the group. Perfect. He needed to tell Ethan the good news about his house. And he would rather not explain his ranking system to the new guy, who looked ready to throw his gloves off.

Mental note: never sleep with Antonio's sisters, no matter how pretty they are or how low they rank.

"Hey, sorry I'm late, guys," Ethan said.

Adam cocked a brow at his best friend. "No, you're not. Natalie just left on tour, didn't she? Which means you were *saying* goodbye—"

"Stop talking," Ethan said. "And yes," he added with a smirk, then took in Antonio. "Hey, I'm Ethan."

Antonio shook his hand, but his furrowed brow remained.

Adam rolled his eyes.

"What did I miss?" Ethan asked.

"Adam was just explaining that he ranks women," Antonio said.

"Oh man," Ethan said with a shake of his head. "I forgot about your tier system."

"You have tiers?" Antonio asked.

Adam exhaled. "Fine. It's like this. There are four tiers," he said, holding up four fingers. "The fourth, or lowest tier, is women who hate me and would never sleep with me."

"The fourth tier is heavily populated," Max said with a grin.

Adam rolled his eyes and continued, holding up three fingers. "The third tier is women who *don't* despise me and *would* sleep with me, but they could never be serious. These are your older divorcees and old schoolteachers," he said with a wink at Ethan, who laughed.

"The second tier is where things get tricky. These are women who *could* be something serious but have a definitive expiration date. Like women you meet on vacation or something. Even if you did like them, it wouldn't go anywhere."

"And the first tier?" Antonio asked.

"These are the women who are smart, and funny, and beautiful, and warm, and are definitely *not* temporary. Long-term types, you know," he said, looking into the distance and thinking how unfair it is that most women fell into that category.

Oh well.

Antonio narrowed his eyes. "So you don't want first-tier women?"

Adam shook his head. "God, no. I like to keep it to third tier. Every once in a while, I get brave and venture into the second tier. But I avoid first tier at all costs."

"Your ranking makes no sense," Antonio said with a shake of his head. "The whole point of tier ranking is to put *your* top picks in the first tier. So your first tier should actually be the women in your third tier. Second tier would remain. Your first tier would be third, fourth stays the same."

Adam shook his head. "No. My rankings, my choice."

"Huh," Ethan said with a squint. "Where did Chelsea fall in your ranks?"

Adam winced, remembering hitting on her and it all going south. God, he wished he hadn't been so stupid. There had been something about her that was just so . . . hard to resist.

"Who's Chelsea?" Antonio asked.

"My girlfriend's sister," Ethan explained. "Adam hit on her. But she's definitely a tier one."

"Speaking of Chelsea," Adam said, hoping to change the subject. "I have some news."

"Me too," Ethan said. "But first tell me why you hit on her."

Adam let out an exhale. "You told me she was selling Monroe Manor. I figured she'd be gone back to Toronto, which put her into category two," he said, remembering the thrill of asking her out and her saying no. He shrugged. "It was risky, and it backfired."

Antonio laughed. "Shot you down?"

Adam shuddered at the awkwardness of her son coming up and calling her Mama and alarms going off in his ears. Kids automatically shot a woman to tier one. He'd taken off like a light and sworn to never go after a two again.

"Yeah, something like that."

Ethan rolled his eyes. "I actually want to talk to you about Chelsea."

Adam's eyebrows rose. "You do? Why?"

Max turned to Antonio. "Come on," he said, "let's warm up."

"Tell him about Float Fest!" Adam called as they took off together in a lap around the ice.

Adam turned his attention back to Ethan as he took a deep breath.

"Natalie hung out with Chelsea and her friend, Jae, a couple of nights ago. She told me that Chelsea is trying to rent the property out to a film production."

The gears in Adam's head started cranking, wondering how filming and construction would work next to each other. He had gone to the property with Ethan and Natalie and the architects a few weeks ago when they completed the contracts to build their house in the spring, and there wasn't that much distance between where Chelsea's property ended and Natalie's began. Two hundred feet at most. "Okay . . . when?"

"I guess they are coming by on Tuesday to see the property."

Shit. He'd planned to stop by tomorrow to get her signature on the insurance papers.

"I was just worried about you, Adam," Ethan continued. "I don't know how many media would come along, if it's a big production."

Adam snapped back. He hadn't thought about that. But it had been so long since he'd received any kind of attention from the media that he never worried about it. One of the many great things about living in Mapleton.

"The thing is," Ethan continued. "Natalie said Chelsea seems to be struggling a little with the property. She's okay, but this would help a lot. I'm just . . . worried about you, I guess. But I also don't want her to miss a chance at getting ahead."

Adam nodded and slapped his friend on the shoulder. He was always thinking of others. "Actually, I'm a little worried about something else. I found out today that your house is being bumped up."

Ethan's jaw dropped. "What?"

Adam nodded. "Something came up in the spring, so we're going to start yours now. The permits came in this afternoon."

Ethan's face split into the grin Adam had been waiting all day to see. Ethan and Natalie were eager to move into their own place and had been disappointed when his dad slotted them in for May.

"Are you serious? It's happening now? I was going to propose before we move in."

Adam laughed. "Well, you better get on it, then. We're breaking ground next week. My dad is going on vacation, so I'm leading the crew."

Ethan's smile faltered. "How is that going to work next door to filming? I don't want to put Chelsea out."

Adam nodded. It had the potential to be a disaster. There were few things on earth as noisy as building a home. "Let's not borrow trouble. Maybe she won't get the contract."

Ethan exhaled. "I hope she does, though. The taxes on that place are ridiculous, and she's got a kid to look after . . ."

"We'll make it all work," Adam said, hoping to reassure, but not fully certain himself. "I can always call in a favour from Uncle David. Let me worry about the house. You worry about convincing a girl you've known for two months to be your wife."

Ethan smiled. "All right," he said, skating off with a huge grin. Just as Adam was about to follow, Ethan stopped and turned back to him, looking more serious.

"What?"

"You know, if Natalie says yes, that would mean Chelsea would be my sister. And Ben would be my nephew."

Adam nodded, worried about where he was going with this. "Right . . ."

"And she lives in town now, next door to me, so you guys will see a lot of each other."

"Uh-huh . . ."

Ethan rolled his eyes. "Could you just be friends with her? Have you seen her since you asked her out?"

Adam winced. He knew it was coming, he just didn't want to hear it. "No, but I have to go over there tomorrow to get some insurance papers signed for the build."

"Perfect. Just ask her to be friends."

Adam stared at Ethan with a blank look. "You want me to say, 'Chelsea, will you be my friend?'"

"Well, not like that. That'll make you sound like a weirdo. Just think of her the way you think of me. Or Amy."

Adam shook his head. "That's impossible. I've already pictured her naked, in my bed, on all fours with her ass—"

"Stop. Stop now."

Adam shrugged. What could he say? His mind moved fast. "I think it's better if I distance myself."

"That's impossible. What's going to happen when I get married? You'll both be at the wedding. Or if I have a kid? You won't come to their birthday party?"

"Of course I'll be at your kids' birthday parties."

"And so will she," Ethan said. "You can do this, Adam. I believe in you."

Adam rolled his eyes. "Fine," he said. "I'll ask her to be my friend, and I'll try not to look at her tits when I say it."

Ethan smiled. "It's all I ask."

They skated off together, talking about the house, but Adam's mind kept conjuring the image of Chelsea and reminding him he'd never, *ever* had a girl that was just a friend.

This was going to be interesting.

THREE

"Look up at the sky, Ben."

Ben tipped his smiling round face up to the heavens, and Chelsea fastened the buckle of his helmet under his little chin, then adjusted the GoPro on top and clicked it on. "There you go, buddy."

"Thanks, Mama!"

He bounded off the porch toward his bike that was waiting on the paved path that wrapped around the side of the house into the gardens. When he reached it, he hopped on, but as he tried to put his feet on the pedals, he tipped over. Luckily, he shot a foot out in time to stop himself from face-planting.

"You keep trying, Ben. I'm just gonna clean up the gardens a bit, then I'll help you, okay?"

"'Kay!" he said, his brow creased in concentration as he stared down his foe.

Chelsea smiled and made her way to the barn. She had questioned her decision to move them into the old house at least a billion times since she inherited the place. It was expensive; it was huge; it was way too much upkeep. But seeing her boy have room to run and play and knowing he would start at a safe school the next day was enough to reassure her.

Now she just had to make it work. Thankfully, she had a plan. And if that plan failed, she had several backup plans already in the works.

She reached the old barn, which Natalie had warned her was full of bats, and slid the door open fast, ducking, just in case they mounted an attack. She swore to herself in that moment that if she ever wrote and directed a horror film, she would shoot it in this barn, among the sharp, rusted farm equipment and bloodthirsty bats.

Her mind whirled back to the screenplay already written, perfected, printed in her desk drawer, but she shook it off. One day, when the time was right, she'd follow her dreams. Right now, she had to deal with her reality.

She stayed low, creeping through the doorway and into the corner of the barn where a shovel, pruners, and wheelbarrow rested against the wall. As soon as she retrieved them, she darted back out and slid the door closed behind her.

A half hour later, after Ben's millionth failed attempt to start his bike, Chelsea had the gardens cleaned up and joined him. Her soft white T-shirt and worn black jeans were covered in dirt and sweat, and her hands were sliced up from the thorns on the dead rosebushes she'd ripped out, but it was worth it. The terraced gardens were now a blank slate, ready for a set designer to come put their touches on it.

Hopefully, that would be the case.

"It's really hard, Mama," Ben said, wobbling from side to side as Chelsea held him with one hand on the handlebar and one hand on his seat. "My scooter is so much easier."

"I know, but biking is what you want. Just keep pedalling. You'll get it."

She wasn't sure that was actually true, but what could you say? Maybe she should look up some videos on the best way to teach a kid to ride a bike. They were days into this, and he was no better now than he had been before. He would either steer or pedal. Not both. And he couldn't stay upright for more than a few milliseconds.

"You gotta keep pedalling, Ben. When you stop, you'll tip," she said, picking up her pace to a light jog.

His little legs started pumping faster until he got to the bend in the pavement where the path curved around the corner of the house, then he started turning.

"Yes! Don't stop pedalling, B—"

The words died in her throat as they came around the corner and saw a person. There wasn't enough time to process what was happening, and not enough time to stop.

There also wasn't enough time for the intruder to get out of the way.

The bike crashed directly into the legs of the guy, and the impact threw Chelsea backwards into the grass. It took her a moment to hop back up, but she was too late to reach for the bike. Ben was screaming, latched onto the handles and pedals like a stunned gargoyle as the bike started tipping away from her.

She scrambled for him, but he was going down fast. He had almost hit the ground when a muscled arm shot out and grabbed the frame of the bike, righting it and holding it still with little effort.

Chelsea lunged forward and pulled Ben from the bike, prying his fingers off the handles and setting him on the ground. She reached for the bike, and that's when she finally saw that the person they'd run down was Adam.

He was lying on his back with his eyes closed, blood gushing down his leg, and papers scattered on the ground all around him.

Chelsea winced. She squatted down next to him, wondering whether he was okay. Maybe she should call someone? He seemed unresponsive. What if he'd hit his head?

She thought for a moment, then made a fist and drilled it into his upper arm, trying to ignore the way his grey T-shirt stretched across his biceps.

"Yo," she said.

He opened one eye. He was squinting so tight she just barely glimpsed green through thick lashes. "Am I bleeding?"

Chelsea looked down at his body. Between his black gym shorts and running shoes, in the middle of his shin, was a sizable gash, probably from a pedal. Most alarming was the puddle of blood forming below him on the pavement.

She swallowed back a shudder.

"Um, a bit."

It was more than a bit. She wondered whether they were going to use her property for a splatter film. If not, she'd need to come out and hose off the walkway before tomorrow.

"It's bad, isn't it?"

She looked again, and a glob of blood pulsed out of his leg.

Her tongue darted out in an involuntary gag.

"There's so much blood!" Ben yelled, squatting down on the other side of Adam. "It's coming out of your leg like . . ." He started making gurgling noises in his throat.

"Ben," Chelsea said, shaking her head.

Adam groaned and sat up, looked down at the carnage, and pulled a face.

"Maybe it looks worse than it is?" Chelsea asked.

Adam looked up and met her eyes. A smile tugged at the corner of his mouth, and she noticed a faded scar on the side of his lip pulling his mouth tight. "I guess that would be the gallant thing to say."

Chelsea snorted. "Sorry, you don't exactly strike me as the gallant type."

"No?" he asked, groaning as he stood, then shifted his weight to his good leg. "What type do I strike you as?"

Chelsea wouldn't dare look back at his face. He was standing too close. She was feeling uncomfortable. She turned and bent, gathering up the papers that had escaped a white binder he'd been holding. When she stood, she forced a smile and shoved the binder at him. "The forgiving type?" she asked, finally meeting his eyes.

She gave Ben a little elbow behind her, and he took the hint. "I'm sorry," he said from behind her leg.

Adam's face softened. "It's all right. Just bad timing."

The awkwardness of their first meeting at the baseball diamonds settled on her like a wet blanket as the silence between them stretched. She looked around, wondering what the hell he was doing there.

Luckily, Ben broke the tension by squatting down to get another look at the blood. "You need a bandage," he said.

Now that Adam was standing, the blood was working its way down the front of his shin in a stream through his leg hair, turning his white sock red.

Chelsea rubbed her forehead. The last thing she wanted to do was invite Adam into her house, but she couldn't very well leave the guy dripping blood everywhere. Besides, he was Ethan's best friend, so he couldn't be *that* bad.

Right?

"Come on," she said, waving toward the door. "I'll get you a bandage, and you can tell me why you're skulking around my property."

Adam smirked. "Skulking?" he asked as he fell in step with her.

"Mm-hmm . . ." Chelsea nodded. "You've got some explaining to do."

FOUR

Adam followed Chelsea into her creepy old house and tried to pretend that he was gallant. But with her ass swaying in front of him and the dirty handprint on the back pocket of her worn jeans making it impossible to look away, he was struggling.

Think of the blood.

Who the fuck was he kidding? A tornado ripping through the place couldn't distract him from that ass. And those hips. And those lips.

"Are you going to die?" Ben's voice broke through his thoughts.

Adam's step faltered as he looked down at Chelsea's kid. He looked just like her: blond hair sticking out from under his helmet and round aqua eyes piercing Adam's retinas and examining his brain.

"Uh," he said, searching for words. It was a question he asked himself daily yet never had a firm answer on. He made a show of glancing at the watch on his wrist. "It's already four, so probably not today," he said.

Chelsea laughed as she walked through the entryway toward the back of the house, oblivious to his internal strife. "Oh, Ben. People don't die from a cut on their leg," she said, then threw a bright smile over her shoulder at him that had his heart ceasing. "They die from medical malpractice. Sit. I'll get the alcohol."

Adam couldn't stop the laugh that bubbled up out of his throat as he sank down into the chair. He looked for a place to put his binder, but the table was covered with drawings, crafts, a Spider-Man backpack, and all other manner of kid stuff. He settled for holding it on his lap.

"We don't have any more of the bandages where Spider-Man hangs upside down," Ben said in a solemn voice, as if delivering news of a terminal illness. "Mama says they're all the same, but she's wrong."

Chelsea turned toward the table with a first aid kit in hand, rolling her beautiful eyes. Then she sat in the opposite chair, her knees resting in the open space between his thighs. She shoved the artwork aside, set down the kit, and flipped it open.

There on the top sat the dreaded brown bottle of alcohol. It was the same bottle his mother had used on him when he was a child. He looked up at Ben, who kept one worried eye on the bottle as if, at any moment, it might come after him.

Smart kid.

That shit stung like a bitch.

"My mom used to tell me all the flavours of Kool-Aid were the same," Adam said, trying to get the worried look off Ben's brow.

"What's Kool-Aid?"

Adam's jaw dropped. "You did *not* just ask that."

Ben's giggle sounded like the tinkling of ice pellets on a window during an ice storm. "Yes, I did."

Chelsea gave an indulgent smile that revealed straight teeth and deep dimples. That, mixed with her thick, shoulder-length, curly blond hair that was glowing from the afternoon sun, made her look like an apparition.

That was until she tipped the brown bottle onto a cotton ball.

"He's very literal," she said, traces of the smile still etched on her features. "Cross your leg over."

Adam slumped his shoulders but did what she said. She held out the soaked cotton ball for him, but he ignored her offering. "How does your kid not know what Kool-Aid is?"

"Too sugary," Chelsea said as she pushed the cotton ball at him, again, no-nonsense. "Take this. It's better if you do it to yourself."

He tried to stop the smirk that took over his face. He really did.

"I think we both know that's not true."

He knew the exact moment she registered his joke, because her creamy skin took on a slight pinkish tint, and her eyelids dropped over the blue of her eyes.

Shy Chelsea was too fucking gorgeous to take.

He reached for the cotton ball, but he was too late. She leaned forward and stabbed it into his cut.

The sting that followed was vicious.

"Fu—"

"No swearing," she said, cutting him off.

"Shi—"

"That's also a swear word!"

He blinked hard and glanced at Ben, who was staring fascinated at the cotton ball turning red.

Take your mind off it.

He jerked his gaze up, and it landed on the camera on Ben's head. "You learning to ride your bike?" he asked through a clenched jaw.

"Yup. I'm not very good, though."

"No one's good at anything the first time they try. You should learn on the beach, though. That's where I learned."

The stinging receded, and his mind cleared. When he looked from the red cotton ball up, he connected with Chelsea's bright eyes. She quickly glanced away, pulling the cotton ball away from his leg and dropping it onto a tissue. Then she pulled out a bandage.

"Isn't it harder to bike through the sand?" she asked.

Adam shook his head. "The sand down there is compacted. Normal bike tires go over it without any problem, and falling on sand is way better than pavement. You should take the pedals off, too, so he can learn to balance first."

Chelsea narrowed her stunning eyes. "How do you know these things?"

Adam shrugged. "My dad taught me."

"And you remember?"

"Well, I didn't learn until I was ten," he said, looking over at Ben. "I was scared."

Chelsea let a smile break as she ripped the paper off the back of the bandage and laid it on his leg, pushing the sticky part into his leg hair. "Thanks for the tips. We'll take all the help we can get."

"No problem," Adam said, staring at the bandage and wondering how much hair it was going to take off with it.

"You got Spider Gwen," Ben said, pointing at his leg.

Adam nodded in approval. "I always thought she was hot when I was a kid."

Confusion came over Ben's face. "Does she shoot fire?"

Chelsea laughed as she cleaned up. "He means he had a crush on her."

"Ohh," Ben said with a smile. "Sophia kissed me," he said, then lowered his voice and added, "on the mouth."

Adam's face cracked into a smile. This kid was hilarious.

"Sophia was in daycare with Ben," Chelsea said to clarify. "He shared his chocolate with her, and she kissed him."

Adam laughed. "Well played," he said, making Ben giggle again with that little noise. He turned to Chelsea. "The kid's got good instincts."

Chelsea's smile faded, and the awkwardness that had been simmering just below the surface of all their interactions bubbled up.

He could feel it. He *knew* she felt it. So he decided to just call it out.

"Are we awkward?" he asked.

Her brows inched up for a moment, then she smiled her half smile, which sadly revealed no dimples, and nodded. "Yup. The awkward alien has invaded."

"Awkward alien?"

Chelsea nodded. "Awkwardness is like an alien invasion. You gotta kill the aliens before they lay eggs. Otherwise, it will just take over, and you'll never get rid of it."

Adam nodded. "Have our aliens laid eggs?"

Chelsea nodded. "Yup."

Adam braced himself. "I'm sorry about how things at the baseball diamonds went," he said, glancing at Ben, who had focused all his attention on sorting the bandages into neat piles. "I just don't . . . I don't date women with . . . I mean . . . I don't date women . . ."

"The shells are cracking," she said with a scrunched up nose. "Hatch, hatch."

Adam laughed, despite the awkwardness. "I don't date," he finally settled on.

Chelsea nodded, then silence fell over them. It was a stupid thing to say, since he had asked her on a date. But he couldn't very well explain that he'd only intended to sleep with her and never see her again. He looked back up at her, and she had busied herself with straightening some of Ben's artwork on the table.

The aliens were out of their eggs now, running all over the goddamn place. He'd need a fucking blowtorch to salvage this.

"Can we be friends?" he asked bluntly, out of desperation.

Chelsea narrowed her eyes at him.

"We have mutual friends now, and it's a small town. You won't be able to avoid me," he said, plastering on an over-the-top smile.

Chelsea rolled her eyes.

"I'm a great friend." He kept his sales pitch rolling along. Maybe it could kill some of the baby aliens. He wanted the awkwardness to end, for sure. But he also wanted to prove to himself, and everyone else, that he could be just friends with a gorgeous woman he was desperate to bone.

Chelsea let out an exasperated exhale. "Fine," she said. "I'll be your friend. Is this why you came lurking around here?"

Adam's smile beamed from his face.

Nailed it.

"Only partly," he said, feeling cocky. "I actually need your permission on some insurance forms to use your driveway for heavy equipment. We're breaking ground on Ethan and Natalie's house next week."

Chelsea stood paralyzed, staring at him for a moment. "Next week?"

Adam nodded and flipped open the binder to the pages he needed signed. "Ethan told me you're hoping to rent your place as a film location, but I think we can work together to get around that."

"Film locations need to be silent. Isn't building a house kinda loud?"

"It's extremely loud."

"How is that going to work?"

Adam pulled a pen out of the binder rings and clicked the bottom, then handed it to her. "We don't work all day, every day. And out here, we can start early or go late since the only neighbour is you. The loudest part is digging the foundation and framing. We can make it work."

Chelsea took the pen and stared at the paper with a furrowed brow, then threw a nervous glance at Ben. "I really need this contract. If I don't get it, I . . ."

She trailed off, breaths coming faster and more erratically.

"Hey," he said, hating the nervous energy that was coming off her. He hadn't realized he'd got used to her playful quirkiness until it was gone. Then he missed it. He wanted to pull her into a hug, but that would have the aliens laying eggs for sure. But then again, friends hugged each other all the time, right?

Still, it was probably best if he implemented a no-touching policy with her.

"We'll deal with problems as they come."

Chelsea slumped into a chair, face drained of hope. It was hard to watch.

Adam took a chance and patted her shoulder with his hand. "Nothing to worry about. I told you, I'm a great friend. I look after my people, and you're my people now. Plus, I can always call in a few favours."

Chelsea looked up at him with a raised brow. "Favours? Who do you know in the film industry?"

Adam smiled. Who did he know? Almost no one.

But everyone knew him.

"I can get a favour if I need one. You'll have to trust me."

"I don't trust anyone," she said, staring at the paper. "But I want Natalie and Ethan's house to get built." She glanced up at him and narrowed her eyes. "You won't damage my driveway, will you? The last thing I need is another problem to fix."

Adam shook his head. "No damage at all. And if there is, we'll fix it. I'd never put you out like that. It's all in the contract."

On a deep exhale, Chelsea scrawled her signature on the three highlighted lines, then closed the binder and passed him the pen. "I hope you know what you're doing," she said with her glazed, aqua eyes.

Adam stared, lost for a minute in the glistening, before letting out an exhale. "Me too."

FIVE

Chelsea sped down her driveway, gravel spitting, and skidded to a stop next to a big black Land Rover. She *hated* being late. But it was unavoidable. Her morning had been a disaster.

It was Ben's first day of school, and although he'd seemed excited to go, when the bus had pulled up, his whole demeanour shifted. Sensing a meltdown, Chelsea told the bus driver to drive on without Ben and brought him to school herself. She bribed him with a lollipop to get him in the car, and when he somehow lost the damn thing, he started crying.

She got him into the school and settled with enough time to stop at Brin's Café for a coffee, but by the time she made it through the lineup and back to her house, she was five minutes late for her meeting.

She hopped out of the car, slammed the door behind her, and took off down the path to the backyard, where she assumed she'd find the location scout. But when she rounded the corner, past where she'd hosed off Adam's blood the night before, she found two people, a woman and a man, roaming around the gardens together, talking and pointing in all directions.

She came up behind them, then cleared her throat. "Hi," she said as the woman turned toward her. "Sorry I'm late, I'm Chel—"

Her voice stopped when she took in the tall, elegant woman's face.

"Chelsea," the woman said with a simple nod. "I'm Lilian Walsh."

Chelsea's brows rose as her smile broadened. Lilian Walsh—*the* Lilian Walsh—was roaming around her backyard.

Chelsea ordered her face to behave.

"It's so nice to meet you. I'm a big fan."

Lilian smiled politely, no doubt used to fawning fans, before she did a half turn and used her hand to gesture toward the gentleman with her. He turned, and she took in his short, stocky build, his deep-brown skin, his black coiled hair, stylishly greying at the temples. He unleashed a smile she'd seen in hundreds—if not thousands—of interviews and magazine articles, and her heart stopped.

Play it cool. Play it cool.

Play.

It.

Cool.

"Allow me to introduce—"

"Vincent Shadd," Chelsea said, her voice cracking. She stepped forward and took his hand, hoping some of his genius might transfer to her through hand-to-hand contact. She hoped she didn't come across like a creep, but she honestly couldn't stop herself.

"I'm Chelsea," she said, shaking his hand up and down. It occurred to her she was being a bit too aggressive, so she let up. But didn't let go. "I'm a huge fan of your work."

Vincent's eyebrows rose, streaking deep creases across his forehead. A bright white smile followed.

"You must be in the industry," Lilian said in a dry voice, earning a playful scowl from Vincent.

Chelsea nodded, keeping her eyes fixed on her idol. "I just graduated from Toronto Film School. I've studied all forty-four of your films, Mr. Shadd."

"Please call me Vincent," he said with a wide smile.

Chelsea nodded. "Vincent." Holy crap, she was on a first-name basis with an Oscar-winning cinematographer whose every word was like gospel to her. She had studied his films, listened to his advice to young filmmakers, and applied everything he said to all of her work.

Jae was going to literally shit herself when she told her.

She stared into Vincent's dark, rich eyes for an eternity, wishing she could jump through them into his brain and somehow know all the things he knew. Imagine all the things he'd seen, the huge amount of experience he had.

"Chelsea," he said.

She blinked and realized that he was no longer smiling. In fact, his face was more of a grimace.

Uh oh.

She'd taken her worshipping too far. She looked down at their still-linked hands and let go, taking a small step back. Famous people loved to be worshipped. But only from afar. He probably *hated* that she was fawning all over him.

"You seem really sweet," he said. "So I don't know how to tell you this . . ."

Her heart dropped. She had acted super weird and made Vincent Shadd feel uncomfortable.

She took two more steps back. "I'm sorry," she said, looking at her feet and trying to gain some composure. "I just . . . I love your work."

His navy velvet loafers came into view as he, shockingly, moved closer to her, and she tried to process what the hell was going on.

An exhale came from his lips, then a rush of words.

"You have a lollipop in your hair."

"I— What?"

"You have a lollipop. In your hair. It's red."

Chelsea's eyes blinked at superspeed as she processed the words. Once they registered, she shot her hand up to her hair and felt around until her fingers found the sticky lollipop mushed into the side of her head.

"Oh, thank God," she said, as she yanked at the red mess.

A chuckle came from Vincent. "You're happy that it's in there?"

She smiled. "Well, I thought I had made you uncomfortable with my fangirling and you were looking for a nice way to tell me to get away from you."

Lilian laughed. "He doesn't get many fangirls. He's loving this."

Vincent smiled wide, all teeth, and nodded. "How long has that been in there?"

"Oh, at least an hour," she said on a deep exhale as Vincent and Lilian both bubbled over with laughter. "And I came into contact with several dozen people, including a super-hot dad at my son's new school."

Lilian laughed. "Annnnd *this* is why I never had kids."

Vincent shook his head, then focused his attention on the hair-covered candy in her hand. "I have two daughters. God, I miss those days."

She could see his minds-eye bringing up an old image of his kids as he stared wistfully at the disgusting mess, and she was pretty sure she would love Vincent Shadd until the day she died. Whoever said you shouldn't meet your idols was obviously idolizing the wrong people.

"Thanks for telling me, Vincent," she said, still giddy to be using his first name.

He clapped her on the back. "Anytime. And I'm sure the super-hot dad will look past it. You're lovely."

Chelsea smiled. How was this real life?

"Now," he said, breaking up the sentimental moment. "Let's discuss your property. What do you think about the lighting?"

Chelsea cleared her throat, tried to be professional. "What are you shooting?"

"A Regency romance based on a book series. Starring Winter Barlowe."

Chelsea forced her jaw to stay in place at the famous actress's name. "I think the lighting is perfect.

The property faces south, so the gardens are always sunny, no weird shadows. Nice open spaces."

Vincent gave a slow nod.

"What do you think, Vin?" Lilian asked.

With a wink at Chelsea, he replied, "I think the lighting is perfect. The property faces south, so the gardens are always sunny, no weird shadows. Nice open spaces."

She would have died of happiness, but a brilliant thought shot through her brain, stopping her: she should try to get a job on set.

She'd opened her mouth to ask whether she could apply for a position when the roar of an enormous engine behind her cut her off. She twisted to look over her shoulder and watched as an eighteen wheeler with an excavator on a flatbed came across the lawn at them.

Shit.

"What the hell is that?" Lilian asked. Her mouth kept moving, but the deafening sound of the truck passing drowned her words out.

Two more flatbeds with enormous pieces of equipment rolled past before a big, rusty white truck came up behind them with Adam behind the wheel. He came to a stop next to them and hopped out of the truck, absently slamming the door behind him as he strode in their direction, all worn jeans, white T-shirt, and steel-toed boots.

Chelsea had to force her face into neutral when his sharp, playful green eyes met hers.

"Hey, Chelsea," he said.

Thank God the lollipop wasn't still in her hair.

"Hi, Adam," she said, turning toward Lilian and Vincent. "This is—"

"Hartley?" Lilian asked, voice unnaturally high pitched. "Mr. Hartley, wow. I'm— I mean, it's a pleasure to meet you. I'm pleased to meet you." She took his hand and shook, not letting go. Much the way Chelsea had done to Vincent.

Adam cleared his throat. "I go by Vale, but I much prefer Adam," he said with a charming smile. "Ms . . ."

"Walsh," she said, giving her head a shake. "Lilian Walsh, executive producer. I've met David a few times. He must be your . . . uncle?"

Adam nodded.

She looked around and raised a brow at his beat-down, rusty old truck and construction equipment. "Do you work . . . here?"

Another nod.

Lilian seemed to remember something, then gave a small nod.

Adam cleared his throat. "It seems we have a bit of a scheduling conflict. I hear you're going to be filming here on Chelsea's property."

"Well," she said with hesitation. "We're undecided," she said, earning an eyebrow raise from Vincent.

"I see," Adam said. "Well, my company is going to be building a house over the next few months, right over there," he said with a jerk of his thumb. "It's for a close family friend."

Lilian nodded. "Of course. Not a problem at all. We can find somewhere else—"

"No. That won't be necessary," he said, cutting her off. "I'm sure we can plan out a schedule. Can I take you out for lunch this afternoon? We can work out all the details?"

Lilian beamed.

Literally beamed.

"Of course," she said. "It would be my pleasure."

"Great. It's settled, then," Adam said with a wink at Chelsea.

What the fuckity-fuck was that?

They discussed the details of lunch while Chelsea stared on, absolutely dumbfounded, until everyone turned to leave and she remembered she was going to convince them to give her a job.

"Um," she said. Less than a stellar opening, but it did the trick. Everyone looked at her. "I was wondering if there are any vacant positions on set that I can apply for."

Vincent smiled, but Lilian hesitated.

"I have some experience. I currently work as a scriptwriter, and I do a lot of editing work on the side. I've also written and directed several shorts."

"Sorry," Lilian said. "We've been filming in the studio for weeks now. We just need the outdoor scenes. All the positions are filled."

Chelsea's heart sank. But she wasn't about to give up that easily.

"What about volunteer positions?" she asked, shifting around the schedule in her mind to see whether it would be possible. She was dying to get some real experience for her resume.

"I don't think—"

Adam drew all the attention of the group by clearing his throat, and Chelsea had to wonder once again who the hell he actually was.

Lilian glanced at him, and he gave her a half smile and a quirked brow.

Lilian looked back at Chelsea. "Sure," she said. "We'll find something for you."

"She can shadow me," Vincent said.

Chelsea snapped her head in his direction. "Really?" she asked.

Vincent nodded. "Absolutely."

"I'm not sure if that can work," Lilian said. She turned to Adam, ignoring Vincent and Chelsea. "See, our director is young. This is his first feature film. I need Vincent's attention on him."

"I can do both."

Lilian looked as if she wanted to protest, but Adam was still looking at her, waiting. "Fine," she reluctantly said, giving Vincent a pointed look. "But you know how Jasper can be."

A loud clashing sound rushed through Chelsea's ears.

Ja—

She must have misheard.

"I can handle Jasper," Vincent said, his voice barely registering as the blood drained from Chelsea's face.

No.

"I'm sorry," Chelsea said, forcing the words out. "Did you say Jasper?"

Lilian smiled widely. "Yes, Jasper Fenton. You've heard of *him*, I'm sure."

Chelsea was at a loss for words. She moved her head up and down in a dazed nod.

Adam's voice, clear and deep, with a touch of hesitation, broke through. "Who's Jasper Fenton?"

Chelsea gave her head a little shake, unable to form words, let alone thoughts.

"He's a brilliant young up-and-coming director," Lilian said, pride clear in her voice. "He was just featured in CUT magazine."

Chelsea rolled her eyes, but the crunching of tires on gravel behind her replaced her sarcasm with nausea.

"Ah, here he is now," Lilian said, then added in a conspiratorial whisper, "I gave him a later time so we could agree on the place before he saw it. He's rejected every other location. We're getting desperate."

Chelsea swallowed. Then swallowed again. Her eyes darted around the space, looking for a solution before landing on Adam's truck. Would it be too bizarre if she jumped in and drove off? Where would she go? Would Vincent think she was a weirdo? She could feel the tension rolling from her head down her arms and pooling at her feet like lava, hardening, cementing her in place.

Adam moved in closer and placed his big hand on her shoulder. The warmth seeped through the thin white cotton into her skin.

"Who's Jasper?" he asked, leaning toward her ear with a low voice, only for her.

She had just opened her mouth to answer when Jasper appeared on the path, his long stride eating up the ground between them at warp speed, and every word died in her throat. She had seen him a handful of times since they'd split, but it was only ever through a car window as she dropped Ben off. She avoided speaking to Jasper. Every time she saw him, she remembered all the times they'd shared. The late nights talking, watching films and laughing, that would so naturally lead to making love.

Their eyes connected, and Chelsea dropped her gaze to the ground in a last-ditch effort to avoid him, but it was useless. Adam moved in closer behind her and kept his big hand on her shoulder.

"Jasper," Lilian said once he was within earshot. "Allow me to introduce Adam V—"

"Chelsea?" Jasper's deep voice cut her off.

Chelsea braced herself before looking up up up and meeting the big brown eyes that had once looked at her with so much love.

"Hi," she said, her voice thick and crackly from not speaking.

Lilian's and Vincent's gazes ping-ponged between them. "You know each other?" Vincent said.

Chelsea nodded, searching her brain for neutral words that wouldn't give away how well she knew him. She was about to say "We went to school together," but Jasper spoke first.

"Of course she knows me," he said, with a shake of his head, as if thinking otherwise was completely absurd. "She's the mother of my son."

SIX

Adam narrowed his eyes at Jasper Fenton as he loomed over Chelsea. Her spine had gone stiff, shoulders had crept up to her ears, jaw had clenched. Something bad must've happened between them for her to be this uncomfortable in his presence. What made little sense was how happy Jasper looked to see her. No signs of tension or apprehension. He looked thrilled, smiling widely as he asked what she was doing there, and whether she and Ben lived there permanently now, and whether he'd started school.

How could this guy not know where his son was living or what school he was attending?

The whole thing seemed super fucked up.

Adam hated how awkward Chelsea had become. And hated how this fucking guy was looking at her, like a present had fallen into his lap. Adam knew it probably wasn't a good idea to get involved, but she was his friend now, and he would have her back.

Always.

Just like any other one of his friends.

Adam reached around Chelsea's back and placed his hand on her opposite shoulder, moving in closer to her side. The move did not go unnoticed by Jasper. He stopped speaking midsentence, his gaze snagging on Adam's hand before connecting with his eyes.

Adam did what he thought would antagonize the douche canoe most: he smiled.

"Who are you?" Jasper asked as he squared his shoulders and tipped his chin up.

"Adam."

"Uh-huh," Jasper drawled out, glancing at Chelsea, then back at him. "And you two are . . ."

Adam smiled again and cocked an arrogant brow that he knew the guy would take as a challenge. He just couldn't help himself.

Jasper exhaled through his nostrils like a dragon breathing fire.

"Friends," Chelsea said.

Jasper clearly didn't believe her. He opened his mouth to say more, but Lilian cut him off and brought the conversation to the film. She told him in no uncertain terms that they would use Monroe

Manor for the film, shook Chelsea's hand, and told her she'd email her the paperwork, then confirmed lunch with Adam before announcing they had much to do and forcing Jasper and Vincent to follow her into the gardens to discuss logistics.

Once they were all out of earshot, Chelsea turned on him. He braced himself, figuring she would demand to know why the hell he was having a pissing contest with Jasper, but thankfully, she had other things in mind.

"Who the hell are you?" she asked, crossing her arms across her chest and tapping her foot.

She looked so goddamn cute when she was demanding things.

He wanted more.

"What the hell was that?" he volleyed back, jerking a thumb toward Jasper.

"*That* is none of your business."

Adam smiled and nodded. "And here I was, thinking we were friends."

Chelsea rolled her gorgeous eyes and turned to walk away from him. He gently grabbed her hand in both of his. She turned and looked at him.

"My mother was Grace Hartley," he said, waiting for her to recognize the name. But she didn't. She just gently shook her head, the tips of her hair dancing along her bare shoulders. "As in Hartley Communications."

Her eyes went wide. "Like the Internet company?" she asked, voice high.

Adam nodded.

"I didn't know Hartley was a name."

"My great-grandfather started the business. It grew over the years into what it is today."

Chelsea looked around, trying to connect the dots. "So . . . but . . . why do you live here? And build houses? And drive a rusty old truck?"

Adam didn't really enjoy telling too many people about his mother's family, but he didn't really see a way out of it. Plus, they were friends now, and friends share things. And he had every intention of finding out about Jasper. It was only fair.

"My mother bought a piece of property on the lake and hired my dad to build her dream beach house back in the eighties. Eventually, they fell in love and had me," he said with a shrug.

"Eventually?"

Adam smiled. "Well, that's how the story goes. My dad grew up pretty poor. He taught himself everything he knows, started his company, Vale Construction, from the ground up. He's very proud to be self made. And my mom was an overprivileged princess with sky-high expectations for her house. It took a while for them to like each other."

"Oh," Chelsea said. "So they had you and stayed here in Mapleton."

Adam nodded. "My dad felt strongly about me growing up 'normal.'"

Chelsea laughed. "You're not normal."

Adam couldn't help the smile. "No?"

She shook her pretty head. "Normal people don't clear their throat and get whatever they want."

Adam feigned offence. "I did that for you."

"I know," she said, tipping her chin down and smiling up at his eyes. "Thank you."

His natural inclination would be to touch her, brush her hair behind her ear, or kiss her. At least pull her into a hug. But he took a step back instead and shoved his hands into his pockets, wondering why he was being awkward with her. If she were any other female friend, he wouldn't have thought twice.

Well, okay, his only other female friend was Amy. And she was more like a sister.

And gay.

And married.

Adam gave his head a shake. "You're welcome. I told you I'm a good friend to have around. I never claimed to be normal."

Chelsea laughed. "At least you're honest. I still don't get how Lillian knows you, if you grew up in Mapleton, and you're not involved with the company."

Adam schooled his features into neutral. He *was* honest, but that didn't mean he had to volunteer information. As much as he hated talking about being a Hartley, he absolutely refused to talk about his past that had sent him running from that spotlight and refusing to return.

"Lillian knows my Uncle David, who runs the company now, and I get recognized because we look alike. But only by certain people who run in those circles. Most people, like you, don't know us at all. The Hartleys are extremely private. They try not to draw attention to themselves."

Chelsea nodded. "I see. And what about your parents? Do they still live in the house they built?"

"Uh, no," Adam said in a shaky voice before clearing his throat. "My mom died when I was thirteen. Pancreatic cancer."

"Oh, I'm so sorry. I didn't know."

Adam nodded. He didn't enjoy dwelling on it. Best to carry on, look for the positives, enjoy what little time you have on Earth. "Thanks. It was a long time ago. I live in their house now."

"Mansion on the beach. Definitely *not* normal."

Adam rolled his eyes. "It's just a beach house. You're a Monroe living in the biggest mansion in Mapleton. Don't reverse-snob me."

Chelsea twisted her head to look at the massive house, then turned back. "That's different."

Adam crossed his arms and thrust out his chest. "I know what real estate goes for around here. Your place is worth at least three times what mine is."

Chelsea folded in on herself a little. "Yeah, well, I'm sure you don't have to work three jobs to afford the taxes on yours."

Her response made him feel like the hugest ass. "Sorry, I didn't—"

She waved him off. "It's fine. I've got it figured out. It won't always be hard for me once I get my career going."

Adam nodded. "Volunteering to work with Vincent is a smart idea. Is that what you want to do? Whatever he does?"

Chelsea smiled. "He's a cinematographer. And, yeah, I guess I would be happy to do that."

"But it's not what you want?"

Chelsea's head tipped from side to side as she glanced across the lawn at Vincent, Lilian, and Jasper. "Actually, I always wanted to be an indie filmmaker. But I need to start somewhere, so . . ." She trailed off, eyes downcast.

"I see. Well, it's good to learn everything you can if you plan to direct one day. My dad made me work with every trade as a teen during the summer. Makes it a lot easier to tell people what to do and to make sure they did it right."

Chelsea nodded and smiled. "Your dad seems like a great guy."

Adam nodded, bouncing on his toes, happy to have a segue land in his lap. "Yup, and Ben's dad seems like a real dipshit."

Chelsea burst into laughter. "You picked up on that, eh?"

"Mm-hmm," he drawled out.

"Well, he is a dipshit."

"What happened to you two?"

Chelsea's eyes widened. "I really don't think—"

"Don't start," he said, cutting her off. "We're friends. I told you all my shit. Pony up."

He was half expecting her to slap him across the face, but she just rolled her eyes and smiled. "Fine. We were friends in film school, started hanging out a lot, started sleeping together, and then I found out I was pregnant."

Adam had to stop himself from wincing. He looked across the lawn at Jasper's back. The guy seemed completely in love with her. Something wasn't adding up. "Then what?"

Chelsea clasped her hands, wringing them a little. "We moved in together. I thought it was forever, you know?" she said, piercing him with those eyes.

Forever. "Yeah."

"But . . . when Ben was three weeks old, I came home from a checkup with him, and Jasper was packing up his stuff. He said he couldn't do it, didn't want to give up his career, and . . . he left," she said, snapping her fingers. "Just like that."

"Brutal," he said, deciding he would be totally justified punching that fucker's face in.

"It's been a struggle."

"Why does he look like he's still in love with you?"

Chelsea shrugged. "He came back, after a few months, and told me he regretted leaving and wanted to get back together, but by that point, I had lost all the love I had for him. I guess abandonment is a hard line for me. The last time I saw him, he told me he still loves me."

Adam stopped himself from cursing. "What did you say back?"

Chelsea flashed a smile. "I told him that the awkward alien invasion made our relationship planet uninhabitable a long time ago."

Adam laughed. "You're a weirdo."

Chelsea laughed. "That I am," she said, looking at Jasper in the distance. "I don't know if he really got what I was saying, though, but it doesn't matter. What was between us was dead and done."

Adam breathed a sigh of relief, then immediately convinced himself that it was for a friend avoiding a toxic relationship with an asshole, and not because he'd just received confirmation that the pretty girl he was dying to see naked was unattached.

"Anyway . . ." she said, shaking off the conversation. "I've got work to do. Thanks again for everything."

"Yeah, no problem."

She smiled before turning to walk away, and he forced his eyes off her ass, reminding himself that she was the reigning queen of tier one and completely off limits to the likes of him.

But it didn't stop him from smiling for the rest of the day, knowing that at least Jasper was out of contention, too.

SEVEN

Chelsea stretched her legs across the couch, trying hard not to wake Ben. His head was on a pillow on her lap, and his little legs were stretched across the couch on top of ice packs she'd given him after a nasty fall from his bike.

The bruises were already impressive, but at least there hadn't been much blood.

"I still can't believe you," Jae said, placing a cup of tea on the coffee table within reach of her. "You're actually going to work for Jasper?"

Chelsea reached for her tea and took a sip. "Vincent Shadd."

"Ugh, I know," Jae said, sinking into the worn office chair they were using as living room furniture. "Still."

"Do you want me to ask if you can come along? Vincent will probably say yes."

Jae's whole face sagged. "I can't. I barely sleep as it is. Editing reality TV is absolute dogshit. I'm going through hundreds of hours of film each week and it's still not enough for my dicky boss."

"Sorry, Jae."

Jae shrugged. "At least I don't have to answer to *Jasper*," she said, sticking her tongue out and making a puking sound.

Chelsea smirked. "I can handle Jasper. Vincent is worth it. I'm just happy that lollipop wasn't still in my hair when Jasper came up."

Jae laughed. "Did Adam see it?"

Chelsea shook her head. "No, but I don't care what I look like around him. We're friends." She glanced down at Ben to make sure he was still sleeping. "There was a super-hot dad at the school that saw me with it, though."

"Ooh," Jae said, leaning forward. "Do tell."

Chelsea laughed. "Tall, nice smile, grey in his beard, no ring, daughter in Ben's class who was also having a meltdown on the first day."

Jae snickered. "And *you* were actually into him?"

Chelsea considered this, then nodded. She wasn't salivating over him as she had been with Adam, but he seemed kind and patient as they silently commiserated with each other. "Yeah, I actually was.

He doesn't appear to be a deserter like Jasper. Or a fuck-boy like Adam."

Jae sipped her tea while staring over the rim of the cup at Chelsea. "You sure you won't get hurt?"

Chelsea shook her head. "Jasper's nothing more than a nuisance. I have to take the bad with the good."

Jae nodded. "And Adam?"

Chelsea paused with her teacup midair and widened her eyes.

"He's good looking," Jae said, mounting her case. "You said so yourself. You also said he's charming and funny. And the vasectomy thing is a plus."

"How?" Chelsea asked, setting the cup down without taking another sip. What the hell did his vasectomy have to do with her?

"Well, you're afraid of casual sex because you might get pregnant. But if he can't get you pregnant, then there's no risk."

Chelsea shook her head. She hadn't really thought about that. But it didn't matter, anyway. "It's not that I'm *afraid* of casual sex—"

Jae cut her off with a look.

"Okay, fine. *Afraid* might be an accurate word. But I'm also not interested in someone who hates children. I'm waiting until I've settled into my career, and then, when I'm ready, I'd like to find someone long term. Adam will never be that."

"What if he wants a relationship, just not babies?"

Chelsea shook her head. "I don't think that's the case. But even if it was, I already have a kid," she said, pointing at Ben in her lap. "It's too late. I think I'd need to find a single dad. Me and Adam would be a disaster."

Jae squinted at her, unconvinced.

Chelsea shook her head. "Anyway, we probably won't be seeing much of each other. He's working across the lawn on Natalie's house, and I'm only going to be there for a few hours in the afternoon on filming days. After the jobs are done, we'll be nothing but acquaintances who run into each other at the grocery store and pretend they're busy so they don't have to stop and talk."

Jae nodded. "I guess I won't worry about you, then."

"Good."

"How are you going to make this work with your other jobs, though?"

Chelsea sighed. It was going to be hell but worth it in the end. "I'm going to have to wake up at five on those days and get most of my work done in the morning while Ben's still asleep."

Jae nodded. "When do you start?"

"End of this week."

Jae's brows shot up. "That fast?"

Chelsea nodded. "I guess they're already behind. They were searching for a location for a while. Jasper kept shooting places down. The production and set crews will be here tomorrow morning. They'll start filming on Friday."

Jae nodded, looking down at her half-drunk tea, and Chelsea knew exactly what was going through her mind.

"You're wishing it was our film being shot on Friday, aren't you?"

Jae nodded again, not making eye contact.

Chelsea felt like shit, but there was really nothing she could do. Lilian had transferred her the location fee after her meeting with Adam that afternoon, but she needed that money in an emergency fund for when she would be between jobs. It provided enough buffer for her to feel at ease about her finances, but it wasn't nearly enough to live off of while making a feature film. Still, she hated that she had abandoned their dreams.

"Maybe we can work on another short?" she said, hoping to appease both Jae and the voice in her head telling her she'd given up.

Jae nodded. "After you're done with Vincent. You're going to be too busy over the next few weeks."

Chelsea nodded. "Okay. I'm going to carry Ben up to his bed."

Jae got up and picked up Ben so Chelsea could stand, then passed him to her.

"Good night," she whispered.

"Good night."

After tucking Ben into bed, she went to her desk to get a head start on the work she'd be juggling next week. It was going to be difficult, but the experience she'd get by working alongside Vincent would be incalculable. Working so closely with Jasper was going to be uncomfortable, but in the end, it would all be totally worth it.

EIGHT

Adam ducked into, what would soon be, Keller's Pub. It was late afternoon, and he had already put in a full day's work between Ethan's build and meetings with the Float Fest event coordinator. Luckily, everything was going great on both counts. Lilian had been so happy to be having lunch with a Hartley that she agreed to work around Adam's schedule, and the event coordinator had dotted every i and crossed every t. All that was left was to show up and have fun.

Adam smiled as he dropped his bag on the old worn bar top and pulled his tool belt out.

"Good of you to finally stop by."

Adam spun around to find Max standing in the doorway, holding a sledgehammer in one hand and covered head to toe in drywall dust.

"Sorry, I've been busy."

"With who?"

Adam reared back. "Um, not *who*, *what*. Ethan's build has taken on a life of its own, and we're coming down to the wire with Float Fest."

Max nodded. "I've been wanting to talk to you."

Adam rolled his shoulders as he slipped his tool belt around his waist and buckled it. "Go on, then."

"It's about Chelsea. I'm worried about you. She's exactly your type."

"Well, fear not, Maximilian," Adam said. "We are only friends. And I don't have a type."

Max raised an eyebrow. "*You* don't have a type?"

Adam laughed and shook his head. "All women who say yes to me are my type."

Max shook his head, but a smile came through the scowl. "Fair enough. But still, you know you like 'em like Chelsea. Quirky, funny, short, blond, lots of curves."

"And all the other ones, too."

Adam pushed past Max toward the kitchen, where they were starting the demo. They were taking the place down to the studs and starting with a clean slate, which was going to be a ton of work but absolutely worth it. He pushed a pair of safety goggles over his eyes before reaching for his own sledgehammer, hoping Max was going to drop the whole

Chelsea thing. He got a few satisfying swings in before Max piped up again.

"The thing is—"

Adam's phone rang from his pocket, cutting Max off. When he pulled it out and looked at the caller ID, he smiled. "I gotta take this, sorry," he said and answered.

"Uncle David!"

"Nephew Adam!" His uncle's voice boomed through the phone.

Max rolled his eyes and began smashing the wall down with a huge, and frankly scary, amount of force.

"How's it going?" he asked as he stepped out of the room, searching in vain for quiet.

"Excellent, as always. I heard you went to bat for a pretty blond."

Here we go again.

"Is there anything you don't hear?"

"When it comes to you? No. Who is she?"

"She's a Monroe from Mapleton, Victor Monroe's niece, with the potential to be Ethan's sister-in-law."

"So . . . not a girl you're trying to impress?"

"Just a friend."

"That's unfortunate," Uncle David said, and Adam could hear his uncle deflate. "I was hoping she would be the one."

Adam rolled his eyes. "Stop hoping things. What do you need?"

"I'm glad you asked. I need to know how you're going to handle this film shoot in your little haven over there."

"Are you worried about me?" Adam asked, trying to inject some sarcasm.

His uncle didn't pick up on it.

"Of course I am."

He rolled his eyes. "I'm thirty-one years old, Uncle David. It's been over a decade since I was in the public eye. I doubt anyone will even recognize me."

"Lilian Walsh and Vincent Shadd recognized you."

Adam exhaled and turned to face the mirror still hanging on the wall above a booth. He had to admit, he was extremely recognizable. He looked exactly like his uncle, and if that wasn't enough of a give-away, the faded scars on his face would remove all doubt.

"I'll lie low."

"It's a big production, Adam. The film crews will be there for weeks, staying in town. I heard Winter Barlowe is the lead. Media will be everywhere. God, Lawrence must be shitting himself."

Adam winced. He hadn't even thought about his dad. He'd *hated* the media attention he got from being married to Grace Hartley. He was extremely protective.

"Actually, he's away on vacation."

Uncle David went silent for a beat, probably recovering from shock. "No kidding. Where did he go?"

"He's driving an RV across Canada."

David laughed. "How very Lawrence of him. Well, at least we don't have to worry about him threatening a reporter with a sawed-off shotgun again."

Adam laughed, wondering how his uncle managed to squeeze that old story into every interaction they had. He was about to ask whether he would ever let it go when a sharp bang drowned out his thoughts and caused a ringing in his head.

"What the hell was that? Where are you?"

Adam blinked away the ear pain. "I'm at the bar. Max and I are demoing. I better run."

"Okay, but promise you'll send someone else into Brin's for your coffee, and order all your meals in, until this blows over. I'll have security monitor things from my end."

Adam rolled his eyes. He really didn't think he would get recognized, but since he didn't have the time to lounge around town anyways, he decided to just humour his uncle. "10-4. Gotta go."

"One more thing, I'm sorry, but I can't make Float Fest this year."

"Oh, that's too bad. It's going to be the best one yet."

"I don't doubt it. Maybe I can come to town soon so we can spend some time together. I'm due for a round at Mapleton Golf Course."

Adam laughed. "Sure, anytime after Float Fest would be good."

"Love you, Adam."

"Love you, too," he said, then hung up and slipped the phone back into his pocket and turned to find Max staring him down.

"Wall's down," he said.

Adam nodded. "Sounded like the roof was crashing in."

"What did Uncle David want?"

Adam scrubbed a hand down his face. "He's worried about the media in Mapleton for the film shoot at Chelsea's. I guess Winter Barlowe is the star."

Max shook his head, clearly unaware of one of the biggest stars in the world and not caring an iota. "He should be more worried about Chelsea."

Adam dropped the sledgehammer on the ground with more force than necessary. "What is your problem?"

Max squared his enormous shoulders and crossed his arms. "I know what you're like."

Anger rose in Adam's throat. The fatigue from the week caught up to him in that moment, and he'd had enough. "You don't know what I'm like."

Max lifted an eyebrow.

"Ugh. I'm capable of being friends with a pretty girl."

"I'm not doubting that. I'm just not sure you can get close to her without . . . torturing yourself. Did you invite her to Float Fest?"

Adam stopped, confused by the direction of Max's questioning, then surprised when he realized he hadn't. "No," he said. "Why?"

"You invite everyone. Why didn't you invite her? Is it because you're avoiding her? Too much temptation?"

Adam rolled his eyes. "Fine. I'll invite her. Want me to call her right now?"

Max waited a beat before continuing, "Come out with Antonio and me next week. His cousin and her friends are in town."

"Fine."

"Fine."

"We good?"

Max nodded.

Adam pulled on a pair of gloves and slipped his safety goggles back over his eyes. "You know, you used to be fun. Ever since the ink dried on that loan you've been downright grouchy. I'm gonna need a beer—"

His phone rang from his pocket again. When he looked at the display and saw his father's name, he wanted to throw it on the ground and smash it to bits.

"Hi—"

"What is this about a fucking film crew?"

Adam was ready to scream when a beer appeared in front of his face. He took the beer from Max, gulped down the cold liquid, then went about reassuring his father that everything was perfectly fine.

NINE

C helsea was in love.

It was only the second time she'd been with Vincent, but she had never felt so strongly about someone in her life.

"See?" Vincent said, moving aside and gesturing to the camera.

Chelsea smiled as she leaned forward and peered through the viewfinder. The camera was on Winter Barlowe's stand-in. She stood perfectly still in the middle of Chelsea's garden, under dazzling lighting, with chaos surrounding her.

The set design crew was hard at work transforming the flower beds. Jasper was ranting and raving at a group of production assistants, and across the lawn, the roar of heavy equipment mixed with country music was coming from Adam's crew.

Today was prep. Tomorrow they would start filming.

Chelsea had asked Vincent at least five hundred questions already that day, and each time, he patiently explained what he would do, then showed why.

He was incredible. She loved him.

"I see exactly what you mean now," she said. "I hope I'm not annoying you with too many questions."

Vincent smiled. "Not at all. It's nice to have someone to pass my experience to. My kids were never interested."

"Really?"

Vincent nodded. "They were only interested in the actors I worked with. You're a film geek, like me. I enjoy talking about all this stuff. Besides, I can't shake the feeling that I'll be watching your films one day and bragging that you learned everything you know from me."

Chelsea laughed. "Hopefully. Maybe," she said, then felt her smile falter. "One day."

An awkward moment of silence passed. "You want to direct, right?"

Chelsea nodded.

"You know what? So did I."

Chelsea's brows rose. "Really? But you've been the best cinematographer in the business for, like, thirtysomething years."

Vincent nodded, gave a half smile. "A teacher found that talent in me and encouraged me to pursue it. After a while, I became known as a solid DP, and now . . ." He paused, shook his head, looking in the distance. "I can't believe how fast the years went."

Chelsea shrugged. "I'd be happy with a fraction of your success."

"Mm, that's what you say now because you've had *no* success. But you should be careful about settling. I think you have the right manner to direct."

Chelsea's smile wavered. "My friend Jae and I, we've written and directed three shorts since film school. I really did love it."

"They any good?"

Chelsea nodded. "Yeah, but they haven't been very successful. You might like them, though. We followed all the advice we could find from you."

Vincent let out a laugh. "Good idea," he said with a smile. "So, is that why you abandoned your plan? Because your shorts flopped?"

Chelsea shrugged. "Not entirely. I have Ben and the house to pay for," she said. "Sometimes there are too many demands to follow dreams. We wrote a few features. One that's pretty good, but we're going to see if my agent can sell it."

"It's going to be tough to sell a screenplay that's only 'pretty good.'"

Chelsea smiled. "Actually, I was being modest. It's really great. It's a dark romantic comedy about two coworkers who are secretly plotting to kill each other, and they fall in love."

Vincent's eyebrows rose at Chelsea's carefully crafted logline, just as she'd hoped they would.

"Can I read it?"

Chelsea's mouth fell open. "You want to read my screenplay?"

Vincent nodded.

"You're serious?"

Vincent laughed. "Yeah. I know some people. If it's good, I'll pass it along."

Chelsea stood in stunned silence for at least five Mississippis before words came. "O-of course you can read it. I'd love that!" she said with way too much enthusiasm but not really caring. "I'll go get it right now!"

"If you've got your shorts handy, I'll look at them, too. See how well my advice does in real life."

A sound of disbelieving delight escaped Chelsea. "I'll be right back," she said, turning abruptly to run home. She took a single leap forward and ran into a hard wall. When she looked up, her eyes connected with Jasper's.

His hands glided up her arms and rested on her shoulders to steady her. "Everything okay, Chelly?" he asked.

The feel of his hands, and the sound of her old nickname, had her grimacing and shaking him off.

He fisted his hands and narrowed his eyes.

"You need help with something, Jasper?" Vincent asked.

Jasper reached a hand up and raked his fingers through his thick, brown hair. A flood of memories hit Chelsea. How many times had she seen him do that exact move when he was frustrated? Too many to count. Every once in a while, she would catch Ben doing the same thing.

"Yeah, I do," he said with enough force to grab Chelsea's attention. "I can't stand those hillbillies over there blaring their redneck music."

Chelsea's eyebrows inched up. She glanced toward the build site where a group of guys were gathered, eating their lunches on the tailgates of four trucks. She picked Adam out of the crowd immediately. In fact, she'd had a hard time *not* looking over at him all afternoon. Mostly because of the vast difference in vibe between the construction job site and the film set. Across the lawn, they looked as if they were having fun. Here, everyone ran around on eggshells.

Just then, Adam tilted his head back and laughed. He was sitting in the centre of the group, wearing a backward ball cap and construction vest, and all the other guys were hanging on his every word.

Seemed about right.

"We're not shooting. What does it matter? Isn't this part of Lilian's agreement?" Vincent asked.

Jasper huffed. "It's so loud I can't even form a thought."

"I'm not entirely sure the music's to blame," Vincent said under his breath.

Chelsea coughed to hide a laugh.

Jasper stabbed a glare at Vincent before turning to Chelsea. "You're friends with that guy, the loud one in the middle. Go over and ask him to turn off the music."

Chelsea gaped at Jasper. There was no way she was going over there and telling them to turn off their music, like some crotchety old hag who was desperate to complain about something.

"No."

"Please," Jasper added through clenched teeth, then turned and walked off.

Chelsea glanced back at Adam, then at the torn-up mud field between them, then down at her white jeans and sneakers. She wanted to ignore Jasper and get the screenplay for Vincent. But she also had a vested interest in keeping the director of the film happy. The last thing she needed was for him to throw a tantrum and pull out at the last minute. She needed the money, and the time with Vincent.

"You don't have to go," Vincent said. "Jasper's in over his head, panicking, and taking it out on them."

"He's always been easily frustrated. Honestly, I'm surprised he landed this position."

Vincent laughed. "Me too."

Chelsea sucked in a deep breath. "It's okay. I'll go. I rented this property for a film set, and I should make sure it's functioning as well as possible. Plus, it's probably best if Jasper and Adam don't interact too much. They don't seem to like each other."

Vincent glanced across the field and smirked back at her. "I can't imagine why."

Chelsea shrugged.

Vincent huffed a small laugh. "I'm just about done with this now, anyway. You can get the script and shorts to me later."

"Thank you so much," Chelsea said.

She sucked in a cleansing breath and braced herself for seeing Adam up close in all his blue-collar hotness, then set out across the muddy lawn.

TEN

Adam was draining his fourth water bottle of the day just as he saw Chelsea break from Vincent and Jasper and start walking across the lawn toward him. He'd have liked to say he'd just noticed her, but the truth was he'd been having a hard time keeping his eyes off her all day.

She was wearing white jeans and sneakers with a pale-yellow cotton shirt that had the tiniest buttons holding it together. The kinds of buttons that would slip open with one good tug. Her shirt stopped just above the waistband of her pants, and when a breeze came, it picked up the bottom slightly, giving him a glimpse of her soft skin and pretty little belly button.

He wanted to drop to his knees and kiss her right there.

His plan to think of her as one of the guys was already failing. He was more likely to be hit by a falling satellite than to look at her and not think of sex.

He mentally slapped himself.

"Hey—"

A catcall screeched through the air, cutting off Chelsea's voice. At first, she looked surprised, gaze searching for the offender. But she gave up quickly, looking back at him with a laugh and a smile that showed her pretty dimples.

Fuck.

"Did I just walk into a real-life cliché?" she asked with a laugh.

"'Fraid so," he said, looking over at Joel, knowing he could whistle like that. "Get coffee," he yelled over the music. Joel gave a sheepish look and a nod before getting into his pickup.

"You're pretty brave coming over here."

Chelsea laughed. "It wasn't my idea. Jasper asked me to come speak to you about turning your redneck music down. Also, he called you a hillbilly."

Adam threw his head back and laughed. It was hilarious how seriously that guy took himself. He glanced over the top of Chelsea's head, narrowing his eyes in on Jasper's pompous scarf. "Redneck music? I'm offended."

Chelsea smiled. "Yeah, you really look it, too. Somehow, I knew you'd like being called a hillbilly."

"It's a badge of honour, and I wear it proudly."

Even as they were speaking, Jasper had his hands flailing through the air as he pointed and yelled at some girl with a clipboard, making Adam seriously question Lilian's ability to hire a director. He shook his head and pulled his phone from his pocket, adjusting the volume down. "I thought you were shadowing Vincent. You shouldn't have to run errands for that clown."

Chelsea rolled her bright, playful eyes. "It's only a few weeks, and you two don't seem to like each other much. It's probably best if I act as a liaison."

Adam smiled, held her gaze. "I'd much rather see you than him."

Chelsea smiled up at him just as the sun peeked out from behind a cloud and a beam of light illuminated her aquamarine eyes. He was lost for a moment until the sound of Joel's truck tires spinning snagged his attention. He hopped off the tailgate and opened his mouth to warn Chelsea, but it was too late. Joel put on the four-wheel drive and hit the gas, spraying them with giant globs of mud.

He jumped forward between her and the truck, trying to shield her, but by the time the truck moved, they were both almost completely coated.

Chelsea whimpered a little and held her hands out as if she didn't know what to do next. Her eyes were closed, with mud on her eyelids.

Shit.

"Don't open your eyes."

Adam lifted the bottom of his shirt up to her face and wiped the mud from her lashes. Luckily, it was thick clay and came off quickly in clumps. "There, you can open," he said.

He twisted the shirt and lifted it up to wipe his own face, certain Chelsea was going to scream at him. Or worse, cry. But when he looked up from the shirt at her, she was staring at his abs with one eyebrow cocked and her mouth slack.

Adrenalin shot through his veins. A thousand images of her flooded his brain. Images he'd had since the moment he'd met her but had tried desperately to repress.

Fuck, he wanted her.

He wouldn't survive knowing she wanted him, too.

He lifted his hand to a piece of muddy hair on her cheek. Her gaze swept up his body, landing on his mouth just as he tucked the strands behind her ear and watched a flush work its way up her neck.

He stared at the skin on her chest turning pink. At the small gaps in the fabric between her buttons.

If he just shifted slightly, he'd be able to see what colour her bra was.

"What's going on?" asked a strange, garbled voice from behind him.

It was on the tip of his tongue to tell the intruder to fuck off when the lusty fog cleared from his brain and it registered whose voice it was.

He jumped back and twisted, finding Natalie and Ethan standing right behind him. "What?" was all he could get out.

Natalie stood with her hands on her hips, looking pissed off, while Ethan stood beside her, holding a bag and hiding a grin. "What's going on?" she repeated.

What's going on?

I'm imagining forty different ways I want to fuck your sister.

That's *what's going on.*

No one answered.

"And why are you all covered in mud?"

"Truck tires," Chelsea said, looking down at her mud-caked shoes and not owning up to her end of the eye-fucking. Best to pretend it never happened.

Ethan cleared his throat. "We have good news."

Adam zeroed in on Ethan. "Wha—"

His voice was drowned out by Chelsea's squeal.

"Oh my God," she yelled, jumping up and down a little. "Is that an engagement ring?"

"Yes, it is," Natalie said, dropping her scowl and replacing it with a beaming smile.

Finally, Adam's brain was getting some blood again. "Wow, you convinced her!" he said, pulling Ethan into a hug. "Congratulations."

Ethan laughed. "Thanks. We wanted to tell you both first. It's lucky you were both here . . . together."

Ethan slid him a look that Adam read immediately, but he answered with a shake of his head.

"Yes," Natalie said, giving him a distrusting look. "We wanted to tell you both because we've decided to elope, and we want you both to be our witnesses."

Adam's eyes bulged from his skull. "Elope?"

Natalie nodded. "Yeah, in a couple of weeks. When I get back from tour." She glanced over at Ethan with love in her eyes. "We're going to go to Niagara Falls."

Adam took a step back. Then another. They couldn't *elope*. He knew it was asshole-ish to tell someone what to do on their wedding day, but eloping was going too far. Connor had already eloped, telling no one, and that was bad enough. He wouldn't stand for another friend getting married without a proper celebration.

Especially not his best friend.

"You can't do this," he said, unable to stop himself. "You can't elope."

"Told you he'd take the news badly," Ethan said under his breath.

"What the hell are you talking about?" Chelsea asked, narrowing her eyes at him.

He ignored her scrutiny. "They can't elope. I'm supposed to be best man."

"You are best man. I'm pretty sure that's what they're asking of you," Chelsea said with an eyebrow up, as if she was looking at the most ridiculous person alive.

Ethan and Natalie nodded.

"But I wrote a speech to say at his wedding when I was thirteen."

"Oh God," Ethan said with a wince.

"And Niagara Falls? No." His head was now shaking back and forth involuntarily.

Natalie tapped her foot impatiently. "I don't care about flowers and cake and all that shit. And I don't really have anyone to invite, anyway. I just want to be married to Ethan."

Chelsea turned to her, tilted her head to the side, and brought her hand to her heart.

He rolled his eyes.

"I'd be honoured to be your witness," she said.

"Thank you, Chelsea," Ethan said, then turned to Adam. "And you?"

He was about to scream when a brilliant thought popped into his head. "Give me a month, and I'll plan a wedding for you."

"What?"

The gears were turning. "I'm almost done with Float Fest. I will have some time on my hands. We could use my family cottage in Muskoka. I'll arrange a limo bus, get a caterer, hire some musicians."

Silent stares from all three of them. How could they possibly think that eloping in Niagara Falls was better than an actual celebration?

"Are you serious?" Natalie asked, then turned to Ethan. "Is he serious?"

Ethan smiled and nodded. "You just don't get him yet."

Adam ignored them. "If you tell me no, then I'm throwing the bachelor party to end all bachelor parties to make up for no wedding. This needs to be celebrated properly."

Natalie rolled her eyes. "Fine. I don't even know why I'm arguing with you. That actually sounds really nice. I've always wanted to go to Muskoka."

Adam smiled. "That's the spirit." He looked over at Chelsea, who was staring at him with narrowed eyes.

"You're really bizarre," she said. "I'm going home to shower."

She turned toward her house without another word, and Adam's eyes immediately dropped to her ass.

Which reminded him . . .

"Wait, Chelsea. You're coming to Float Fest, right?"

She turned back toward him. "Umm . . ."

Silence hung in the air between them, reminding him of when he'd asked her out and she'd shot him down. "Just, you know . . ."

A blank stare.

". . . like, as friends?"

God, why was he so fucking awkward when he asked her things?

"I don't know," she said, then turned without another word and walked away.

Natalie and Ethan followed her, leaving Adam standing alone in the mud, berating himself for touching her face. It was one thing to mentally lust after her; he'd succumbed to the fact that he wouldn't be able to stop that. But skin-to-skin contact was too dangerous. If she showed up to Float Fest, he'd keep a safe distance where touching wasn't even on the table. And yes, he'd probably think of her naked the whole time, but thinking and touching were two different things.

It wasn't as if she could read his mind. He was allowed to think whatever he wanted.

ELEVEN

Chelsea stepped out of her car in the marina parking lot and grabbed her straw beach bag, wondering for the millionth time why she had even come. She was having serious FOMO, knowing Vincent was shooting at that very moment, but he'd insisted she should go have fun and wouldn't take no for an answer, so what could she do? Besides, she was desperately curious to see what a festival that Adam had created would be like.

She was betting it would be fun and a little ridiculous, just like him.

She threw the bag over her shoulder and set out toward the boats. She'd never been to a marina before. Never been on a boat, either. Unless you counted a canoe one year at summer camp, which she figured no one would. She had relied on Jae to dress her, borrowing a lime-green bathing suit that had cut-outs on the sides and went so high up her hips it was almost as if she wasn't wearing bottoms.

When she'd turned in the mirror and seen how much of her butt was hanging out, she'd almost called the whole thing off. But Jae had just shrugged, said, "Sun's out, buns out," and insisted she looked hot, so she threw a pair of cut-off jean shorts and an open button-down white linen shirt over it and pretended to be the kind of person who regularly walked around marinas and spent time on boats with her ass cheeks exposed.

She searched for the number on the post that Natalie had given her as she slipped a pair of sunglasses over her eyes and pulled her hair up into a bun on her head. She found the number, walked through the little gate, and nearly tripped over her own feet.

Adam was standing on an enormous boat.

No, not a boat.

A yacht.

Okay, maybe not a *yacht*.

Whatever the hell it was, it was impressive.

But it still didn't hold a candle to the sight of Adam. He was wearing blue swim trunks with an open Hawaiian shirt revealing an unbelievably ripped torso. She had glimpsed his stomach two days before when he'd wiped mud out of her eyes, but this was different. She tracked her eyes up from his waistband over his chest to his neck, then caught on his mouth.

When she realized he was facing her and probably watching her mentally devouring him, she blinked up at his eyes. And found him looking at her the same way.

"Hey," she said.

"Hey."

Sensing another eye fuck coming, she added, almost absentmindedly, "Your boat has an upstairs."

Adam blinked and looked up, then back at her. "Yup. There's a downstairs, too." He stepped to the dock and held out a hand, ushering her aboard.

"Thanks. What's downstairs?"

Adam smirked and wagged his eyebrows. "Bed."

Chelsea felt her mouth drop open and a laugh bubble up. "What—"

"Sorry," he said, cutting her off with a shake of his head. "That wasn't . . . I shouldn't say things like that to you. I'm just having a hard time not—" He snapped his mouth shut and reached a hand up and rubbed his scratchy jaw. "Want a beer?" he asked, turning toward a kitchenette area in the back corner of the boat.

"Sure," she said, trying to pretend she didn't know exactly what he was thinking. Of course she knew. It was the same thing *she* was thinking.

And it involved that bed and no swimsuits.

"Chelsea!"

Chelsea spun around to see Ethan and Natalie stepping on the boat, followed closely by Max and Antonio.

"Hey," she said, trying to wipe the image out of her mind.

Adam walked over and handed her a can of beer, then introduced her to Max, a giant, tattooed, broody type, and Antonio, a suave-looking Italian doctor. The four guys got to work untying the boat from the dock as she and Natalie watched on in silence.

She glanced at Natalie and discreetly fanned her face with her hand while pretending to pant. Natalie burst into laughter and nodded.

Those four men were fucking hot.

"Help yourself to the fridge, Natalie," Adam called.

"'Kay, thanks!" she called, then looked at Chelsea. "A cold drink is just what I need."

They got the boat untied, then Adam smoothly backed out of the marina. He headed to the middle of the calm blue sparkling lake toward a barge surrounded by a giant circle of boats tied to one another. There was a large space between the boats and the barge for people to swim, and it was already filling up with floating swans, flamingos, and lamas.

"Is that a band setting up on the barge?" Chelsea asked.

"Yup," Adam said, moving past her to toss a rope to the guy on the boat next to them. "Shania Twain cover band."

Adam stepped over the edge onto the boat next to them, shaking hands with them and saying hi to the entire group of people on it as if they were best friends.

"Is there anyone he doesn't know?" Chelsea wondered aloud.

Ethan laughed. "Not in Mapleton. He put an addition on that guy's house."

Chelsea watched him laughing and joking with the family in the boat and wanted that bed even more than before. There was something about him that she hadn't been able to put her finger on until right then. She finally realized that the reason he was so attractive wasn't his solid chest or his wide, easy smile that made her panties flame.

It was how altruistic he was.

He was the type to do anything for anyone, no questions asked. No paybacks necessary. It's why he'd offered to plan Natalie and Ethan's wedding, and why he put on a festival. He just seemed to live his life to the absolute fullest. And it was fun to watch.

Max stood from beside her, causing the boat to shift and pulling her attention away. "Another?" he asked, nodding at the beer in her hand.

"No thanks. It's a little early for me," she said. "Which reminds me, why is this festival at noon on a weekday in September? Wouldn't it make more sense to be on a weekend? In the summer?"

When no one answered, Chelsea looked at Ethan, who was staring at Natalie's hand engulfed in his on her lap. Antonio was looking out at the horizon. Max was reading the side of his beer can.

"Who died?" Adam asked, stepping back onto his boat.

Silence.

"What did I miss?" Chelsea asked.

Max rolled his eyes. "Chelsea asked why Float Fest is in the middle of the week in September."

Adam winced. "Uh, well . . . there are already a lot of festivals in the summer."

"Okaayy . . ."

Max huffed out a breath. "Adam doesn't want kids at his festival. Weekends in summer mean kids will come. He hates kids."

Chelsea stared at Max in disbelief, waiting for him to smile and say "Just kidding!" but he didn't.

Right.

And all the reasons she wouldn't be going to that bed downstairs with Adam came roaring back. She couldn't let herself get sucked in by his larger-than-life personality. He hated kids. She had a kid. Her brain brought up the image of his face at the baseball diamonds looking at Ben for the first time, and she had to shake her head to get rid of it.

The worst part about it was that, for a split second, she wondered whether things would be different if Ben weren't in the picture. The flood of guilt that followed *that* thought made her nauseous.

"Hey," Adam said, placing a hand on her shoulder. "I don't hate kids," he said emphatically. He looked around, as if he was going to drag her somewhere more private to talk, but his friends had already moved to the kitchen area.

"It's okay, Adam. It's not like this is news to me."

Adam shook his head. "I like kids. I really do. I just don't want to have them."

Chelsea wanted to ask what his reasons were, but the conversation was making her feel as if she was being rejected. Again. It made her skin crawl. She felt hot. She glanced over the edge at the water and decided she needed to cool off.

"I don't need an explanation," she said, taking her shirt off her shoulders. "We're friends. Right?"

He was running a hand through his wavy, sandy hair, and stopped, still as a statue, when she tossed the shirt on her bag and started unzipping her jean shorts.

"Friends," he all but breathed out.

"I'm hot. I'm going to swim." She slid the shorts off, pulled her hair from its elastic, then turned and stepped on the edge of the boat. She had just leaned forward when she heard a commotion behind her.

"Wait!"

"Stop!"

"No!"

There was a split second for her to wonder why everyone was yelling at her, but it was too late. She was already in the air above the water.

• • • • • • • • • •

Splash.

The warm lake water hit Adam in the face, and his friends started yelling at him, but none of that was working to clear the image of Chelsea's bare ass from his mind. He stared down at the water, dumbfounded, waiting for her to pop up.

"Why did you let her jump?" Ethan asked, coming up next to him and looking into the lake.

"What's going on?" Natalie asked.

Adam winced.

Max piped up. "The first two people in the water have to compete in the Float Fest Cup."

Natalie shook her head. "Just when I was thinking this was a normal festival."

Chelsea emerged from the water, blond hair slicked back, tits looking in-fucking-credible in that lime-green cut-out bathing suit.

"What's wrong? What did I do?" she asked.

Adam opened his mouth to explain, but Max cut him off.

"Where's your phone?"

Adam jerked a thumb over his shoulder. "On the counter."

"Good."

Max's hand landed on Adam's shoulder, and before Adam even registered what was happening, he was over the side of the boat.

He swam to the surface, about to yell at Max, but Ethan was lying on the boat horn, announcing that someone was overboard. Cheers went up, and people began jumping into the water and swimming toward their floats. The event coordinator came on the mic on the barge, announcing that the competitors had been chosen.

"Adam," Chelsea's voice came from beside him. She was treading water, looking nervous. "Competitors? What the hell is going on?"

"First two people in the water have to compete in the Float Fest Cup."

"Why?"

Adam shrugged. "Because it's *Float* Fest. Not *swim* fest."

Chelsea huffed out a disbelieving laugh. "I'm afraid to ask, but what's involved in the Float Fest Cup?"

Adam started swimming toward the barge. "Come on. You're about to find out."

TWELVE

Chelsea Davenport was a cheater.

A dirty, rotten cheater.

Adam couldn't believe her innocent blond hair and pretty dimples had fooled him. He should have known better. As soon as the gun had gone off in their floating mat race, she tripped him—tripped him! He fell with a splash into the lake, to the tune of her maniacal laughter, and she won handily.

He was on to her in the second event, a complex minute-to-win-it challenge that involved twirling several times on the barge, hitting a baseball into the water, and retrieving it.

She'd bunted, even though it was against the rules, and would have beaten him if he hadn't been such a fast swimmer. He'd dove off the barge and swum like a fiend to make it back before her. It was nice seeing the shock on her face when he pulled himself onto the barge while she was still in the water.

All those morning runs and swims had paid off.

They were all tied up, and it came down to the last event: a scavenger hunt around the boats. The first person to collect all three hidden rubber duckies won. He figured it would be easier for him, banking on all his friends in town helping him out. But it turns out they were more interested in helping the sweet, half-naked girl.

He never stood a chance.

Adam shook his head again, side-eying Chelsea as she stood on the barge next to him grinning ear to ear. The event coordinator handed her the trophy, and she hoisted it above her head, as if it were the goddamn Stanley Cup. When a round of applause and boat horns roared up, she hopped up and down and hugged him.

It was hard to stay mad with her warm arms wrapped around his neck and her tits pressed against his chest.

"This is the best festival ever!"

Adam laughed. "Because there's no ref calling you on all your penalties," he said, leaving an arm around her shoulders as they walked over the boat decks back to his boat.

Chelsea tipped her chin up. "I don't know what you're talking about."

Adam snorted. "You tripped me."

"I slipped."

"And you bunted."

"I'm just not a very good hitter."

Adam narrowed his eyes. "And I *know* Jane threw you the last rubber ducky."

Chelsea's shoulder lifted and dropped. "I can't help if people want to help me."

They made it back to his boat, and everyone was waiting for them. They hugged and congratulated Chelsea as she beamed from ear to ear.

She looked so happy.

Her dimples were so pretty.

Her eyes matched the lake.

"You look pained."

Adam blinked away from Chelsea to Max, who was standing in the kitchen area prepping some burgers.

Adam ignored him, bent to the cabinet, and pulled out two towels. "I'm fine."

"You're white-knuckling it," Max said, then looked pointedly at Adam's hands. "Literally."

Adam looked down at his fists in the towels and ordered himself to relax. He shook his head but didn't say another word, knowing how bad a liar he was.

He walked to Chelsea and passed her a towel, disappointed when she wrapped it around her body, covering up.

"I'm going to make a video of this," Chelsea said, wiping her hands off to make sure they were dry, then taking her phone from her bag. "I wish I had my drone. Can I go upstairs?"

Adam nodded, watching her turn and climb the stairs. She was up there for a minute or two, then came back down.

"I need a shot of the guys jumping into the water," she said. "Will you do it?"

Adam smiled. "Sure," he said without even thinking, wondering whether there was anything she could request that he would say no to, and coming up blank.

"Antonio, Max, would you help me out? Ethan, you too!"

Chelsea gathered them up, had them each take off their shirts and stand on the edge, backs facing her.

"I'm going to count down. Then everyone jumps together."

"Is it going to be three, two, one, jump, or three, two, jump on one?" Antonio asked, as Ethan took off his glasses and handed them to Natalie.

"Three, two, one, jump."

"So we're counting down from four," Ethan said.

"Fine," Chelsea said. "Three, two, jump on one."

"That seems wrong to me," Max said with a smile.

"Okay, then. We'll do four, three, two, jump on one. Everyone happy?"

"No," Adam said with a smirk.

Chelsea tipped her head back and laughed. "Quit fucking with me. Ready. Four, three, two, jump!"

Adam squatted down, launched up, and did a twist in the air. Max and Ethan both did somersaults. Antonio attempted a somersault and failed miserably. They all popped out of the water, laughing. They swam to the back, climbed the ladder onto the boat, and towelled off.

Then Ethan said, "Your turn."

Adam hid the excitement on his face by towelling off his hair.

Chelsea dropped her towel, and Natalie pulled off her dress. They stood on the edge of the boat, holding hands, and Adam nearly died.

He knew his jaw was dropped. Knew that anyone looking at him could see he was staring at Chelsea's ass where the green fabric dug into the middle of her cheeks. Fuck, he wanted her. Would it really be so awful if they had sex? Just once? Maybe she would be down for that. Then it would be out of his system, and they could focus on being friends.

Ethan counted down before Chelsea and Natalie jumped off the edge, still holding hands. When they climbed back aboard, Chelsea towelled off, then put on her jean shorts and shirt.

The move made him sad, but he'd see if he could get them back off her later. He knew when a woman was interested, and Chelsea was definitely interested. They could probably find a way to make it work.

"I better get going," Chelsea said.

Adam's brain skidded to a halt. "Going?" he asked.

"Yeah," Chelsea said, reaching her hands up and gathering her hair onto her head. "I want to be home to have dinner with Ben."

Shit. He'd totally forgotten about Ben as soon as she dropped her shorts. Was that bad?

Probably.

Chelsea looked around at the water, a frown taking over her face. "How do I leave? Do I have to swim for it, or . . . ?"

Adam was still trying to get his brain to catch up to real time when Ethan elbowed him in the ribs.

"No," Adam said, giving his head a shake. "I'll borrow a Jet Ski. Just a sec."

He went to the next boat, borrowed a set of keys, went to the back of the boat where two Jet Skis were docked, and got on one, then drove it over to his boat. Chelsea said bye to everyone, then climbed on behind him, pressing her warm front onto his back.

He suppressed a moan. "Hold on," he said, and her hands came around his waist.

He hit the gas and drove her back to the marina. It was only a two-minute drive, but her hands on his stomach and her chest against his back were pure torture. When he pulled up, he got off, then held out a hand for her to take.

She stepped off the Jet Ski and into the shallow water on the ramp. "Thanks for inviting me, Adam. I had a really great time."

"I had fun, too."

They stared at each other for a moment. He wanted to kiss her. He wanted to hug her. Honestly, he would take any form of physical contact she'd give him at this point. He didn't want her to go. He wanted to look at her ass again. He hadn't had enough yet.

He had just opened his mouth to ask her when he'd see her again when a hand landed on his forearm.

"Hi, Adam," came a breathy voice.

He wrenched his eyes off of Chelsea's and came eye to eye with a girl he'd slept with a few months ago. He couldn't remember much about her except she had vocal fry and her name ended with *ah.*

"Hey," he said, trying to sound dismissive and hoping she'd take the hint.

She didn't.

Her eyes took on an overly dramatic, worried look. "You're not leaving already, are you?"

"Uh, no," he said, wondering how he could get rid of her.

"Good," she said, running her hand up and down his arm. "I was hoping we could catch up."

Adam moved his arm out of reach. "I'm actually kinda busy right now."

She slid her gaze to Chelsea for a split second, then back to him. "Okay," she said. "Come find me later. I'm on the huge white swan."

She turned and walked away, but when he turned back to Chelsea, she'd already taken off toward the parking lot.

"Wait," he said, trying to follow.

She didn't stop.

"Chelsea!"

She turned around but kept walking backwards. "I gotta go. I'll see you around," she said, then turned again and picked up speed toward her car, leaving him standing in the ankle-deep water, wondering why he'd ever thought it was a good idea to make the festival on a weeknight in September.

THIRTEEN

"I'm okay!"

Chelsea winced as Ben hit the ground, and his bike landed on top of him. He was so used to falling at this point that he was reassuring her he was okay while still in the air. Chelsea jogged to him and pulled the bike off him. She started dusting off the dry sand, but he was already taking the bike from her and mounting it again.

"He's okay?" Jae asked, coming up and passing a coffee to Chelsea.

Chelsea took a big swig of coffee. "Yeah. His determination is admirable."

They watched as he hobbled on and off the bike down the beach as the sun got a little higher in the sky. It was an enormous hazy ball hanging low over the lake, still shaking off the pinks and purples of sunrise.

"This beach is so beautiful," Jae said. "It must be even better from a boat."

Chelsea smiled, remembering the afternoon she'd spent at Float Fest. "Next year, you'll have to come, too. We'll get a babysitter for Ben. Or you can go on your own."

Jae cocked a brow. "Not a chance I'm going without you. I'm pretty sure Natalie will drown me."

Chelsea burst into laughter. "She's not a murderer."

"She hates me."

"She doesn't. She's just . . . standoffish until you get to know her. And she's protective. Like Charlize Theron's character in *Mad Max: Fury Road.*"

Jae sipped her coffee, unconvinced. "I'd roll the dice with her if it meant being on a boat with those guys. God, those videos you took," she said, adding a low whistle. "The things I would let them do to me . . ."

"Them?"

"Yup. All of them. All at once."

Chelsea nearly snorted out the sip of coffee she'd taken. "If you're including Ethan in that, then you probably *should* worry about Natalie."

The mental image of the guys on the boat came back to her mind, but she could hardly see anyone but Adam. He stood out from the crowd, at least for her. But she knew she wasn't the only woman who felt that way. The stunning brunette who'd thrown herself at him was obviously suffering from the same affliction.

If it were just his looks that she liked, she'd get over it. But she was starting to get to know him and realizing he was so much more under the surface. He was kind. And smart. And caring.

The type of guy who would make a good partner.

And a good dad.

But he had no interest in being anyone's partner or having kids. He was only interested in being her friend and casually sleeping with stunning brunettes.

Chelsea let out a sigh she hoped would go unnoticed and searched down the beach for Ben. He was headed back toward them on his bike, with his feet pushing him along like Fred Flintstone.

"Holy fucking fuckballs," Jae said, elbowing Chelsea in the ribs.

She shot Jae an annoyed look before her eyes landed on a dripping wet god emerging from the surf, and she schooled her features to neutral.

Jae's panting was audible. "Look at this fucking dude," she said, panting. "I'm going in."

She dramatically stuck her leg out toward him in a big step before Chelsea grabbed her by the shirtsleeve and held her in place.

"That's Adam."

"What?!" she yelled.

Chelsea half expected her head to spin like Regan in *The Exorcist*.

"*That* is Adam?"

Chelsea hummed. "Didn't you look at his face in the video?"

Jae shot Chelsea an incredulous look as if to say "Of course not!"

"That video did *not* do him justice. My panties are wetter than that lake," Jae said before snapping her mouth shut as Adam came closer.

He reached down to adjust the bottoms of his swim trunks that were clinging to his thighs, then combed a hand through his hair, pushing it off his face and making his pecs stretch and his abs tighten.

They both whimpered.

"Hey," he said with a perfect white smile.

Chelsea tried desperately to play it cool. "Hey," she said.

His smile brightened before he turned to her friend. "You must be Jae. I'm Adam."

"Uh-huh," Jae said, mouth slack.

"It's really nice to meet you."

"Yeah," Jae said.

Chelsea glanced in Jae's direction and rolled her eyes at the dreamy look on her face as she mooned over Adam.

"So . . ." Chelsea said, hoping to move on from her friend drooling all over her . . . other friend, "this is why you beat me at minute-to-win-it, even though I bunted." She waved a hand at his soaked body.

Adam's eyes narrowed. "So you admit you bunted?"

Chelsea shrugged as a smile took over her face.

Adam laughed and shook his head. "Most mornings I run that way," he said, jerking a thumb down the beach and making his biceps bunch up. "Then I swim back."

"I see. So you live . . ." Chelsea trailed off, looking around.

"Just there," Adam said, pointing to a house behind her.

Chelsea turned, eyes widening when she saw the navy-and-white house with a huge glassed-in deck. It was smaller than the neighbouring houses, but it looked like the set of a movie, right down to the gorgeous white deck furniture, giant potted palms, and the tall grasses emerging from the sand below and swaying peacefully in the breeze.

"Wow. Your mom definitely had a vision. It must've been amazing to grow up on a beach."

Adam nodded. "Yeah. It was. But we left after she died. My dad . . ." He trailed off, looking at the sand. "He couldn't stay."

Chelsea wanted to know more. Wanted to know everything. Wished there was something she could do to bring the easy smile back to his face. "When did you decide to move back?"

"Uh," Adam said, tipping his head to one side. After a long pause with Adam looking uncomfortable, or at least unsure of how to answer, Chelsea shook her head.

"You don't have to answer."

Adam shook his head. "I moved back once I fully recovered from my accident."

Chelsea's brows rose. She was just about to ask "What accident?" when she heard Jae gasp from behind her followed by a crashing noise.

"I'm okay!"

Chelsea spun around to find Ben sprawled back out on the sand, pushing the bike off himself. She jogged over, with Adam beside her. Jae was already there, having wandered away from them without her realizing.

She'd have to remember to ask Jae not to give them any privacy going forward.

"Hey, Ben," Adam said, "you hurt?"

"No."

"Benny, you need to let me hold the seat until you learn to balance."

Ben's eyebrows bunched up. "No."

Chelsea pinched her lips together. His determination was admirable. But his refusal of any help was driving her wild. She needed to find a balance between the two, but she had no idea how.

"You need a hockey stick," Adam said.

Chelsea, Jae, and Ben all looked at him with eyebrows quirked.

"Is he having a stroke?" Jae asked. "This is a bike," she said, raising her voice to help him out.

Adam laughed. "You put the end of the stick in the back, above the tire, then you hold the stick. That way, you can stop him from tipping, but you're not holding the bike up for him."

"Above the tire?" Chelsea asked, bending down to look at the bike. "Where?"

"Hold on, I have an old stick in my garage you can have."

Adam jogged up the beach and disappeared between the houses.

"God, his back . . ." Jae whispered, mouth gaping open again.

"Okay. You need to stop," Chelsea said, but she glanced at his muscles bunching, bigger around his shoulders, then narrowing in a V shape toward his waist.

"And those shoulders . . ."

Chelsea shook the thoughts from her mind. "Seriously, Jae," she said in an annoyed tone, even though she'd been thinking the same thing.

"He seems so nice, too. Doesn't he?" she asked, voice all soft.

"Well, he *is* nice. I think he just really loves helping people. He's planning Ethan and Natalie's wedding."

"Aww," Jae said, her eyes going all misty.

Chelsea rolled her eyes. "Get a grip."

Adam came jogging back a minute later, wooden hockey stick in hand. "Like this," he said, pushing the stick through the metal bars on Ben's bike, then wiggling it to make sure it was in place. "Hop on, Ben," he said.

Ben climbed on and started to pedal, with Adam holding the stick and the rest of them following behind him.

"See, when he falls, you just hold him up. When he gets better, just take out the stick. Done."

Chelsea stared on, watching Adam walking behind Ben. A flood of emotion and guilt hit her. She wished Ben had a dad in his life. Wished Jasper weren't such a dickwad. Wondered whether she should have forgiven him so that Ben could have a dad. Wondered whether she should try to find a man that would fit into their lives.

Wondered whether Adam could ever be that man.

"Do I need to tell *you* to get a grip?" Jae asked.

Chelsea blinked, shaking the thoughts out of her head. She and Ben didn't need Jasper, or Adam, or anyone else. But maybe it would be nice to have someone to do life with. Someone who wanted to build a family with her.

Or maybe she just needed to get laid. She could always hit on that hot dad at the school Monday morning.

Adam passed the stick to Jae and stood next to Chelsea, watching in silence for a moment before breaking it.

"I was going to call you today."

Chelsea's brain stopped working.

"Oh?" Chelsea said, trying hard not to show any kind of reaction.

"Yeah," he said. "I was going to ask for your help with Ethan's wedding, now that Float Fest is over. I don't know what kinds of flowers or colours or what kind of cake Natalie likes."

Chelsea couldn't help but roll her eyes. "Why didn't you just let them elope?"

Adam feigned offence, pretending to clutch a set of pearls. "How could you say that? Getting married is a big deal. And big deals need to be celebrated."

"Eloping is still celebratory."

Adam shook his head, the mood shifting slightly. "Life's too short to let happy times slip by. You gotta stop and soak them in."

Chelsea glanced back at his house, then up at his green eyes staring a hole through hers. The mystery of Adam was clicking into place.

He lost his mother young, avoids the media spotlight, and just mentioned something about an accident.

"Why are you looking at me like that?"

Chelsea smiled at his playful green eyes. "I'm trying to figure you out."

He laughed and shook his head. "Good luck with that."

She wanted to know more, but he swiftly moved the conversation along.

"Do you have time to talk about the wedding right now?" he asked, nodding his head toward his house. "I don't think it will take too long."

Chelsea's eyebrows rose. "You don't think it will take long? To plan a wedding?"

Adam shook his head with a cocky smile that made Chelsea laugh. She glanced over his shoulder at his house and tried to imagine what it was like inside. Maybe with a look at his personal space, she could connect more dots.

She looked over her shoulder at Jae and Ben, then back at him.

"Okay," she finally said. "Just let me tell Jae."

She turned to walk toward Jae and Ben, trying to hide her giddiness, when Adam's voice grabbed her.

"I'm just gonna grab a quick shower first," he said. "Let yourself in through the patio doors and help yourself to whatever you want from the fridge."

Before she could say a word, he turned and jogged off toward his house, leaving her on the beach feeling incredibly uneasy about letting herself into his home, but at the same time, unbelievably excited.

• • • • ● • ● • • • •

Chelsea crept up the wood stairs leading to Adam's house and crossed the deck. When she got to the door, she reached her hand up and knocked, feeling weird about walking into his house alone as if she owned the place. When he didn't come, she reached for the handle and reluctantly let herself inside.

"Hello?" she called, as she closed the door behind her.

No answer.

She took a few steps and listened, making out the sound of the shower running from somewhere deep in the house. She toed off her sandals, then stood awkwardly by the door, looking around.

The house was open and bright, with mostly white walls and hardwood floors. A massive white kitchen sat to her right, looking picture perfect, and she wondered whether he ever cooked himself meals. In front of her was a dining room table and chairs that looked as if no one ever sat at it, and to the left was a sectional sofa in front of an enormous TV.

Other than a pair of sneakers by the door and a tea towel on the counter, his house showed zero signs of life. It was the exact opposite of her house, which was brimming with kid stuff.

She scanned the room, her eyes falling on a sideboard table with a few picture frames. She listened for the water, which was still running, before tiptoeing over and bending down close.

There were three pictures in total. The first was one of those souvenir shots taken on a roller coaster at Canada's Wonderland with Ethan and Max. They were teenagers when the photo was taken, all so young looking and wearing matching expressions of terrified glee. The second photo was of him and his dad in hockey skates standing next to each other on a skating trail in a stunning snowy forest.

But the third photo really caught her attention.

She lifted it up, wishing it was a phone so she could scroll in to get a closer look. It was Adam as a small child, probably around Ben's age, standing in the messy kitchen with an apron and a toothless smile, holding a plate of awful-looking cookies. Behind him stood his mom, hugging him and smiling into the camera with a face that looked identical to his.

She'd pulled it closer and closed one eye, trying to get a better look, when the water suddenly stopped. She placed the picture frame down exactly as it had been and tried to look casual; although, it was impossible as she imagined what he would look like at that very moment stepping naked out of the shower and reaching for a towel.

Shaking her head, she walked over to the fridge, paused for a moment, then shrugged and opened the door. Inside the fridge was much like the rest of the house. Empty. There were condiments, drinks, beer, and some apples and carrots. She grabbed a can of pop and closed the door, then stood awkwardly in the kitchen, waiting for him to come out and hoping he'd be fully clothed.

She didn't have to wait long. A few seconds later, he walked into the kitchen wearing gym shorts and a T-shirt, his hair still wet and his skin flushed.

It must have been a hot shower.

"Hey," he said with a smile as he opened the fridge and pulled out his own drink. "Thanks for coming and helping me out."

Chelsea nodded. "Well, I am technically maid of honour. It's the least I can do."

He smiled and opened a drawer, pulling out a pad of paper and a pen and walking to the dining table. "Is here good, or would you rather sit on the deck?"

Chelsea looked out the three big French doors that led to the sunny deck. "Let's sit outside."

Adam nodded and led her to the doors, opening one set and following her out. She sat on a big, cushioned swivel chair and set her drink on the table in front of her. Adam followed suit, sitting in the chair next to her.

"Okay," he said, twirling his chair toward her and flipping the pad open. "What do we need for a wedding?"

Chelsea laughed. "I think you're in over your head."

Adam shook it off. "No, I've been in over my head before. This I can do. Let's start with what we know. Does she have a dress?"

Chelsea nodded. "Yes. She texted me a photo the day she bought it. And she ordered a dress for me, too. It's pale blue. I'm going to have a fitting next week."

Adam scribbled down the information. "Usually, people in weddings match, right? So I should wear pale blue?"

"Yeah."

"Okay, anything else? Music, food, cake, photographer?"

Chelsea's mind fixed on photographer, and she thought it would be amazing if she could make a wedding video for them. Maybe that could be their gift, since funds were too tight for much else. She'd love to make it a surprise, but how would she film it? Maybe she could ask Ethan's mom or sister to record it or use a photo montage set to audio. She knew she could get great audio from a set of tiny microphones that Jae had. If she weaved them into the bouquets, she could record them saying "I do" without them knowing.

Brilliant.

"What are you thinking?"

Adam's voice broke her thoughts.

"I was thinking about flowers," she said.

"Okay, which flowers should we go with?"

"Oh," she said, racking her brain, wondering whether Natalie had ever mentioned what types of flowers she liked and coming up blank. "I don't think she's ever said anything about flowers before."

"Well, what kinds of flowers do you like?"

Chelsea met his eye and stared for a moment. She'd never been given flowers before, but she wasn't about to admit that.

"Umm . . ." she said, breaking eye contact. "Well . . . my grandma, Elizabeth, had huge gardens at the manor when I was a kid, and my favourite flower was a peach-coloured rose that grew on a trellis and smelled like honey. She used to pick a few when I was coming and put them in a little vase on the coffee table."

When she glanced back up at him, he was staring at her, then quickly blinked away.

"Peach roses it is," he said, writing it down.

Chelsea shook her head. "I don't know if she likes those."

Adam shrugged. "Well, she hasn't given us much to go on. Besides, roses are much better than going with *my* favourite flowers."

"What are your favourite flowers?"

Adam smiled. "Dandelions. I used to pick them for my mom."

Chelsea couldn't help but smile. "That's very sweet."

"I don't get why everyone hates them so much. If it weren't for dandelions, I would never have been able to give my mom flowers."

Chelsea stared at Adam, her eyes going misty.

"Hey," he said, patting her knee. "It's okay. I'm sure Natalie would rather have roses than dandelions."

Chelsea blinked, trying to clear the emotion away.

Focus on the wedding.

"I can order the flowers and pick them up. There's a florist in Mapleton, right?"

"Yeah, just let me know when you order them, and I'll stop by and pay."

"Thanks," she said, wishing she could insist on paying but knowing that was impossible. She looked over at him, diligently scribbling down notes to himself about the flowers, and couldn't help her feelings from deepening.

How many guys would take on planning their friends' wedding?

None that she'd met, that's for sure.

She shook her head again, reminding herself that Adam was not, and never would be, someone she could be with. He was just a friend.

A very attractive friend with a good heart.

Focus on the wedding!

"Do you think the peach flowers will look okay with the blue dress?"

Adam turned his attention to her, then his gaze drifted from her head down to her feet and back up, finally settling on her eyes. "Honestly, I don't think there's anything that would look bad on you."

Her eyes widened as her heart stopped and her brain went dead.

Why did he say things like that to her? It was like at Float Fest when he made that bed comment, but somehow, this was worse.

More emotional.

More intimate.

She blinked away from his stare, and the first thing her eyes landed on was Ben on his bike in the distance. That's what she needed, a reminder that he was no good for her.

No good at all.

She reached toward the table, hoping to distract herself by taking a drink, when a drop of rain hit her on the nose.

Then another.

She looked up at the darkening sky that had been perfectly blue a moment before.

"Is that a storm?"

Adam cleared his throat.

"Yeah. Storms come on fast at the lake. They pass quickly, too, though." He tipped his head up at the sky before turning all of his attention back on her.

"Do you want to call Ben and Jae in? We can wait it out."

Oh, no.

There wasn't a chance in hell she was going back into his house filled with personal things that only endeared her toward him more.

She needed distance. And a lot of it.

"Thanks, but we should probably get going."

Adam nodded. "Okay, well, thanks for the help and for taking on the flowers."

"No problem," she said as she stood. "Thanks for the hockey stick. That was brilliant."

He nodded, holding her eyes with his for a long moment before asking, "Is it okay if I stop by your place this week after work? To talk about the wedding?"

She wanted to say no. She wanted to say yes. In the end, she just nodded wordlessly.

Adam's face transformed into a heart-stopping smile that tugged at the scar above his upper lip. "Great. I'll see you soon, then."

Chelsea broke eye contact by turning away from him and setting out across the deck. The sky was dark grey now, with ominous clouds rolling in over the lake. She walked down the steps toward Jae and Ben, putting her hand up in a little wave. "See ya," she said.

He stood still, watching her. "Bye, Chelsea."

She held her smile until she turned, then it dropped.

God, she liked him. A lot. She wanted to spend more time alone together, getting to know everything about him.

But that was normal for a friend, right?

Maybe not.

Maybe she'd let her feelings for Adam cross the friendship line. But was that really the worst thing in the world?

Chelsea reached Ben, and he hobbled over and hugged his arms around her waist. She pulled him in close and hung her head.

Yeah.

It was.

FOURTEEN

Adam squinted as a sudden burst of sunlight shot through his back doors and filled his house with warmth. He glanced over his laptop screen from the dining table and scowled out at the deck and the now clear blue, sunny sky.

Fucking storm.

As soon as he'd come out of the water and seen Chelsea on the beach, his entire morning had started looking up. He'd seen it all unfold in his mind; Jae and Ben would bike on the beach while he and Chelsea hung out. Maybe they'd go for a swim, then he'd offer to order in lunch on the deck.

But then that storm started rolling in like hellfire, and she ran off at the first raindrop.

Why? He didn't know.

Probably because he ogled her every chance he got.

He huffed out an annoyed breath and slapped his laptop closed. He'd been answering emails since she left, but it wasn't distracting enough. He just kept circling back to Chelsea, wondering how he could fix the mess he'd got himself into.

He really enjoyed hanging out with her as a friend. Truly, he did. And he was determined to keep her as a friend. But he'd asked her out before, and made that bed comment at Float Fest, and probably stared into her eyes one too many times, so there was some work to be done.

No problem, though. He could still turn this around.

He drained his coffee, pulled out a notepad, then shifted his attention back to Ethan and Natalie's wedding, trying to ignore the image he'd conjured of her in a pale-blue dress with peach roses. That was not helpful at all.

He shook his head and grabbed his phone, dialing his Uncle David. He was always good for a diversion. Plus, he needed to find out whether anyone would be at the cottage in two weeks.

As usual, he answered on the first ring. "Adam!"

"Uncle David! How's it going?"

"Same as always. How was Float Fest?"

A green bathing suit and tons of soft skin flashed in his mind, and he worked to clear it. "It was good. Fun."

His uncle's tone changed. "I'm sorry I missed it."

"It's okay. There's always next year. And I was considering the possibility of changing it to the summer."

"Really? I never thought I'd hear you say those words."

Adam rolled his eyes. "Well, it's getting bigger every year. It isn't just me and my friends anymore. It'd probably be good for the town to have it on a weekend. More tourist money coming in."

Adam gave a satisfied nod at his own words. They all sounded completely rational.

"Anyway, I was calling because I need a favour."

"Anything."

Adam smiled. "I was wondering if I can use the cottage."

His uncle's pause was heavy. "You don't have to ask permission to use the family cottage, Adam. It's *your* cottage, too."

"Well, I'm hoping to go in two weeks. Actually, I was going to invite a group up for a wedding. Probably about ten to twenty people."

Silence fell between them. He thought the line had disconnected. He pulled the phone down and looked at the display, then put it back to his face.

"Hello? You there?"

"You're having a wedding?" his uncle asked.

"Yeah. Ethan talked this beautiful girl into marrying him. He proposed last week. They were going to elope, but I—"

"Ethan?" his uncle asked, cutting him off.

"Yeah."

"So *you're* not getting married."

Adam laughed. "Of course not."

"Why do you say it like that?"

"I'm never going to get married, Uncle David. I've told you this before."

"Yeah, but I thought you were just . . . I don't know, too young to be thinking about it. You're not that young anymore, Adam. Your friends are getting married. Soon they'll have kids. You always wanted to get married and be a dad."

"No," Adam said with exaggerated patience. "I always wanted to be *like my* dad."

"That's not true. Before your accident, you were ready to get married to that Surrel girl."

Adam squeezed his eyes shut tight.

"Well, things obviously changed. I don't want that anymore. It doesn't matter how old I manage to get."

"How old you *manage* to get? Adam, I know you think—"

"Look," Adam said, knowing a lecture was coming. "Forget about me getting married. It's not going to happen. I'm going to invite everyone to the Muskoka cottage for *Ethan's* wedding in two weeks. Do you know if anyone else will be there?"

Uncle David audibly sucked in a breath and blew it out before moving on. "Probably not this time of year. But there's plenty of room either way. I'll email you the name of a caterer and a band that I used for a party up there this summer. They were excellent."

"That's perfect. Thanks."

"No problem. Anything else you need, just let me know."

"I will. I better get going."

"When will I see you, Adam? It's been a while," he said in his worried voice.

Adam softened. "I'm not sure. I've been really busy with dad away and Max's pub. I'll see if there's a time I can come over."

"Anytime. I'll make room in my schedule for you."

Despite being mildly annoyed, Adam knew his uncle loved him and worried about him, so he softened his voice. "Sure thing. Talk soon."

He hung up and set the phone down on the counter, staring at it for a long while. It would be weird, now that his friends were getting married. They would have kids, too. He shook off the unease that filled him whenever he thought about it. There was nothing he could do. He'd just have to make the best of a bad situation.

A knock on the door sounded through his house, and he'd never been more grateful for a distraction. He answered the door to find Max standing on his porch.

"Hey, can I borrow your truck?"

"Sure," he said, swinging the door open wider for Max to step in. "Do you need my help with something or just the truck?"

"My sister needs her stuff moved."

Adam stopped and looked at Max. He was grumpier than usual. In fact, he looked pissed right off. "Is it the boyfriend?"

Max pulled a murderous face. "Yes."

"I'm coming with you. You look like you're going to land yourself in jail."

Max's hands fisted. "I'd like to grab that little prick by his permed mullet and bash his fucking face in."

"Then I'm *definitely* coming with you. Where is she?"

"I picked her up in the middle of the night and brought her to my place. I just need to get her stuff out of his apartment."

Adam nodded. "Just give me a minute."

Max followed him inside. "You missed a good party last night. Why did you cancel on us?"

Adam's step faltered. "I just wasn't up for it."

"You weren't up for dinner and drinks with pretty girls from out of town?"

Adam bent into the closet and grabbed a pair of running shoes, then started pulling them on, wishing he were a better liar. "That's right," he said. "I've been busy. Tired."

"What did you do this morning?"

Adam looked up at Max. "Why all the questions?"

Max cocked a brow. "You're so into Chelsea you can't even see straight. You can't lie to me."

Adam stared Max in the eye. "She's my friend. She's cool and fun. I really like her as a friend."

Max nodded. "I know. That wasn't a lie. She *is* your friend. But you want more."

Adam tied his laces. "No. I don't."

"Lie."

Adam stood, grabbed his keys off the console table. "I just need time to push her further into the friend zone."

"Have you considered—"

"Fucking her out of my system? Yes."

Max laughed. "That's not what I was going to say. Although, she is beautiful. And she would probably be an amazing lay . . ."

Adam felt his body go still. He could see an alternate universe where Max hit on her at the baseball diamonds instead of him. Could see how she'd be into him like most other women were. Could see how a relationship with Max would be far better for her and Ben.

It made him a little sad, but mostly pissed off. Now he was ready to bash *Max's* face in. "Don't."

"Don't what?"

"Don't . . . anything."

Max cocked a brow. "I would never. I just wanted to see how jealous you'd get."

Adam shook it off. He *was* jealous, and he hated it. But there it was, all the same.

"Let's go," he said, walking past Max to the truck.

Max followed but didn't let it go. "Have you considered telling her why you feel the way you do about kids? Maybe she'd be okay with it."

Adam shook his head as he started the truck. "It's not how she would feel about it. I can't do that to her. Or to Ben. We've been through this."

Max nodded and looked out the window. "Sorry, man," he said.

Adam swallowed. "It is what it is," he said, then pulled out of the driveway.

FIFTEEN

Chelsea was sitting on a wicker loveseat on her huge front porch, with her computer in her lap and headphones covering one ear. They'd wrapped up filming a little early that day, and she had already finished her work that morning, so while waiting for Ben's bus to arrive, she caught up on editing the videos she'd taken of Ben biking and of Float Fest.

It took her no time at all to put together Ben's biking video from the GoPro footage she'd collected, and she thought it turned out pretty good. She kept Adam in it and beeped out all his swear words. But when she turned her attention to the Float Fest pictures and short videos she'd taken, she had a harder time. She paused certain frames to make Adam look directly at her with his easy, sunny smile.

She had just zoomed way, way too far in to the shot and leaned forward to the screen to count his abs when she heard a throat clearing.

She looked up and saw Adam's smiling face just on the other side of the porch.

"Hey, whatcha doin'?"

Chelsea had a mild panic attack, sat back, and started closing tabs. She looked over her shoulder, wondering whether he'd have been able to see his abs on her screen when he came around the corner of the house. It was hard to tell.

"Uh, I'm just editing some videos."

Adam stepped forward and leaned against the railing with a smirk. "What videos?"

He knew.

"Ben's biking video when he crashed into you. And Float Fest."

Adam laughed. "Can I see?"

She hesitated but didn't want to seem even more suspicious, so she casually said, "Sure," and patted the seat beside her.

"I'm pretty dirty," he said, climbing the stairs. "Is that okay?"

She looked him up and down. His worn jeans, dirty work boots, thin white tee.

Fuck yes.

There wasn't a single thing about him that wasn't okay.

"It's okay," she said. "It's just outdoor furniture."

Adam sat down beside her, taking up all the space, and then some. He was much closer than they'd been on his deck when they had armrests between them. His jeans pressed up against her bare thigh, warming her skin. She tried to ignore the sensation by slipping off her headphones and passing them to him. But when she saw how dirty his hands were, she twisted around and put them on his head herself.

Once the headphones were on, she made the mistake of looking down at his eyes. He was watching her. His smile was long gone, and his warm green eyes were moving all over her face. They finally settled on her eyes before he blinked.

"Uh," she said, breaking eye contact with a hard blink and turning back to her laptop. "I'm still working on the Float Fest one, but you can watch the biking one."

She twisted the laptop in her lap toward him as he leaned in closer to her, then she opened the video and hit Play.

The video was only a minute and a half, but it had turned out great. She had a brief interview with Ben at the beginning before he started, then GoPro footage of him falling repeatedly. She put it in slow motion just before Adam came into the frame and added the theme from *Jaws* before the crash.

Adam was smiling while watching, then burst into laughter when the foreboding music started. He was still laughing when it was done but started shaking his head.

"There's no way I swore that much," he said.

Chelsea laughed. "I guess you're not very self-aware, then."

"You added extra beeps," he said, gently elbowing her ribs.

Chelsea couldn't stop laughing. "Maybe a few. For effect."

His laughter settled into a handsome smile. "Can I see what you have so far with the Float Fest one?"

"Sure."

She closed the biking video, opened the Float Fest one, and clicked Play. It was only forty seconds long and ended on the guys standing on the edge of the boat, Adam looking back at her with a smile right after he'd said no.

"Can I have a copy when you're finished with it?" he asked.

Chelsea shrugged. "Sure. What's your email?" she asked, typing what he told her into her notes file.

"You said you and Jae made short films, too. Can I watch them?"

Chelsea's brows shot up. "Right now?"

Adam nodded.

She looked at her watch. Still twenty minutes before the bus would get there, and she had one film that was only ten minutes long she thought he'd like. "Okay, just one."

They sat together in silence, watching the first film Chelsea and Jae had made. It was a ridiculous comedy about a bird that fell in love with a rat, so she lived her life as a rat. They'd created the entire thing alone, and she could still remember spending hours each night after Ben went to sleep sewing the costumes and searching Google for woods and streets in Toronto to film it.

When the credits started rolling, Adam slipped the headphones off and passed them back to her.

He sat silent for a moment, as if in thought. "Are you the bird?" he asked, then looked over and held her stare.

Chelsea shook her head. "It's just a movie," she said, wondering whether it was only obvious to him because he knew her history with Jasper or whether she had just been so depressed when they created it that her emotions bled through the screen.

Adam shook his head. "Jasper's the rat."

Chelsea's eyebrows rose, and she cleared her throat. "Okay, that's enough of the psychoanalysis of my film."

She closed her laptop and tried to change the subject. "Should we finish talking about the wedding?"

Adam's eyes narrowed in at her. "Why aren't you dating anyone?"

Chelsea's mouth gaped open. "What?"

He shifted in his seat to face her. "When I asked you out, you said no, no matter how much I tried to convince you."

Chelsea rolled her eyes. "Adam, you asked me out, then ran off when you saw Ben. I'd never date anyone that didn't like my son."

Adam winced. "I mean, before that. And just for the record, I do like your son."

Chelsea shook her head. "I just don't . . ."

"Just don't what?" he asked after a few beats. "You must get hit on all the time," he said, dropping his gaze down and back up. "You're gorgeous. And funny. And kind. And you have this quirky fun . . . ness about you."

"Fun . . . ness?"

Adam nodded.

Chelsea tried desperately not to be flattered but was failing. So she went for a deflection. "Why don't you have a girlfriend, Adam? Why do you have this weird fear of children when you keep insisting that you like them?"

Adam sat back in his seat and crossed his arms. "You first."

Chelsea was about to open her mouth and tell him to go away. The only problem was that she was so curious about why he'd run away from her at the baseball diamonds that she was willing to be open with him in exchange for his story. Plus, he'd already figured her out from the bird rat film, so she didn't have all that much to lose.

"Fine," she said. "I don't date because it's too risky. I'm trying to build my career, and I can't afford another setback like last time. If I got pregnant again, it would be a disaster."

"But most men don't walk away from their girlfriends and babies, Chelsea."

Chelsea shrugged. "Too risky."

She could see the gears turning, knew exactly what he was going to ask before he probably even knew.

"So casual sex is off the table for you, then?"

"Yes."

A look of absolute horror came over his face. "Does that mean that Jasper was the last time you—"

"Enough of this," she said, cutting him off and holding her hands up as if she were warding off a demon. "Your turn."

It took Adam a few minutes to recover, but he finally cleared his throat and composed himself.

"I got in a bad car accident when I was twenty-two."

Chelsea stared on, waiting, hooked. Wondering whether that was all he was going to give her to go on. Finally, he started speaking again.

"I moved to Toronto after high school for university and started dating a girl whose family was connected to mine. We left a party one night. We'd all been drinking, but my friend insisted he was okay to drive. Obviously, he wasn't, because he smashed into the corner of a building. I was in the front passenger seat and hit it square on. Everyone else in the car was fine."

"What happened?"

"I was in pretty awful shape. They put me in a coma for three months. They didn't think I was going to live. I almost lost my right eye. But I made it through, started my recovery, moved back to Mapleton, and haven't left since."

"What about school?"

Adam shook his head. "They diagnosed me with a traumatic brain injury. I had to give up on school. I couldn't keep up with the courses."

"And your girlfriend?"

Adam took a moment before answering. "She broke up with me. It seemed for a while that I would never recover at all from the brain injury. It took me six months of speech therapy just to talk coherently again."

Chelsea gaped at him. A million thoughts raced through her head, but the first one was, *That fucking bitch!*

"Anyway, I don't blame her. She had to look out for herself. We were all so young, and she . . ."

"What?" Chelsea asked, on the literal edge of her seat.

"She wanted to get married and have kids. With me. And I . . ."

Another long pause.

"You what?" Chelsea asked, feeling like she was going to explode.

"I have a low life expectancy," he finally got out. "I'll be lucky if I make it to my forties. They said I'd have a stroke and die in the first few years after the accident. It's a miracle I've lived this long."

Chelsea stared at him in shock for a long moment. She started sentences in her head repeatedly, not able to come up with something to say.

Adam cleared his throat. "Anyway, that's why I steer clear of kids, and girlfriends, and wives. I'd just end up dying and leaving them all alone."

All alone.

Chelsea didn't know what to say. She knew what it was like to be left all alone. She hated watching Ben grow up without his dad.

Silence dropped between them like a curtain coming down on a stage until Adam cleared his throat.

"So, wedding."

She had still said nothing. Wondered whether she was no longer capable of speech.

Adam reached a hand up to her shoulder. "It's okay, Chelsea. It was a long time ago. I've come to terms with it."

Chelsea nodded, trying to come to terms with it herself.

"Chelsea?"

She was still trying to form a thought, trying to stop the tears that were pricking her eyes, when Jasper's voice broke through her thoughts. She blinked up to see him standing on the other side of the porch, looking at Adam with a murderous stare.

SIXTEEN

This fucking guy.

Adam stared at Jasper's face and wondered whether he'd get sued if he jumped over the railing and punched him in the nose. It might actually be worth it. He wanted desperately to break that motherfucker's nose. It annoyed the crap out of him he was sniffing around Chelsea again. The guy clearly had a thing for her still.

And it wasn't jealousy.

Not at all.

He just thought Chelsea was way, way, way too good for someone like Jasper. Adam had always been protective of his friends, and that included her.

"What are you doing here?" Jasper said, meeting his eyes with a scowl.

Adam stared at him, gave a smirk. "What do you think I'm doing here?"

Jasper bared his teeth.

He could almost hear Chelsea's eyeballs rolling. "What do you need, Jasper? I thought everyone had left for the day," she said.

Jasper looked at her face and dropped his scowl. "I had a meeting with the higher-ups. It was very important."

Adam snorted. He couldn't help it. This guy was just so desperate to look better than everyone else. He'd probably been on a phone call with his dog walker or something.

Jasper shot a glare at Adam before looking back at Chelsea. "I wanted to talk to you. In private."

Adam's hands fisted.

"Oh, I'm busy," Chelsea said, looking uncomfortable. "And Ben will be here any minute."

Run off, you scummy little rat. She isn't interested.

"I think you'll want to make time for this," he said with a gross smile.

Chelsea let out a sigh. "Fine. What is it?"

Jasper glanced at him, then back at her. "I have an extra ticket to the premiere of *Loop* at TIFF this weekend. I wanted to see if you'd like to come with me."

Adam smiled to himself. There was no way she was going to agree to go with him to the Toronto International Film Festival. He couldn't wait to hear her tell him to take a fucking hike.

He waited.

Waited.

Waited.

Finally, he turned to her and saw a look on her face that stopped his blood from circulating. She was looking at Jasper . . . wistfully.

"Are you serious?" she asked.

Jasper smiled. "Of course. Jeroen Peck gifted them to me."

Okay. One more name drop, and that was it.

"Uh," Chelsea said, seeming to weigh her choice.

He couldn't believe she hadn't already said no. Was she actually considering saying yes? There was no way she should go with him. It would probably be an event in the evening. They might stay overnight together.

In a hotel.

His head began to shake. He couldn't let that happen. What kind of friend would let their friend make such a terrible decision?

"She can't," he said before she could agree.

Chelsea and Jasper both swivelled their heads toward him, and he smiled.

"You speak for her now?" Jasper asked.

Chelsea snorted beside him, so he smiled wider.

"She can't go with you, because she's already coming to the premiere with me."

Chelsea frowned at him while a laugh came out of Jasper.

Then another laugh.

Finally, the little rat started cackling, head tipped back and arm across his stomach.

"You expect me to believe that you, *you*, have tickets to the hottest premiere at TIFF? The event of the year?"

Adam nodded, while Chelsea cringed.

"They don't even sell these tickets. It's invite only. Not that someone like you could afford it anyway," he said.

Adam's smile grew.

"Enough, Jasper," Chelsea said. "You're making an ass of yourself. I'm not going with you. Even if I wasn't busy, it would still be a no."

Yes!

Chelsea stood up and started walking across the porch toward the stairs. "Go home," she said.

He wasn't sure whether she was only talking to Jasper or whether she was addressing him, too.

Jasper huffed, then turned and walked off. Adam hopped up and jogged to catch up with Chelsea, who was now marching to the end of the driveway to meet the bus. It wasn't lost on him that Jasper wasn't even going to stay to see Ben.

That guy was such a fucking douche.

"Chelsea, wait!"

Chelsea slowed but kept walking. "What now?"

"What time should I pick you up? For the premiere. Do you know what time it starts?"

Chelsea came to an abrupt stop, turning toward him. "Wait, were you serious?"

Adam nodded. "Of course."

Her brows rose over her pretty eyes. "You can get tickets?"

Adam smirked. "I can get almost anything."

Now he felt like an overly cocky douche, but at least he had the clout to back it up.

"I thought you were just helping me get rid of Jasper."

Adam nodded. "I was. But you seem like you'd really like to go, and I offered, so I'd like to take you."

She stared at him for a while, seemingly unsure how to respond, and he threw up a silent prayer that she would say yes.

"Why?" she asked.

"I just want you to have what you want," he said, running a hand through this hair.

Her face softened into a surprised look that made him wonder whether anyone ever put her first. The thought caused a mixture of anger and sadness.

"I can get the tickets for you and Jae, if you'd rather," he said, hoping she'd say yes to something. Anything.

The bus pulled up, red lights flashing, pulling their attention to the road for a moment.

"Okay."

Adam snapped his eyes back to hers.

"Okay? Good," he said with a smile. "I'll get them and drop them off for you guys."

"No. I mean, okay, as in we can go together," she said.

Adam had to stop himself from jumping in the air. He couldn't stop his smile from growing, though. "Cool," he said.

Chelsea smiled, and he saw the dimples. She turned and jogged toward the bus, stopping just as Ben climbed down the stairs. He was wearing a backpack almost the same size as he was that bounced from side to side as he ran to Chelsea's open arms.

Adam waved to Ben, and when he waved back, he wrenched his eyes off the two of them, turned, and walked back to his truck, pulling his phone out along the way.

SEVENTEEN

Chelsea pulled up the zipper on the back of her lacy black dress and turned. She took in her reflection in the full-length mirror of her hotel bedroom, assessing herself from all angles, and wondered what was more unbelievable, that she was in the fanciest two-bedroom penthouse suite downtown Toronto offered, or that she was going to the most talked about movie premiere with Adam.

Was this real life?

She picked up the macaroni bracelet Ben had made for her to wear that night and fastened it to her wrist. It was too big and half-covered in red fingerpaint, but it made her feel more like herself in the glamorous dress Jae had given her to wear.

She wasn't really a glamorous type, but she felt a million times better knowing she was doing this with Adam. She had told Jae about Adam's offer for the two of them to go instead of him, but Jae had insisted Chelsea go with him and wouldn't take no for an answer. She even encouraged Chelsea to "jump Adam's no-risk bone."

She shook away her smile and slipped into her—Jae's—shoes, grabbed her bag and took a deep breath, then walked out into the living room to meet Adam.

He was standing in the middle of the room, beer in one hand, remote in the other, watching sports highlights on TV. And he was wearing a suit.

He turned when she walked in and stared at her in his usual way. Which was fine because it gave her more time to stare at him.

His suit was navy and impeccably fit, with a white shirt and black tie. He'd gone to the barber while she was in her bedroom of the suite getting ready, and his hair was cut short in the back, longer up top, and perfectly styled, as if he'd spent the day on a photo shoot.

His neck looked delicious.

He cleared his throat. "You look beautiful, Chelsea."

Friend.

He's only a friend.

Don't think about his bone.

Or how good jumping it would be.

"Thanks," she said, trying for a casual tone. "You too."

He set down the beer and turned off the TV. "The limo is waiting downstairs. We should get going."

Chelsea nodded and headed for the door. They rode the elevator down in silence, took the three-minute ride to the premiere in silence, and stepped out of the limo onto the red carpet.

And then the world exploded.

The second Adam's foot hit the carpet, a hundred people started shouting his name, practically climbing over each other to get his attention. Chelsea was not prepared for him to garner such a huge reaction. She almost wanted to laugh. She couldn't think about Adam in any way other than the cocky player construction guy who liked country music and drinking beer out of the bed of his truck.

He took her hand tightly in his grip and started toward the door, sparing only a slight nod of his head at his adoring fans. No wave. No smile.

He was acting so guarded, so different from himself. He was *never* without a smile and a wave. He loved chatting up people in Mapleton. She'd expected him to hop out of the limo, yell "Hi!" and start dancing toward the theatre doors.

Instead, he dropped his gaze to the floor in front of him and moved briskly, never breaking his stride.

It wasn't until they'd stepped into the theatre and the doors had closed behind them, shutting out the world, that his whole body relaxed.

"You okay?" Chelsea asked.

"Yeah," he said, taking a deep breath but keeping hold of her hand. "I was hoping they wouldn't recognize me."

Chelsea looked back out the door at the crowd, cameras aggressively trying to photograph him through the glass.

"I'm sorry. I didn't realize this was going to be hard for you. You're so . . . outgoing. I thought you'd bask in this sort of thing."

Adam shook his head. "When I was younger, I did. That was part of the problem." He raised his hand to run through his hair, then made a face when he remembered it was styled. "Haven't you googled me?"

Chelsea smiled and shook her head. "No. Honestly, I forget that you're a somebody. I just think of you as this over-the-top small-town guy with lots of friends who lives to have fun."

"That *is* who I am. Out there is just my name. And my past." He glanced out the window, a frown marring his brow. "The press shadowed me relentlessly after my accident, they got footage of me in the hospital, used telephoto lenses to show my injuries and scars, they even followed my ex around and gossiped about our breakup. It was brutal."

Chelsea sighed. She wanted to hug him but settled for squeezing his hand a little tighter in hers.

"Anyway," he said, shaking his head to clear the bad memories. He smiled down at her before reaching his free hand up and scratching his stomach through his custom-made designer suit. "Do you think they've got popcorn at these things?"

Chelsea laughed as he melted back into the man she'd come to know, and the tension between her shoulder blades eased. "Let's find out."

* * * * * * * * * * *

Chelsea was stunned when the credits started rolling and Adam leaned in and told her he'd got them on the list for the most exclusive after-party of the festival. Possibly even more stunned that he'd be willing to go. She loved parties and thought it would be amazing to be in a room full of that many industry people.

He'd told her he was happy to go with her as long as she didn't walk away and leave him alone with them, and she emphatically agreed.

She didn't really want to be there without him, anyway.

They arrived at the party by limo, and although there were still cameras vying for Adam's attention, it was far fewer, and they weren't allowed in the room.

The moment she stepped into the loft, she was floored. The room was entirely marble, from floor to ceiling, with purple lighting up the walls. There was a DJ set up in the corner and servers with platters milling about the room, offering the rich and famous tiny little bites of food.

Chelsea walked through the room with wide eyes, watching big name producers and directors make their way to Adam and introduce themselves to him. He'd politely say hello, then immediately introduce her, and she would do everything she could not to embarrass herself as she'd done with Vincent when she'd first met him.

They made their way around, all the while tightly gripping each other's hands, until Adam leaned in close to her ear and whispered, making her skin tingle all over.

"There's someone I want you to meet," he said, warm breath fluttering over the shell of her ear and trickling down her neck.

She hadn't recovered from the sensation yet, but he was already walking, gently tugging her along.

They weaved through the crowd all the way to the other side of the room before Adam finally stopped and Chelsea came around him to see a man's back.

When Adam tapped the man's shoulder and he turned around, Chelsea's jaw dropped.

She was looking at Adam.

Only . . . old.

"Adam?" the man said, first in shock, then repeated it so loud it drew the attention of the crowd.

Old Adam let out a disbelieving laugh, pulling Adam into a bear hug and holding it for at least thirty seconds before letting go. "What are you doing here?"

Adam laughed and sounded more like himself than he had since the car ride from Mapleton. Chelsea found her shoulders relaxing, breath coming easier.

"I'd like you to meet Chelsea Davenport," he said, stepping aside and gesturing toward her. "We went to the premiere of *Loop*. Chelsea, this is my Uncle David."

Uncle David turned to her, giving her all of his attention. The shock from seeing Adam slowly receded from his handsome face, and he smiled, staring into her eyes.

"Chelsea," he said, taking her hand between both of his and squeezing gently. "It's very nice to meet you."

The charm oozing from the man had her stunned. "Hi," she said, unable to break eye contact. She was entranced. Is this what Adam would look like when he was older?

If he was older.

A sadness washed over her, and she glanced away.

Uncle David let go of her hand, but his fingers stopped, and he looked down at her macaroni bracelet. "Ahh," he said. "Adam's been doing arts and crafts again, I see."

Chelsea looked down as Uncle David slid her bracelet up her wrist. She laughed and smiled back up at him. "He tried his best. Measuring is hard."

Adam slid a look over at Chelsea as his uncle laughed. "I knew you two would get along," he said.

Chelsea smiled back at David. "My son made this for me."

David's jaw dropped. He cast a quick glance at Adam. "You have a son?"

Chelsea nodded. "His name's Ben. He's going to be five in a few weeks."

"I see," David said, locking eyes with Adam and raising his brows a bit as if asking a question.

"We're just—"

"Sorry," a glamorous woman in a silver jumpsuit drowned Adam's voice out. "Forgive me for interrupting," she said, only looking at David. "I *must* introduce you to someone, David. This is Jasper Fenton."

From behind the woman came Jasper, wearing a suit just as impeccable as Adam's and the rest of the men in attendance.

"Jasper," David said politely, shaking his hand. "A pleasure."

"Likewise," Jasper said. He took a breath to continue but glanced to the side and caught Chelsea's eye, then Adam's, and his jaw hit the floor. "Chelsea?"

David beamed. "You two know each other?"

Jasper nodded in silence, then looked over at Adam with his mouth gaping open like a dead fish. "You . . . How . . . ?"

An awkward silence stretched on for an eternity.

"Do you also know my nephew, Adam?"

Jasper's eyes went wide. You could see the blood drain from his face as he realized he'd been calling one of the richest men in Canada a hillbilly and treating him like crap.

"We've met," Adam said in an icy voice.

Chelsea's eyes darted to Adam. She'd never heard that tone come from him before. David clearly picked up on it, too, because he stood a little taller.

His face went a little more serious, and he took a step toward his nephew.

If Jasper were anyone else, Chelsea would have felt bad for him. There was a lot of hostility coming from Adam and his uncle. But she didn't feel bad. She felt as if the universe, which had been tipped entirely in his favour, was righting itself.

"Maybe you should excuse us," David said.

Jasper didn't utter another word. Just turned and walked off.

David turned to Adam. "Why don't you like him?"

"He's a selfish little rat," Adam said. "Don't trust him."

David nodded, wheels turning in his eyes. He looked at Chelsea. "You own Monroe Manor, don't you?"

"Yes," Chelsea said.

"I've done some business with Victor Monroe. And I knew Elizabeth. I'm sorry for your loss."

"Thank you."

"And you're working with Vincent Shadd?"

Chelsea smiled. "Yes."

"I wish I'd known you two were coming," David said. "I'd like to spend more time with you, but I'm booked all day tomorrow."

"It was a last-minute thing," Adam said.

Another person came to speak with David, then another. Finally, David said he had dinner reservations with someone and had to go. He hugged them both, told Chelsea again how pleased he was to meet her, and left.

Chelsea looked around the room, then at Adam. "Do you want to go?"

"I'd love to, but Drake just walked in."

Chelsea's brows rose. "Drake? Like *the* Drake?"

Adam rolled his eyes. "How many Drakes do you know?"

Chelsea smiled at him. He was so impossible not to like. She really didn't care about Drake. She just wanted to get away from all the people and be in the hotel room so she could hang out one-on-one with Adam. Maybe test the waters and see how he would feel about a one-time bone-jumping. How bad would that really be? And, as Jae pointed out, zero consequences. If she was going to scratch her new-found itch with someone, wouldn't it make sense to do it with a guy she really liked who couldn't possibly get her pregnant?

She smiled, her mind made up. "Maybe we can say hi on the way out."

Adam returned her smile. "It would be rude to just walk past, wouldn't it?"

Chelsea laughed and nodded.

They walked together toward Drake, still holding hands, and Chelsea smiled to herself as she realized they hadn't let go of each other the entire night.

EIGHTEEN

Adam stretched his neck from side to side to relieve the tension in his jaw from laughing for the last hour straight. He finished his beer and put his feet up on the coffee table. They'd both changed into comfortable clothes after returning from the party and had ordered almost everything off the room service menu. The food was delicious, and the minibar was running out.

Chelsea sat forward, reached down, and pulled off the oversized hoodie she was wearing. She had a thin crop top underneath, and definitely no bra. He thought he might die. She stretched out beside him, put her feet out on the coffee table next to his, and dropped her head onto his shoulder.

It was a friendly move. Something that only friends would do. He couldn't even count the number of times Max had dropped his head on his shoulder while they were watching a Leafs game.

Actually, he could.

It was zero.

"I can't believe you actually did that," she said. "It must have been fun growing up with you."

She snuggled her head in more, twisting and cuddling into the side of his body. But she couldn't really cuddle in properly, because he kept his arm stiffly against his side, blocking her.

He felt like a robot.

He hadn't been this awkward since the *first* time he'd been on a couch with a girl.

Maybe this was just how Chelsea was with her friends, more touchy-feely. Some friends were like that, right? Or maybe that's just how guy-girl friendships worked?

He pulled his stiff arm out from under her, then draped it along her shoulder and down her arm as she snuggled into his chest.

He took a deep breath, his brain filling with the sweet scent of her hair, then slowly exhaled. This was fine. Nice. Actually, it was more than nice. It was downright enjoyable. He ran his hand up her arm to her shoulder and back down to her elbow. When she shivered a little, he wondered what she would do if he slid his hand up her spine into her hair.

Or up her thighs.

His thoughts were going in an extremely *un-*friendly direction.

Maybe touching each other in a friendly way was predicated on each party *not* having unfriendly thoughts. If that was the case, he was failing miserably.

He couldn't stop thinking about her lips. Or how soft her skin was. Or how squishy her tits would be when he buried his face in them.

"Don't you think?"

A record scratched to a stop in his mind.

Fuck. Was she talking this whole time?

"Mmm . . ."

It was a panic answer. He knew it. She knew it.

She stopped and turned toward him, leaning away from his body and piercing him with those jewel eyes. Her pink lips stretched into a smile. "You weren't listening to me."

Adam shook his head. "No."

Chelsea laughed. "Why not?"

I was thinking about your tits, was probably an unacceptable answer. He looked down at her lips. That would be a less offensive answer without him having to lie. His eyes grazed down her body to her little plaid shorts. *I was thinking about your thighs,* was a creepy thing to say.

He shrugged, lost, then looked back up at her face. But when he saw her eyelids had grown heavy, and her pretty lips had parted, and her chest was heaving as if she'd just been chased by a pack of wild dogs, he gave up his search for a reply.

He knew he'd never be able to find one while looking at her.

She lifted her hand and slowly brought it to his thigh, resting it there for a moment, then moving a millimetre higher toward the outline of his dick in his grey jogging pants.

Jesus.

He was lost. His brain was gone. He had absolutely no idea what to do next.

The comforting thing was that she was right there with him, locked in this weird trance, searching for an exit but hoping to never find one. If she was going to touch him, it only seemed fair that he could touch her.

He placed a gentle hand low on her back, slid it up her spine. Just as he imagined, her eyelids dropped, and she let out a shiver-sigh that brought him an inordinate amount of satisfaction. He wanted to do everything to her. Learn everything that she liked. Make her happy.

"Adam?"

He slipped his hand up the back of her neck and put his fingers in her soft hair. "Yeah?"

She tipped her head back into his hand, exposing more of her neck, pushing her chest closer to his face. She moved up to her knees, then slid one leg over his thighs and straddled his lap, settling down right on top of his out-of-control erection.

Then she moaned.

And her eyelids fluttered closed.

And her neck was close to his lips.

"I'm not sure friends touch each other this much," he said, unable to stop his internal thoughts from pouring out. "This feels like a line crossed."

Chelsea chuckled a little. "Adam, I'm sitting on your erection. The line is a dot in the rear-view mirror at this point."

"So you *don't* touch your friends like you were touching me?"

Chelsea smiled and shook her head. She shifted forward, leaned down, kissed his neck just below his ear.

He dropped his head back on the couch cushion. "Should we be doing this? We can still stop. We can drive back across the line. You only felt my dick through clothing, so technically, we're still only friends."

Chelsea laughed as she kissed up his neck, along his ear. "If you want me to stop, tell me to, and I will. I'll pretend like none of this happened."

Adam squeezed his eyes shut. The warmth from her body covering his was fucking heaven. "You're putting the ball in *my* court? That's a mistake."

She rolled her hips, sucked the lobe of his ear into her mouth, and he was toast. Shivers cascaded down his body as he shook out his fists, placed his hands on her calves, and glided them up her smooth legs, cupping her ass. He'd wanted his hands on it from the moment he saw her, and now that he had an opening, he wasn't going to waste it.

Every care, worry, and what if seemed irrelevant, and when he squeezed her butt in his hands, the justifications for his actions started flooding in.

Why shouldn't they have sex? They were both consenting adults. And it was no one's business but their own. And how could sex really ruin anything? It would only make their friendship stronger. Friends with benefits sometimes worked out. And they would definitely be the ones who would make it work.

Since they were such good friends.

And had mutual respect.

And mutual friends.

Adam slid his hands up Chelsea's hips, over the waistband of her shorts, onto her soft, warm skin, lifting her top until her breasts were exposed, then he leaned forward and rested his face in the valley between them. "Fuck me," he said, pressing kisses on her skin. "Why did I think this was a bad idea?"

Chelsea laughed. "Not sure. This might be the best thing I've ever done," she said.

She reached her hands up in the air, and he slid her shirt up and off, discarding it on the floor. When she leaned back down, she brought her soft pink lips to his and kissed him.

His heart galloped, but the rest of his body slowed to a halt. She took his mouth with hers, slowly, gently kissing his lips, gliding her tongue along his.

Everything in his body screamed at him to speed things up. He couldn't remember the last time he'd taken his time like this. Maybe never. It was usually a race to get the girl to finish so he could finish and find some relief.

But this was different.

He wanted to bask in this. Wanted to feel her every touch.

He slid his hands up and down her back, up to her hair, down to her butt, along her arms, up to her face. He took in every soft inch of skin as they made out on the couch. And he loved every fucking minute of it.

Eventually, she broke off the kiss and stood. Her cheeks were pink, lips red and swollen. "Take off your clothes," she said.

He smiled and reached behind his neck, grabbing his shirt in his fist and pulling it over his head. Then he lifted his hips and slid his pants and boxers down in one fluid motion. He was pretty certain he would do whatever she told him to. Without question. Without hesitation.

He raised his brows, waiting for the next demand.

Chelsea gave a little laugh but no other words. Slowly, she slipped her shorts off but left on her lacy red panties. Then she came back to his lap, straddling him so his erection rested between their bodies.

He tipped her chin up with his thumb so their lips would meet once more and kissed her at the same speed she set. She ran her hands along his shoulders, over his back, into his hair. Every so often, she would press her body forward to feel his dick against her stomach.

He was a fucking wreck.

He put it off as long as he could, kissing, caressing, dreaming of the heat coming from between her legs . . .

"Chelsea," he said between kisses. "I think I'm dying."

Chelsea laughed and moved to stand, but Adam stood instead, taking her with him. She wrapped her legs around his waist, arms around his neck. He hugged her to him, nestled his face into her neck, and wrapped both arms around her back, taking his elbows in his hands to lock her to him.

She smelled good. Felt good. He was completely disoriented, like waking from a dream, and didn't know where he was going. But he didn't care. He just saw a bed and headed for it.

He laid her down, came over her, kissed her again. Now that she was lying beneath him, he could feel more, see more, do more.

He kissed down her body to her panties, then slipped them down her legs and tossed them on the floor. He kissed back up her legs, watched her squirm as he settled between her thighs. He stayed there a while, not touching, even though he could tell she was desperate for some relief.

"Adam, please," she said.

His name on her lips caused a rush of sensations. "Fuck, I love when you say my name," he said.

She pressed her hips up toward his mouth. "Please."

He moved to her side and knelt on the bed.

"What are you—"

"Shh . . ." he said, knowing that going down on an angle would get her there fastest. "Trust me."

He leaned down and took her into his mouth finally, licking, sucking, tasting. She was so fucking sweet.

He knew the exact moment when she was going to come. She rose on the pleasure, letting out a few strangled moans and gasps before her back arched off the bed and her whole body tightened with the orgasm rocking through her.

It took a while for her to recover and open her eyes, and when she did, she pulled him to her and kissed him. Adam reached his fingers between her legs.

He kissed her, caressed her, brought her back to the point of desire before he moved to kneel between her legs. He was so entranced that he'd positioned his dick in his hand before he remembered a condom.

"Fuck," he said. "Just a second."

He leaped off the bed, searching around the room, before realizing they were in her room. "Shit."

"Here," Chelsea said, getting up and going to her overnight bag. She opened it up, pulled out a fistful of condoms, and passed them to him, then gave him a sheepish smile.

"Jae packed them . . . I didn't, like, plan . . ."

Adam took the condoms with a grin, already ripping one open as she was lying back down on the bed. He put it on and came above her once more, kissing her and teasing her before finally pressing himself into her.

He nearly came right there on the spot. It had been a while since he'd had sex, and she was impossibly perfect. And so warm. So, so warm.

He fell forward, face in her neck as she wrapped her legs around him. She tugged him forward and back, urging him on when he slowed his pace.

"Please, Adam. Please."

Adam kissed her again, sped up. Nearly came. He couldn't seem to rein himself in.

He reached between them, teased her more, brought her back to where she started stiffening, then sped up. Once he felt her orgasm rip through her, convulsing around him, he let himself go, burying himself deep, never wanting to stop.

His orgasm came hard, exploding through him. As it finally ebbed, and his brain came back, he realized how rough he had been. Not sure what to expect, he pulled his face back quickly to look at her, make sure she was okay, but she was smiling at him with her sea glass eyes.

"Y . . . you okay?" he asked with a thick voice.

Chelsea let out a long exhale, her smile growing. "Mmm . . . never been better."

Adam exhaled. He relaxed on top of her, keeping one arm out so she wouldn't take his full weight. He kissed her neck, up to her ear.

"That was . . . too much," he said.

Chelsea leaned up, kissed his shoulder. "It was good."

Adam picked himself up. "Good?"

Chelsea's smile grew. "It was the best sex I've ever had. Happy?"

Adam smiled. "You've only had sex with one other person."

He got up, went to the bathroom attached to her bedroom, and got rid of the condom. Then glanced in the mirror. His hair was going in every direction, mouth bright red. Dick already wanting more Chelsea. He realized it was the best sex he'd ever had, too.

Hands down.

Without a single doubt.

It was way fucking better than good.

He came back into the room to Chelsea stretched out like a starfish on the bed, a smile still on her face. He glanced at the door, but he didn't want to leave. So he lay down next to her and pulled a cover over them both, hoping she wouldn't tell him to go.

"Why didn't we do this weeks ago?" Chelsea asked, rolling onto her side and snuggling in.

Adam laughed. "I'm surprised by you. I thought you've been avoiding casual sex for like five years."

"Almost six, actually."

"Six years," Adam repeated, shaking his head. "What made you change your mind?"

"You," she whispered. "I never really felt like I was missing out on anything until you came along. I think I'm too attracted to you."

"Obviously," he said with a laugh.

She kissed his nipple, sending fresh want stirring in his veins.

"And you can't get me pregnant. So that's a bonus," she said with a laugh.

Can't get me pregnant.

That was a weird thing to say.

"Well, no," he said. "I always wear a condom."

"Yeah, I know," she said. "But I mean, because you've had a vasectomy."

Had a what?

Did she say *vasectomy*? He must have heard wrong.

"What?" he asked.

Chelsea sat up on her elbow, braced her head on her hand. "Sorry, I know it's probably weird that I know that."

He stared at her for a moment, trying to understand why she thought that he'd had a vasectomy. When he said nothing, she continued.

"Natalie told me. She . . . we were talking about you. About Ben, and about how I'm afraid to . . ." She paused, blew out a breath. "Are you mad?"

"I'm not mad," he said. "I'm confused. Chelsea, I haven't had a vasectomy."

He could literally see the blood draining from her face.

"You haven't?"

Adam shook his head. "No. I thought about having one. A few years back. But I . . ." He stopped speaking. Mostly because he didn't want to say why he didn't go through with it. But also because she was no longer listening.

She'd stood from the bed and started pacing the floor. "Oh no. No. No."

She carried on like that for a while. It was at the thirtieth time hearing "Oh no" that he got a little offended.

"Did you only have sex with me because you thought I'd had a vasectomy?"

She stopped, cocked an eyebrow, and stared at him as if he was clueless.

What did that mean? Clueless for thinking that? Or clueless for only realizing it now?

He got off the bed and went to her, pulling her into his arms. "Everything's okay. Let's not implode here. I think you're just having a bit of post-nut clarity," he said, trying for a joke to break the rising tension.

It didn't work.

"It's not okay. I don't do this. I can't have a baby with you. Oh, God . . ."

It was like a punch to the heart. He tried to shake it off, knowing she was just upset right now. But there was too much truth in the words, too much feeling, too much loss.

He stepped back, nodded. He'd just had the best sex of his life with the coolest girl he'd ever met, a girl that was quickly becoming one of his best friends, and she regretted it. Because she might end up pregnant with his baby.

He could almost hear his heart cracking.

"Adam," Chelsea said, placing a hand on his arm. "I didn't mean it like that. And I didn't have sex with you because I thought you'd had a vasectomy. I'm just . . ."

When she trailed off, he filled in the blank. "Scared."

Chelsea stared at him as if she was surprised that he'd say that, which was weird. Because she looked terrified.

"I think I just need a minute alone. Like, just to process. Is that okay?"

"Of course," he said, walking to the door. Before he left, he stopped and glanced back. "I'm sorry."

Chelsea shook her head. "There's nothing to be sorry for."

Adam turned and headed for his room. He sat down on the bed, put his elbows on his knees, face in his hands. Alone with his thoughts was the last place he wanted to be, because that's when the what ifs would come.

What if she got pregnant?

What if I die before I meet my kid?

What if my kid finds me dead one morning, and he's trying to wake me up, but he can't?

What if he screams?

What if they call an ambulance?

What if he never recovers from that?

What if?

What if?

What if?

NINETEEN

Chelsea removed a lens from Vincent's camera, placing it in a large black carrying case. She selected the one he'd asked for and twisted it in place, then turned the camera on and adjusted. He was busier than usual that day and had given Chelsea a list of things he'd needed help with.

She didn't mind.

It was amazing to see his process, to understand why he was doing what he was doing. And it gave her something to do to keep her eyes from drifting across the lawn and staring at Adam.

It had been two weeks since the boning, but when she closed her eyes, she could still feel him. Still hear him. Still taste him.

She'd thought she was just worried that she might be pregnant, so she'd gone to the dollar store, bought ten pregnancy tests, and took one each day, just to be certain. When the first test she took came back negative, she thought she'd be relieved.

But she wasn't.

Which was why she was wondering whether it was the sex, or the man himself, that was causing her to still be flustered after fourteen entire days.

She glanced across the lawn toward Natalie's house, now with walls covered in paper stuff and giant cut-outs of plastic where windows would eventually be, and found Adam, standing by his truck, staring back.

She was about to look away, but he raised a hand and waved. So she returned it, then awkwardly looked away.

They hadn't really spoken since that night. The drive back to Mapleton the next day had been more than a little awkward, with sparse conversation about the wedding and long stretches of silence. Adam had texted her plenty of times since, asking her opinions about music and ties and hairdressers, but they hadn't had a conversation in real life.

She was too scared to.

Which made her wonder how the hell she was going to survive another weekend away with him. He'd rented a limo bus to take everyone up to his family cottage together and bring them back the next day. So she would be stuck on the bus with him the whole time.

At least they wouldn't be alone.

She'd just have to keep reminding herself how awkward this was so she wouldn't climb into his lap when the ridiculous notion inevitably roared back.

His lap was just so inviting.

And his mouth.

And his hands.

"All set?"

Chelsea nearly dropped Vincent's seven-thousand-dollar lens. He took it from her, placed it into the case, and zipped.

"I'm so sorry," she said.

"No harm, no foul. You okay?"

"Yes. Yeah. Yup. Absolutely," she said, nodding.

Her head jerked wildly up and down before she realized she was still nodding and stopped. Her eyes swept back across the lawn, and Adam was still there, looking at her.

Fuck.

Vincent followed her line of sight. "Something wrong with the Hartley kid?"

Oh, where to start?

Chelsea shook her head, trying to play it cool. There was no way she was going to spill all her personal business to Vincent. Although something told her he would be the perfect person to tell things to.

"Not much to that house, eh?" he said.

Chelsea's shoulders sagged at the change in the subject. "No. They want it to be mostly windows. It reminds me of that glass house they shot *Twilight* in."

Vincent made an impressed face and nodded, then looked back at her. "I imagine that's what Andie's and Oliver's boss's house would look like, only in the city. What's his name again?"

"Marcus," Chelsea said without thinking. Then realization came, and her universe stopped. She turned to him fast. "You read my script!"

"Of course I did."

"I can't believe you actually read it, though."

"I said I would," he said, a crease coming between his eyes.

"Yeah, I know. But people just say things all the time."

He cocked a brow. "I never 'just say things.'"

Chelsea bit back a squeal. "And this is why I love you."

Vincent laughed and shook his head. "It was good, Chelsea. Better than good."

Chelsea had to force her breath in and out. "Really?"

"Yes. You already know that."

Chelsea nodded. "I'm really proud of it. I'm glad you liked it."

"I actually really connected to it. I could see the characters, the setting, the tone. I called around, spoke to some producers about it. I understand your agent is working to get it sold."

Chelsea nodded. "Yeah. There's been some interest," she said. But no offers yet.

"I threw my name out there, to DP if it's green-lit."

Chelsea stared at Vincent. "Are you ser—"

"Remember, Chelsea. I don't just say things."

Chelsea smiled. "Oh, my God. If you're on board, it's as good as sold. This is amazing. Thank you! Thank you!"

Chelsea ran forward, pulled Vincent into a wild hug that was completely unprofessional. But he knew how she operated by now.

When she finally let go of Vincent, his face went more serious. "I gotta ask," he said, then entered a lengthy pause.

She was expecting a question about how she researched for the script or a comment on how twisted she must be to write about murdering people. So it surprised her when he finally found his words.

"Are you sure you want someone else making your movie?" he asked.

Chelsea blew a breath up into her bangs and looked down at her feet. Of course she would rather make it. But it was just too risky.

"I mean, no," she said with a smile. "But I can't make it myself, and I need the money. So it's better for it to get made than for it to sit in my desk drawer."

Vincent shook his head. "I know it's a risk, but the payoff could be huge. This is career-launching material. You told me you want to direct."

"The timing is bad. I'm broke."

"You can find investors."

"What if it flops?"

Vincent shrugged. "Then it flops. Investors know the risks."

Chelsea looked around, not sure how to tell her idol to stop pressing her. It would all just be too hard. And she was sick of hard. She wanted something easy. She'd started forming a new excuse in her mind but was ultimately spared when Jasper came up.

"Chelsea, can I speak to you?"

"No," she said, then went about ignoring him and packed up her things for the day.

She looked up at Vincent as she worked. "I have to take tomorrow off. My sister's getting married out of town. I won't be back until Sunday."

Vincent nodded.

"Thanks for," she paused, glanced at Jasper, who hadn't left. She really didn't want him to know she was selling a screenplay. "Everything," she said.

Vincent nodded. "See you next week."

Chelsea turned and started for home as Jasper fell in step beside her. "What could you possibly want, Jasper?"

"Why didn't you tell me that guy is a Hartley?"

Chelsea rolled her eyes, kept moving. "You're being an asshole again. Go away."

She could hear him grumble under his breath beside her. "Can I start over? I wanted to talk to you about us."

"No *us*. Only *me*," she said, marching on toward the side door that led to the kitchen. She wanted to talk to Jae before going to the end of the driveway for Ben.

"Can you just stop for a second?"

Chelsea rolled her eyes and stopped. She crossed her arms and gave him a bored look. "What could you possibly want?"

"I want us to get back together."

She stared at him for a long while before she actually believed he'd said it. "What?" she said, just to make sure he actually meant what he'd said.

"You and me and Ben. I want us to be a family again."

Chelsea shook her head. "We were never a family."

"We were. For a little while."

Chelsea nodded. "Yeah. For about three weeks. Then you bailed on us."

"I can see that you're still angry about that," he said.

She huffed out a breath and turned, marching even faster this time. She couldn't wait to get to the door so she could walk in and slam it in his face behind her.

"But maybe you should forgive and forget. Think about how happy Ben would be."

Her eyes went wide. She couldn't believe the words he was saying. "You've never thought of Ben a day in your life. All you care about is you."

"That's not true," he said with more force than she expected. "I think about you and Ben all the time. I made a mistake."

"Jasper, you've been here for weeks, and you haven't even *tried* to spend time with Ben."

"I'm just too busy right now."

This wasn't working. He wasn't understanding that the moment he'd walked away, she was done. And she would never, ever think of him as anything more than a selfish deserter who would always put his own interests before everyone else, including those he claimed to love. She had to clarify that she was not, nor would she ever be, interested in getting back together with him.

Before she could get the words right in her head, he started speaking.

"Please, Chelsea. Remember how much fun we used to have? Just us, watching movies on the couch, staying up all night talking, debating who's better, Scorsese or Coppola?" He smiled the smile she once loved so much.

But she would never look at him the same way again.

She changed tactics. Obviously, being rude wasn't working to get him to understand, and she needed him to forget about her and move on.

"Jasper, there was a time when I loved you. More than anything. But that's gone now. You ruined me. I could never, will never, think of you as a partner again. It can't get any more over. Dead. Gone. Good-bye. Capisce?" she said, holding her fingers out like a gangster in the movies they used to watch.

Jasper blinked down to his toes. "Are you saying no because you're with Adam?"

She stared at him in shock. "Are you only wanting me because you think I'm with him?"

She turned and walked toward her house without waiting for a reply. She already knew the answer, anyway. Luckily, he stayed where he was. The second she was in, she turned and locked the door, then breathed a sigh of relief before running up to Jae's room to tell her that Vincent Shadd loved their screenplay.

TWENTY

Adam started up his uncle's boat on Lake Joseph and, after a final check that everyone was on board, backed out of the marina.

There were only ten of them: Natalie; Ethan; Max; Ethan's parents; Ethan's sister Amy and her wife, Jaclyn; Adam; Chelsea; and Natalie's friend Jess from England that they'd picked up from Pearson Airport on their way.

It was going to be a great wedding.

He'd checked in with the housekeeper, caterers, band, photographer, and hair/makeup people the day before, just to make sure everything was in order. And it was. Everything was perfect.

Everything except the vibe between him and Chelsea.

That was very much off.

They'd texted back and forth about wedding details and occasionally waved at each other across the lawn, but they hadn't actually interacted in over two weeks.

Sixteen days, to be exact.

He knew his friends were suspicious because they kept looking at him as if he were harbouring stolen jewels. He felt like a criminal. Why did he do it? Why did he think things would be normal?

Nothing was normal.

He told himself not to look at her. When that seemed impossible, he started monitoring how often. He'd give himself a goalpost, like, once they were out of the marina and into the lake, then he could look. Once they were past the halfway mark, then he could look. Once they docked at the cottage, then he could look.

It was fucking torture.

All he wanted to do was get her alone for ten minutes and clear the air that had thickened into a dense fog. But what would he say? How did one go about doing that?

He was lost.

He got out into the lake, then felt some relief and looked at her. And caught her staring at him. At least he wasn't alone in the fog. The thought was comforting. And frustrating.

He smiled, and she stood, walking over to him at the wheel. Maybe she wanted to get back on track just as much as he did. What track, though? Did they have a track?

"Hi," she said, squinting up at him.

"Hey," he said in a thick voice.

He wanted to hug her. Kiss her. Take off his sunglasses and slip them on her face so the bright sun reflecting off the water wouldn't hurt her pretty eyes.

He gripped the wheel tighter. "Everything okay?"

Chelsea nodded, looking back at the other passengers in the boat.

He followed her eyes and found them all watching him like a movie, as if they'd each paid their fifteen bucks and wanted to get their money's worth.

He shook his head at them, and they all looked off in different directions.

"Things are weird," she said.

Adam snorted. "That's putting it lightly."

He glanced back down at her, and she was smiling, on the verge of laughter. "What?"

"Before we . . ." She trailed off with a pointed look.

"Yeah . . ."

"I had myself convinced that we would be totally cool afterward."

Adam laughed. "Same."

"The thing is, I knew that was unlikely, even when I was thinking it. But I wanted it too bad to care."

Adam let out a long breath. "Same."

Chelsea smiled, but only one dimple came out. "Do you think we'll get past it? Or is the invasion too dire?"

Adam smiled, remembering her alien invasion analogy. "I'd like us to be friends. I like you. Your friendship, I mean."

Chelsea laughed, and he calmed down a little. What was it about her that made him so . . . content. Was *content* the right word?

"Cool, I like your friendship, too."

They fell into a slightly less awkward silence as she peered into the distance at the cottages passing by. "Wow," she said. "Would you really call these *cottages*? They're mansions."

Adam nodded. "I know. It's kinda surreal."

Chelsea looked up at him. "This is like the premiere. You don't feel you belong here, do you?"

Adam shook his head. "No."

She nodded, looking around, and he wanted to explain why, even though she didn't push. Maybe that's why he liked her so much?

"After my accident, I just felt like all of this was so fake," he said with a shrug. "It was impossible to tell who actually liked me and who just wanted to be friends with a Hartley. None of my 'friends' even came to visit me in the hospital. I lost touch with all of them."

"I'm sorry."

Adam shrugged. "Don't be. I have great friends in Mapleton. Ethan came to all of my speech therapy sessions. He would sit with me for hours, going through pages and pages of text and helping me relearn it all."

Chelsea's eyebrows rose. "Wow," she said, glancing back to where he and Natalie sat together, holding hands.

"Max, too. He brought me to every single one of my physical therapy sessions, since he's big enough to catch me if I fall. But he wasn't as patient as Ethan. He yelled a lot more."

Chelsea laughed. "I can see that."

Both dimples. He loved those dimples.

"He's a good friend. He yells because he cares," he said, getting a giggle from her. "Anyway, I mostly ignore this side of myself, except for my Uncle David. He wouldn't let me ignore him."

Chelsea smiled. "He loves you."

Adam nodded. "The feeling is mutual. We're here."

Adam brought the boat around, steering toward the dock.

"Oh, it's actually smaller than I imagined," Chelsea said. "Not that it's small."

Adam cocked an eyebrow, not sure what she was talking about. The Hartleys had the biggest cottage on the lake in a prestigious area dubbed "Billionaires Row." He leaned down to her height to look from her vantage point.

"No," he said. "You're looking at the boathouse."

"The boathouse?"

He pressed a button, and one of the garage doors opened. "Yeah, that's the boathouse." He pulled around a little more until the cottage came into view. All three stories, five million windows, and multiple decks.

Chelsea's jaw dropped. "Oh my God."

"No judgment, remember. You own a mansion."

She snapped her mouth closed. "It's nice," she said.

Adam laughed and pulled the boat into the boathouse, then hopped out and started tying it up, Max and Ethan helping. Everyone got off the boat, including Chelsea, holding a box filled with peach-coloured roses arranged into bouquets and boutonnieres that she'd picked up that morning from the florist in Mapleton. They were her favourites, but Natalie seemed pleased with them, too. He hoped she'd like the cheesecake they'd chosen for dessert because it was Chelsea's favourite, and the champagne cocktail they'd drunk at TIFF.

"You can leave that, Chelsea," he said, watching her struggle to lift the giant rectangular box. "We'll bring it up."

Chelsea clung to the box. "No, I'll bring this box," she said.

Adam narrowed his eyes at her. "I'm going to bring it to the kitchen so it can go in the cooler."

Chelsea looked down at the box, then up at the cottage. "Where's the kitchen?"

Adam laughed. "You'll get lost trying to find it. Just leave it with me."

She seemed to debate this, looked up into the air, then shrugged. "Fine. That's fine." She put the box back down but bent over it for a moment, fiddling with the bouquets.

The housekeeper came down to meet them on the dock. "Mr. Hartley, welcome back."

Adam gave a polite smile. "Thank you, Ms. . . ."

"You can call me Shirley."

"Thank you, Shirley. Is everything set?"

"Yes, the spa just finished setting up. Anyone interested can follow me."

"Spa?" Chelsea said, whipping around.

Adam nodded. "Uncle David set it up. It's his wedding present."

Natalie walked to him, pulled him into a tight hug. When she pulled back, her eyes were misty. "Thank you so much. For everything, Adam. This is amazing."

Adam nodded as relief washed over him. "You're welcome."

Chelsea and Natalie skipped off with Shirley; along with Ethan's mom, Gayle; Amy; Jaclyn; and Jess. The moment they were out of earshot, Max started in on him. He'd been expecting an inquisition from Max, but even still, it was impressive how little time he wasted.

"You slept with her."

Adam clamped his mouth shut. He looked over at Ethan, who watched on with the patience of a saint, and Mark, Ethan's dad, whose eyebrows disappeared into his hairline.

"No," he said, turning away to pick up the box of flowers. When he turned back around, Max was staring at him, hands on his hips.

"I knew this would happen."

"Nothing happened," he said. He glanced at Ethan, took in his expression, and winced. No one was buying the lie.

"It's not a big deal, and it's none of your business," he said. "And you definitely didn't *know* it would happen. I didn't even know it would happen."

"So it happened, then? You slept with Chelsea?"

Adam huffed out a breath but stayed silent. Whatever came out would just be a lie.

"Leave it," Ethan said to Max. "It's none of our business."

Max shook his head. "He's in love with her."

Adam stopped moving, kept his eyes trained on the soft peach petals in the box.

"Are you?" Ethan asked.

Was he? He'd known the answer to that question for a while now. Just never wanted to admit it to himself.

"I knew this would happen," Max repeated.

Adam rolled his eyes. "You knew we'd have sex?"

"No, I knew you would fall in love with her. You fall in love so easily."

"What? No, I don't," he said.

"You fell in love with my dog when we were twelve. Bawled your eyes out when he died."

"Well, who wouldn't? That was sad as fuck."

"And Vanessa Surrel?"

Adam cringed. "Ugh, that was just . . . poor judgment," he ground out. "Chelsea and I cleared the air. We're friends. That's it."

Max rolled his eyes. "You said you didn't want anything permanent. It's why you made your stupid tier system. What are you doing to yourself?"

"Why are you so pissy with me lately?"

"I just . . ." Max took a deep breath, blew it out. "I'm worried about you. And her, too. She reminds me of Cara."

"What? Why?"

"They're the same age."

Adam's eyes went wide. There was no way Chelsea was the same age as Max's little sister. Adam looked over at Ethan, who nodded a confirmation.

Shit.

"I just get the feeling that you're going to torture yourself later about her. And her son."

Adam let that sink in. Was it possible that he was right? Yeah. Of course he was right. He was trying his damnedest to be just friends with her, but there was something about her that drew him in and wouldn't let go.

"Do you love her?" Ethan asked.

Adam's shoulders slumped, and he nodded.

"Only as a friend?"

Adam shook his head. "No. But I'm going to fix it."

Mark cleared his throat. "Can I offer a word of advice, Adam?"

"Yes, please," Adam said, putting all his attention on Ethan's dad, hoping for some sound steps to fall out of love.

"Don't complicate simple matters," he said.

Adam stared, waiting for Mark to continue, but he didn't.

"I'm going to the spa," Mark finally said. "Call me if you need me." He took off in a jog to catch up to the rest of the spa-bound guests, leaving Adam dumbfounded.

"What the hell is simple about this?" Adam asked his friends.

Ethan and Max shrugged as they picked up the rest of the boxes and headed toward the house.

Twenty-One

"Are you being good?" Chelsea asked Ben over the phone while putting in a pair of crystal chandelier earrings Natalie had given her as a maid of honour present.

"Yes, Mama," Ben said. "Aunt Jae and I are filling out my birthday invitations."

Chelsea sighed. She hadn't been seeing as much of Ben as she usually did ever since he'd started school and she'd begun working a million hours a week. And now she was at a fancy cottage in a fancy dress, drowning in mom guilt.

"That sounds like fun," she said, wishing she were with him instead, then feeling sister guilt creep in.

She couldn't win.

"I better get going. I love you, Benny."

"Love you, Mama!"

Jae came on the phone briefly to order Chelsea to get more Adam action. Chelsea rolled her eyes and checked her lipstick.

There wasn't much left to do. The ladies at the spa had given her a complete glow up. She'd had a pedicure, manicure, full body sugar scrub, massage, facial, and waxing. The makeup artists and hairstylists had them all looking red-carpet perfect, and the dress Natalie had chosen for her made Chelsea look like a water fairy.

Chelsea twirled in the mirror, smiling at the way the pale blue chiffon floated around her legs. It had two slits that went obscenely high up her thigh but only showed when her legs moved just so. The top was crisscrossed across her chest, and the back of the dress, because Natalie had picked it out, was backless. Her ears sparkled. Her hair fell in soft waves around her face. She felt amazing.

She walked out of the room, eager to show Natalie the completed look, and stopped short when she saw Natalie standing in the room's sunlight in her sleek white satin gown.

"Holy crap," Chelsea said. "You look incredible."

Natalie smiled and did a slow spin. Her dress was backless, too, down to her butt, with a single strap of crystals down her spine. "Isn't it gorgeous?"

Chelsea nodded, speechless. "I do."

Natalie and Jess laughed.

Chelsea settled onto an upholstered chair and picked up a glass of champagne from a shiny silver tray before looking around the room. "Have the flowers come?" she asked, hoping it came across as casual.

Natalie shook her head. "Adam said he'd bring them to the ceremony."

Chelsea inwardly cursed. She'd been worried about the bouquets ever since Adam had insisted she leave them with him. She'd miked them that morning and hoped she had enough recording hours to make it work.

"Which one is Adam?" Jess said with her eyebrows drawn. "Blue Collar Billionaire or Scary Big-Dick Energy?"

Chelsea's jaw dropped as Natalie snickered.

"Blue Collar Billionaire," Natalie said. "Scary Big-Dick Energy's name is Max."

Chelsea smirked at their exchange. "I don't know. Adam's dick is pretty bi—"

"Chelsea. God. No," Natalie said with a scowl.

Chelsea laughed again. She'd come clean that morning about sleeping with Adam. It was pretty unavoidable. Apparently, everyone could tell on that boat that something was up between them. But she hadn't expected Natalie to be so revolted by the whole thing. She knew it was coming from a place of concern, so she reassured her over-protective sister that it was a one-time thing.

Case closed.

"Fine, I'll stop. I have to check something anyway," she said. "I'll be right back."

She stepped out of the pretty room and into the hallway before pulling the speaker app up on her phone. The mics she'd used to rig up the bouquets were powerful, but undetectable, and only started recording when they picked up sound. So when Adam had told her to leave the bouquets with him, she'd figured it was safe to turn them on. They had little recording time, but if they were going to be in the cooler anyway, it was probably fine.

She just wanted to check to be sure the caterers hadn't had an hour-long meeting close by that was recorded and filled up the space on the hard drive.

She pressed Play on the recording and was surprised to hear Adam's voice playing through the speaker. Of course, he'd brought the flowers to the kitchen and had probably talked with Max and Ethan while they went.

She was about to hit Delete when she heard her name.

. . . Chelsea and I cleared the air. We're friends. That's it.

You said you didn't want anything permanent. It's why you made your stupid tier system. What are you doing with her?

Tier system? What?

Chelsea hit the Pause button. Obviously, this was a private conversation. She shouldn't be listening.

But she wanted to so, so badly.

Her eyes darted between the Play button and the Delete button. In the end, the dark side won.

She listened to the back and forth between Adam and Max before Ethan's steady voice entered the conversation.

Do you love her?

Chelsea held her breath, waiting in silence. No answer came.

What the fuck? Did she lose the connection? She held her phone in a viselike grip, staring at the screen, wishing she had put hidden cameras in the bouquets, too. Finally, Ethan's voice came again.

Only as a friend?

Chelsea gasped a little before Adam finally spoke.

No. But I'm going to fix it.

No? But what was his first answer? Did he nod? Did he shake his head? Maybe he didn't love her as either?

Maybe both?

Chelsea stared at the phone. Heard Mark advise Adam not to make simple things complicated. Wondered what the hell was simple with all this.

The door swung open, and Chelsea jumped and fumbled the phone but recovered.

"You ready?" Jess asked. "Ethan just texted. It's time to go."

Chelsea nodded. The three of them walked together down the fancy hall lit with a long line of elegant sconces to the wall of white French doors where they met up with Gayle. Tearfully, she passed the pretty bouquets to them and slipped out onto the deck. Jess followed. Chelsea took a deep breath.

No. But I'm going to fix it.

Her heart was slamming inside her ribcage, beating unnaturally fast. Could he really love her? Did she love him? She'd never even bothered asking herself.

"Gotta go now," Natalie said, shooing her.

Chelsea nodded. "Sorry, I'm having a bit of a freak-out. I'm supposed to be the one keeping you on track."

Natalie shrugged. "I already did all my freaking out. I love Ethan. I'm just getting it in writing now."

With a smile, Chelsea braced herself and stepped out of the door onto the patio. The first set of eyes she found were Adam's. He'd glued them on her, and she couldn't look away. They held each other's gaze for the complete walk down the aisle to where he was, standing next to Ethan and the officiant.

He'd lost all expression, his face serious, and she didn't have to wonder anymore whether he could love her.

From the way he was staring at her, she was pretty certain he did.

. . . .

Chelsea stood smiling as Natalie and Ethan thanked Adam for the twentieth time that night, hugged her, then left the deck, holding hands and looking blissfully in love.

They were completely alone. For the first time since the ride of shame after TIFF.

Adam stared for a moment but seemingly caught himself and looked down. Chelsea could feel his eyes raking down the front of her dress. It was just as painful as his arm had been draped behind her back during the photos, or when his rough hands had touched her skin during the dances.

She could hardly take it. It left her wondering whether she should take Jae's advice and throw caution to the wind.

"Do you want me to walk you to your room?" he asked.

Not as good as "Do you want me to take you to bone town?" but it was probably better this way.

Chelsea nodded, then realized he was avoiding eye contact and hadn't seen. "Sure."

They took a few steps together before she also realized she'd forgotten to take the mics from the bouquets. "Oh, just a sec. I gotta grab the mics."

She went back to the bouquets and startled at Adam's voice behind her, drifting over her head.

"Mics?" he asked.

Oh shit.

Chelsea winced. "Uh, yeah. I miked the bouquets. I'm making Natalie and Ethan a wedding video."

Silence stretched.

"Why didn't you tell me?"

"It's a surprise."

Maybe he wouldn't realize she'd recorded him talking with his friends on the boat. Maybe she wouldn't have to tell him she'd heard it.

She had untangled the tiny mics from the bouquets and turned to find him frowning at them in her hand.

"Is that why you wanted to take the flowers off the boat?"

Uh-oh. "Yeah."

"When did the recording start?"

Double uh-oh.

She went for casual and started walking while she answered. "I turned them on before I left the boat."

Adam stayed in place for a second before jogging to catch up with her. "Uh, so . . ." he said, then whispered, "fuck."

"It's okay, Adam," she said, hoping that ignoring it would make it go away.

It didn't.

"I wish you had told me you were recording me. Everyone."

Chelsea took a deep breath. "I wanted to bring them in myself, but you didn't leave me a choice."

"You should have told me," Adam said.

Chelsea stopped walking. She turned to Adam, and he looked downright distraught.

"Listen," he said. "There are some things that I said. I said some things. With Max and Ethan on the boat, and maybe you could just . . . not listen. To any of it. Please."

Chelsea's heart stopped. She felt like the biggest asshole. She looked out at the dark lake shining under the moonlight and wondered whether she could just dive in and swim away.

"I already—"

Adam's eyes cut to her, intense, waiting.

"Did," she finished.

"Fuck."

"I'm sorry. I heard my name, and I listened, and it was private, and clearly an invasion, and I shouldn't have done it, and I'm sorry."

His shoulders slumped as he nodded his head.

She was the worst human on Earth.

"We can just forget about it, Adam. You didn't say anything. I didn't hear anything. Okay?" She turned and walked without waiting for an answer as her heart broke a little. It hurt, but it would be best if they forgot about it.

Moved on.

Her heels clicked away on the deck for a few steps before he caught up to her. They walked into the house, through a huge, beautifully appointed living room and down a hall before he spoke.

When he finally found his voice, it was soft, deep. Intimate, like that night in the hotel.

"I can't forget it," he said.

She stopped and looked at him, ready to apologize again, when he reached a hand up, untangled a lock of her hair from her crystal earring. Shivers raced along her neck, and all the thoughts tumbled from her head. He stared at her, his eyes moving back and forth between hers, then dropping her lips.

He tucked her hair gently behind her ear before a frown came over his face.

"I tried. I keep trying. I can't stop myself from looking at you. And wanting to talk to you, and touch you, and see your smile. It's only getting worse."

She cleared the flutters occupying her heart, forced herself to steep her brain in reality. He was frowning, almost angry. It wasn't a normal way to tell someone you liked or loved them. She was so put off by his inner torment that she shook off the intimate moment.

"You look really unhappy about your feelings for me," she said. "That's kind of fucked up."

She started walking again, not really sure where she was going but needing to move. Once again, he caught up to her.

"I don't want a relationship."

She stopped dead in her tracks, twisted, stared at him. "You know you're a terrible liar, right?"

Adam exhaled through his teeth and nodded. "Okay, I refuse to be in a relationship. Better?"

Chelsea rolled her eyes. "If by *better* you mean you're telling the truth, then yes. But I wouldn't call that *better*."

She kept walking. "Would it help if I told you I don't love you?" she asked.

"Yes!" he nearly shouted.

Chelsea rolled her eyes. It was on the tip of her tongue, but she hated to lie. So she just told him the truth. "Well, I can't. My like for you is bordering on love."

He fell silent beside her. His face was a mix of frustration and something else she couldn't quite figure out. But mostly frustration.

She decided that since she'd come clean about listening, and they desperately needed a change of subject, she'd ask him something that had been bothering her since she'd heard that recording.

"What's this tier system?"

Adam tipped his head up at the ceiling. "You heard *that* too?"

"Mm-hmm . . ."

"If I tell you, you'll think I'm a dick."

Chelsea stared at him. He looked tortured. More pieces were clicking into place. "I could never think that, Adam."

Adam exhaled, resigned. "I rank women," he said. "I do it to avoid the ones I'm most likely to fall in love with."

Chelsea narrowed her eyes. "Like me?"

Adam nodded, as if he was confirming something truly horrible.

"Okaayy . . ."

That *was* a little dickish. But she knew his reason behind it and understood why he felt the need to do it.

But still . . .

"I don't want to hurt you," he said. "I couldn't live with myself."

Chelsea looked away from his pleading eyes and picked up the pace. They turned a few more corners, walked down a long hallway, and finally arrived at her big wooden bedroom door. In the silent walk, Chelsea had decided she was going to lay it on the line. She wanted Adam. But not just for one night or as friends with benefits. She wanted him in her life for real, as a permanent fixture. She knew he came with baggage, but so did she. And she knew about his medical problems, but to her, losing someone who loves you is a lot different from someone deciding to walk away.

The problem was that he was incredibly skittish, and if she framed it that way, he would run for the hills.

So she tried to use some tact. "Maybe we could just take things slow."

"What does that mean?"

"Well," Chelsea said, summoning some courage. "We're already in this . . . situationship."

His brows rose, and his half grin came out.

"It's like we're keeping each other in our shopping carts, not sure if we should hit Checkout or Delete Item."

Adam laughed.

"What if we just slowly fill out our address and credit card information? See how it goes?"

He dropped his head. "I wish that didn't make sense."

Chelsea smiled. "Can I ask you something?"

Adam stayed in place, silent. She took that as a yes.

"Why *didn't* you have a vasectomy?"

He finally moved. Dropping a kiss on her cheek, he wrapped his arms around her back, pulling her into his warm, hard chest. They stayed like that in the darkened hallway for a while before he answered. She wasn't sure whether it was to avoid eye contact while he confessed or whether he just needed the comfort of a friend.

"I was scheduled to have it done. Which was super fucking awkward since my friend's mom is the nurse at the clinic and I had to hand her a cup of my jizz."

Chelsea laughed. He let out one chuckle, then swallowed and went still.

"At the last minute . . . I just couldn't go through with it. Maybe I selfishly hoped that . . ."

She could feel him shake his head above her, tortured.

"That what?" she asked, voice muffled in his heavenly scented arms.

He squeezed tighter. "That somehow I might accidentally get someone pregnant. And I wouldn't have to feel like an asshole for bringing a child into the world, because it wouldn't have been a decision I made. And then I would get to be a dad, guilt free, for the rest of my life."

Chelsea wanted to cry for him. She held him tight, ready to one-click buy him, despite all the bad reviews and red flags. He had such a big heart. And he cared so much for the people in his life. He would be an amazing dad.

"I'm super fucked up," he said in a low voice.

Chelsea pulled back, looked into his eyes. "I know."

He looked down again, gave a single resigned nod.

Chelsea reached a hand up to his cheek. She rose onto her toes and held his gaze before taking his lips with hers.

He stopped breathing. Went perfectly still. After at least five seconds, he drew a breath and deepened the kiss, pulling her closer to his body. He reached gently for her hair, ran his rough hands down her soft back, then up again.

This kiss differed from the last time. When they'd had sex in the hotel room, it was a little faster, a little more rushed. She'd climbed into his lap almost immediately, desperate to scratch the itch that only he seemed to be able to create in her.

But this was something else entirely.

Adam took his time, with soft kisses and gentle touches. It felt as if he was slowly covering her with his love. And she did the same. He pressed forward, nudging her against the wall. Suddenly, his hands were everywhere.

"You feel so good," he said. "I never want to stop."

"Same," Chelsea breathed.

"I was clinically dead for at least a minute when you walked out on that deck."

Chelsea laughed.

"I saw a light," he said between kisses.

She loved that he could make her laugh while he was making her insides melt. She reached her hand behind her and pressed the door handle down, backing into the room and pulling Adam with her. In a few steps, the backs of her legs hit the mattress, and she fell back.

Adam came down on top of her, putting one hand down to stop from crushing her; the other was still on the back of her neck, holding her just so. Not too hard, not too soft.

Just exactly so.

God, he was great at this.

He trailed kisses down her neck, across her collarbone, over her shoulder, back up her neck. Tingles surged from the top of her head, rushing outwards to the tips of her limbs. His hands spread the yards of soft fabric around her legs, separating where the slit was so he could get to her silky skin. He groaned as he slid his hand up her thigh, and she knew it was because her skin was extra soft from all the waxing and scrubs.

He took his time, moving around her body, kissing her, telling her how beautiful she was, and she lay there in ecstasy, soaking up the sensations. She'd never felt this way before.

She felt adored.

He moved lower, kissing up her legs, higher and higher, his five o'clock shadow between her thighs creating the most divine contrast with the soft chiffon against her skin. When he reached the apex of her thighs and kissed her through her lacy white panties, every nerve ending in her body went haywire.

Her heart was racing as he caressed her through the soaked fabric. She wanted to rip everything off of her body and stop time so this would never end.

Nothing made sense anymore.

Adam slid her dress up to her waist, then tugged on her panties. She lifted her hips off the bed, and he glided them down her legs and discarded them on the floor. When his body heat didn't return immediately, she sat up, wondering why he left, and found him grinning down at her, holding out his hand. She took it and stood, her eyes locked on his, wondering what he was going to do to her next. He looked cocky, like a man with a plan.

"You look like you could walk on water in this dress," he said, reaching to her shoulders, gently turning her around. He came closer, moving her hair and kissing her neck as he took the zipper, and slowly, almost painfully so, drew it down tooth by tooth.

"Adam, please."

She knew she was begging, but she couldn't stop. No more than she could stop her belly from contracting every time his outdrawn breath danced across her ear.

"Shh . . . I want to give you everything," he said, his lips slowly drifting across her neck and back and shoulders. The zipper was short, only going from her waist down to her butt, but it was taking a century for him to get it down.

"Faster," she said, those two syllables almost impossible to get out through the sensations.

Adam ignored this, continued dragging the zipper down. Once it was finally unzipped, he slid his hands up her back to the straps over her shoulders and slowly drew them down until the dress was too loose and floated off her body into a puddle on the floor.

She turned, but he kept his hands on her shoulders, stilling her.

"You said we should take things slowly," he said, gliding both hands down her back to her hips and finally cupping her butt.

Chelsea groaned. "I meant our situationship. I want to undress you."

Adam gave a sharp inhale, one final butt squeeze, then twirled her around, taking her face in both his hands and slowly kissing her. He seemed determined to set a glacial pace.

She gave in, kissing him slowly while working to undo the buttons on his shirt, unbuckle his belt, unbutton his trousers. His pants hit the floor hard under the weight of the belt. Running her hands up his firm stomach and over his chest to his shoulders, she took his shirt down his arms, drifting her nails gently in its wake. She pressed her body into his, his body heat warming her tingling skin.

Suddenly, she was airborne.

Adam lifted her up, bringing his hands under her butt, and slowly kissed her, taking his time before bringing them both to the bed. She rolled on top of him, causing him to protest, but she shook her head.

"I haven't finished yet," she said, reaching for his black briefs that were straining. She lifted them, taking them off, watching him spring free. He studied her carefully as she discarded them, then came back and pressed a wet kiss to the head of his cock, along with a gentle suck.

A bead of moisture formed immediately, and he dropped his head back onto the bed. "Chelsea, don't. I'll come immediately."

Her heart raced. She wanted to take him in her mouth, watch him fall apart. But she also wanted this to last, and she wanted to feel him on top of her again, shoulders bunching, hair falling onto her forehead. God, she wanted it. Now.

She hopped up and grabbed a condom from the stash she'd packed for the hotel. Then ripped it open as she came back to the bed. She hadn't expected she would have sex again, but she was thankful she hadn't thrown them out.

She rolled the condom on, feeling him stiffen further. He sat up as soon as she'd finished, moving unexpectedly fast. He flipped her over so her face was pressed into the soft down duvet, then he grabbed her hips and pulled them until she was kneeling.

She felt exposed, indecent, and more turned on than she'd ever been in her life.

"Oh fuck," he growled out, and she almost came.

He knelt behind her, pressing against her. She swirled her hips to get some friction.

"I've dreamed of this," he said. "I've imagined this every fucking day since we met. This is so much better."

Chelsea was barely registering what he was saying. She was desperate to feel him inside her. She pressed back toward him, and he gave her ass a smack. Not too hard, not too soft.

Just.

Exactly.

Right.

Her whole body relaxed into the pleasure. She put her butt higher in the air, giving herself over to him, knowing he was more than capable of taking care of her needs.

"Fuck yes," he said in a low voice.

She let her eyes flutter closed and became hyper-focused on every touch, every sensation.

He pressed into her, slowly, as if time no longer existed, and slid his hands under her body, cupping her breasts. She was so highly tuned that when he slowly drew all the way out and softly reentered her, she came so hard she could hardly breathe. He held her still, hands gripping her hips, groaning as if the feeling of her convulsing around him was too much. She knew he was fighting off his own orgasm. He stayed still for a moment, waiting for hers to wane. As soon as her body relaxed again, he drew in and out slowly, bringing her right back to the brink of another orgasm.

"Oh God," she breathed, feeling it build again. "Please, Adam."

He slid his hand around her hip, reaching for her and making gentle, slow circles while kissing her neck.

And she came again.

This time slower, with a long build that seemed to roll on forever. He sped his pace fractionally, in and out softly, repeatedly, until he finally gave in to his own orgasm.

They stayed together, connected for a long moment, before he gently pulled himself free of her and rolled down beside her. He tucked her into his big spoon, and suddenly, her back was fully engulfed in his warm body. Her eyes fluttered closed, her breathing steadied, and she fell into a deeply relaxed state. The last thing she heard was Adam's soft voice telling her he loved her, before she slipped into a peaceful sleep.

TWENTY-TWO

Adam was in the limo bus with Chelsea, waiting for the rest of their party to join them before heading back to Mapleton.

They'd opted out of breakfast that morning, choosing instead to stay cuddled up in bed. Actually, Adam had tried to drag Chelsea out of bed to meet everyone for breakfast, but she had stayed put, saying she wanted more alone time and pulling him under the covers with her.

How was he supposed to say no to that?

He'd swiped a couple of blueberry muffins and two cups of coffee from the kitchen on their way to the bus, and they had just finished them when the first passengers arrived. Gayle and Mark.

"Mornin'," Mark said, giving a pointed look at Chelsea's hand wrapped in his and resting on his thigh.

"Good morning, Mark," Chelsea said, sending a smile his way.

So far, so good.

Jaclyn and Amy got on the bus, followed by Jess. Finally, Ethan and Natalie.

"Oh, you guys are already here," Natalie said. "We missed you at breakf . . ." She trailed off, taking in their clasped hands. "What's this? What are you doing?"

"Natalie," Chelsea said in a warning tone.

Natalie threw a glare at Adam before turning her face away to look out the window. He felt like absolute shit.

Everyone seemed uncomfortable or pissed about them holding hands. They were all figuratively circling Chelsea, trying to protect her from him.

How could he blame them?

Chelsea squeezed his hand, and he looked at her. She gave him a reassuring smile that soothed him and made him feel that what he was doing wasn't wrong. As long as he was only looking at her pretty blue eyes, everything felt right in the world.

Suddenly, the bus rocked to one side as Max climbed the stairs. He gave Ethan a nod, then his eyes zeroed in on Adam's lap, and his permascowl deepened. "What are you doing?"

Natalie hummed. "That's what I'd like to know," she said under her breath.

Adam wondered whether Natalie and Max were long-lost twins or some damn thing. They were the same scary, opinionated person.

Adam opened his mouth to say . . . something, when Chelsea piped up.

"Our situationship is none of your business, Max. It's no one's business," she said, giving Natalie a pointed look.

Max stared at her as he sank slowly into his seat. "You sound like Cara."

Adam winced. He knew Max compared Chelsea to his little sister to make Adam uncomfortable.

"Who's Cara?" Chelsea asked.

"My little sister. Same age as you."

Adam glared at Max. Max glared back.

Max had always been overly protective of women, so Adam tried not to take it personally. He'd been raised by a struggling single mother and had had to step up to take care of his younger sister when he was a teen. But comparing Chelsea to Cara, who'd just got out of a pretty abusive relationship, was way out of bounds.

"Careful," Adam said in a low tone that came out more aggressive than he would have liked. Part of him wanted to throw Max out the door. But the bigger part wondered whether he was being defensive because Max was right. The truth was often hard to hear.

He would never mistreat Chelsea. Never. But now that he was in the light of day, surrounded by the criticism of people who cared about both of them, he was wondering why he thought being with her was a good idea. He loved her, no doubt. But would he really date her? Be her boyfriend? Would he ever be more than that?

Maybe.

Maybe not.

Probably not.

Fuck.

She was a long-term relationship type. She didn't do casual sex—she'd told him as much. She wanted a proper marriage and more kids, and he could never offer her that. Would never. So why was he even starting something with her? Was he just stringing her along? He didn't want to lie to her. But he honestly didn't even know what the truth was.

Chelsea's voice broke through his thoughts as the bus lurched forward. Her tone was one he hadn't heard before. Authoritative and cold.

"I'm not interested in your opinion, Max. You're not my brother and I make my own decisions."

Max stared at her, his face softening slightly, as if he was worried. Then he hid his feelings, gave a curt nod, and casually stretched out his legs, crossing his ankles over each other under the opposite seats.

"How was breakfast?" Chelsea asked the rest of the group, voice softer.

Amy piped up with a full recap of the menu, and Adam wanted to hug her. The rest of the ride back to Mapleton was pleasant, with everyone chatting and avoiding bringing up anything even close to Chelsea's hand in Adam's lap.

But Adam barely spoke a word, and everyone clearly noticed his voice was absent. He normally couldn't shut up in social situations, but he was way too deep in his head to even follow the conversation. He just kept wondering why he was doing this and feeling like a selfish prick.

By the time they had dropped everyone off, and Chelsea and Adam were the last ones on the bus together, he'd realized that whenever he was alone with Chelsea, his brain just shut down. Being with her felt so good that he didn't consider her future. She deserved to have what she wanted, not to be hung up with some guy who would never, ever commit.

"You okay?" Chelsea asked after the doors closed behind Ethan and Natalie and the bus started toward Monroe Manor.

Adam squeezed his eyes shut. What a fucking mess he'd made. "I'm not sure." God, that was so fucking douchey. Maybe she'd tell him to go fuck himself, and the balance in the universe would be restored.

Unfortunately, she did the opposite.

She slid in closer to him and rested her temple on his shoulder. "Don't listen to them. Who cares what Max and Natalie think?"

When he didn't respond, she sat up and turned toward him, kissing his cheek, then looking at him with those eyes. God, he loved those eyes.

"Do you want to hang out for a while?" she asked with a smile. "Maybe we can watch a movie?"

He wanted to scream yes. There was nothing he wanted more than to spend more time with her. But he couldn't even force himself to nod. He just stared back at her, completely lost between wanting to love her and wanting to run before he hurt her.

The bus made a right, pulling into the Monroe driveway, and Adam's stomach dropped.

What the hell was he going to do?

"It's just a movie, Adam," she laughed. "It's not like I'm asking you to move in with me."

He nodded without thinking. Just stared at her eyes and nodded.

She smiled, and he got her dimples as the bus came to a stop. "Come on."

He stood and followed her off the bus, but as soon as he set foot on the gravel, her front door swung open and Ben came flying down the stairs toward Chelsea.

"Benny!" she yelled, dropping to a squat and opening her arms. "Oh, I missed you!"

"Mama!"

He smashed his cheek into hers, his little hands spread out on her back.

Adam couldn't look away. He was frozen in place.

Chelsea pulled back, then looked at his hand. "What's this?" she asked.

"An invitation," Ben said. He turned to Adam and walked over. "This is for you."

Adam took the outstretched blue envelope from Ben, then turned it around. On the front, in thick blue marker, was the word *Abam*.

He looked back up at Ben, who was smiling back. "I'm having a Spider-Man birthday party. Aunt Jae said I put the stick on the wrong side of the circle."

Adam stared down at the *b* in his name, then back at Ben, then back at the *b*. If he thought he was lost before, that was nothing. Now he was lost without a compass or directions, out of gas, the sun was setting, and a pack of hungry wolves was after him.

What the hell was he doing here? Why was he inserting himself into their lives? How could he do to Ben what had happened to him?

He couldn't.

He had to end this now.

The bus started up behind him, and he panicked.

"Sorry," he said, avoiding eye contact with Chelsea. "I can't stay." He knew that as soon as he looked at her, everything would make sense again, and he'd dig himself further into this fucking hole he was in.

So he quickly turned, flagging down the bus and hopping on fast when the doors opened. In the back of his mind, he knew it was a dick move, but he couldn't think. He'd just go home, regroup, find some way to end things where no one got hurt and they could still be friends.

But not *too* close of friends.

More like acquaintances.

Awkward acquaintances.

"Fuck."

He dropped his head in his hands, then realized he was still holding Ben's invitation, now wrinkled up in the corner and clammy from his sweaty palms. He looked at the *b* again and sighed.

He'd fix this.

TWENTY-THREE

Chelsea pulled a garbage bag from the cupboard under the kitchen sink and began filling it with empty Spider-Man cups and plates left over from Ben's birthday party.

Ben was playing on the floor in the living room with Jasper, building a Lego set he'd got from him. Jae was staring at Jasper with a scowl, keeping a close eye on the intruder in their house. If it were up to them, Jasper wouldn't have been there. They would have passed him off to spend a few hours with him as they normally did. But Ben wanted to invite his dad, so they went with it.

Jasper had been on his best behaviour until an hour into the party when he'd pulled Chelsea aside and asked whether Adam was coming. It was just a question, but it had rattled her nerves.

She'd started the day hopeful that he would have calmed down in the last week since Ben had given him the invitation and he'd run off, but that didn't seem to happen. She'd texted him earlier in the week and got no answer. He hadn't even been across the lawn.

He'd literally disappeared.

She gathered some plates with half-eaten cake and melted ice cream and shoved them into the bag, imagining her situationship going right along with them.

She wasn't mad at Adam. He'd told her repeatedly, in no uncertain terms, that he would never have a long-term relationship. He'd never lied to her. But she knew he felt the same about her as she did about him, and she foolishly clung to the hope that he would change his mind.

She glanced over at Jasper laughing with Ben on the floor and patiently handing him piece after piece of Lego. It really warmed her heart to see them together. She wanted Ben to have a father in his life.

Just then, Jasper stood and stretched his hands up. He pulled his phone from the back pocket of his jeans and gave it a quick glance before slipping it back in.

She braced herself, both wanting him to get the hell out of her house and wishing he would stay longer to be with Ben.

He tousled Ben's golden head, leaned down and said something, then turned and made his way to her.

"I gotta get going," he said.

Chelsea nodded. "'Kay."

He glanced at Jae, then back to her. "Can we talk?"

"About what?"

"Us, Ben, work," he said.

"Work?"

He nodded his head. "Walk me out?"

Chelsea followed him to the front door, shrugging at Jae's horrified expression as she passed. They stepped onto the porch, and she closed the door behind her. Jasper turned to face her but looked as though he was still working out what to say.

"Are you with Adam Hartley? Just tell me yes or no."

Chelsea rolled her eyes and sighed, refusing to reveal to him that she had no idea.

He ran his hand through his hair. "I think you know I want us to get back together. But I need to know if you're already dating someone else."

"We aren't ever going to get back together, Jasper."

Jasper blew out a breath, and she felt a rush of memories take over her mind. It was something he always did when he got news he didn't like. His chin stayed down, but his big brown eyes tipped up to her. "You're never going to forgive me, are you?"

Chelsea shook her head. "No."

"Not even for Ben?"

Chelsea's heart squeezed. She always felt guilty that Ben didn't have a dad in his life. But it wasn't her fault. She'd been one hundred percent all in with Jasper, till death did them part.

Then he'd walked away.

"Don't do that, Jasper. I'm not to blame for this."

And you're still that same selfish person.

Jasper shook his head. "Of course you're not. But I was young and stupid. I just wish I could go back in time." He glanced over her head through the glass in the door, presumably at Ben on the floor. "If you're not seeing anyone, maybe we can spend some time together. We used to have fun," he said with a smile. "Remember that time we went—"

Chelsea cut him off before he could remind her. "Was there something about work?"

Jasper closed his eyes for a second, blew out another breath. "Our second AD quit this week. I was hoping to hire you."

Chelsea's jaw dropped. "Really?"

"Yeah. You already know everyone and understand how we operate. We have a big day this week, if the weather cooperates, and I'll need all hands on deck."

Chelsea wiped the shock off her face. She was just offered an actual paid job on a film set. Too bad she would have to be Jasper's second assistant. But at least the filming was only a couple more weeks, and the experience would be a great addition to her resume.

"That's great," she said, trying to stay calm. "I can do it."

"Cool," Jasper said. "And maybe you can think more about us?"

She stared at him, unsure how to react, when he stepped forward and pulled her into a hug, causing her to stiffen in shock. Her brain refused to process that she was in Jasper's arms. Then the memories that she'd been suppressing for five years came back.

How they used to go to each other's dorms to watch movies, just as friends. How his floppy hair would mix in his eyelashes as he turned to talk about the camera angles the director chose. How all their friends suspected they were more than friends before they even had their first kiss. How she'd *wished* they were more than friends. The nerves she'd felt when she finally kissed him for the first time. How relieved she'd been when he put his arms around her and kissed her back.

Her eyes drifted closed in his embrace, and she melted a little, arms coming up around his back. It was then that she realized how fucked up it was that the man she wanted nothing to do with was pursuing her, when the man she wanted everything to do with was pushing her away.

It felt good to be wanted. But this wasn't Adam.

This was Jasper.

Jasper.

She dropped her hands by her sides, cleared her throat, and stepped back. The last thing she wanted was to hug Jasper. She wanted nothing to do with him.

Plus, he was technically her boss now.

Ugh.

"You better get going," she said.

"Uh, yeah," he said, staring into her eyes for a moment before breaking contact. "I'll see you on Monday. I'll email you the contract."

Chelsea nodded, turned, and walked back inside without another word. When she closed the door behind her, Jae was staring at her, arms crossed, toe tapping.

"What are you doing?" she asked.

Chelsea leaned back against the door, hands coming up to her face. "I don't know what's going on."

"What did he say to you? And why did you *hug* him?"

Chelsea shrugged. "Momentary insanity?"

Jae nodded. "You're lonely and missing Adam."

"He asked if I was with Adam, said he wants to get back together, and hired me as his second AD."

Jae let out a long whistle. "There's a lot to unpack there. Are you with Adam?"

Chelsea dropped her hands. "No. I don't know," she added, slumping forward. "I *want* to be."

"Then why are you hugging Jasper?"

"I . . ." Chelsea was having way too many thoughts to speak an answer. She wished Adam were there. She wished she didn't fall for fuck-boy men.

"Chelsea, you can't keep doing this," Jae said.

"Doing what?"

Jae sighed. "Okay, I've been thinking for a while now about your situation and the choices you've been making lately, and I'm sure you don't want to hear this, but . . ."

"Hear what?" Chelsea asked, completely lost.

"You keep compromising."

Wheels were turning in her brain, but she was coming up short. "Huh?"

"You don't see it."

Chelsea stared at Jae, wondering where the hell she came up with that.

Jae seemed to brace herself before speaking. "You're compromising with Jasper, when you want Adam. Just like you're compromising with a second AD position for, what? Like, two weeks, when you should be directing our film." She paused for long enough to look up and shake her head. "You're like a master settler."

Chelsea stared at Jae, unable to really believe the words. "No, I'm not."

Jae just nodded. "You're heading down a path where you're going to compromise so much, you won't even recognize your own life."

Chelsea shook her head. Where the hell was this coming from? "Jae—"

She couldn't even get the words out before Jae cut her off.

"Just think about it," she said, then turned and walked away, up the stairs and into her room.

Honestly, she didn't even know what words she would have said. She thought they'd agreed about their screenplay, but apparently, Jae wasn't over it yet.

Was she right? Did Chelsea compromise too much? She did a little, but sometimes there just wasn't a choice.

And she *wasn't* compromising with Jasper. She wasn't getting back together with him. She wanted to be with Adam. That much she knew for sure.

But was she settling for being Adam's "situation" rather than his girlfriend, like she wanted?

Ugh, probably.

Chelsea lumbered through the house to the living room, where Ben was playing on the floor. She sat down with him for a while, playing, talking, laughing, distracting herself by asking him what his favourite part of the day had been. When it was time for bed, he protested.

"I'm not sleepy," he said, his eyes rimmed with red.

She kissed his nose. "Yes, you are."

"My tummy hurts."

"You probably ate too much sugar," she said, standing up and holding his hands, pulling him up off the floor. "Let's give you a bath and read some books."

He held his stomach a little, winced.

"Poor little guy," she said, rubbing his back and leading him up the stairs. "You had too much fun. You'll feel better in the morning."

He tucked himself into her side, and they walked up the stairs together. Chelsea looked down at his sweet little face and totally brushed Jae's opinion about her career choices away. There was a difference between compromising on her dreams and putting her son first. She prioritized building a solid foundation for her and Ben, and that wasn't compromising. That was smart decision-making.

But maybe Jae had a point about Adam. Chelsea now knew that she wanted someone in her life. And she wanted that someone to be Adam.

Now she'd just have to make him understand that she didn't care about his medical problems; she just wanted to be with him. Hopefully, he could come to terms with that.

TWENTY-FOUR

A dam's stomach rolled with the waves lapping against the side of his boat. He pushed aside empty bottles on the table in front of him, and set his half-drunk beer down, then slumped across the seat.

It was five o'clock in the evening, all the beer he had on deck had been drunk, and the marina was getting busier. Boats were coming in from an afternoon of fishing, and families and couples were gathering and getting ready for an evening on the lake.

Adam glanced around, noticed a few other boaters waving to him, and decided now would be a good time to hide below deck. Maybe he'd take a nap. As long as he didn't have to see anybody, he'd be fine.

He stood, his vision swirling, and took a step toward the stairs when Max appeared out of nowhere and came aboard.

Adam thought he might puke. He sat back down on the bench, put his head between his knees.

"I've been calling you," Max said, his voice hard.

Adam didn't have to look up to know he would find Max's signature scowl and crossed arms. "And I've been ignoring you."

"You're drunk?"

Adam shook his head. "No. I was drunk a couple of hours ago. Now I'm hungover."

Max sat on the bench next to him. Before Adam realized it, Max had swiped the blue envelope from under the bottles and flipped it over.

"Abam," he read.

Adam squeezed his eyes closed and slumped. "He put the stick on the wrong side of the circle."

Max opened the envelope, pulled out the Spider-Man invitation, and scanned it. "This was today. Two hours ago."

"Yeah." Adam glanced around the marina, wondering how fast it would get around town if he hung over the edge of the boat and puked into the lake.

Probably fast.

But did he really care?

"You didn't go?"

"No."

Max put the invitation back into the envelope and placed it on the table. "You let things get out of hand with Chelsea."

Adam nodded. There was no sense in denying it now. "Way out of hand."

"And now you hate yourself."

"Yup."

"Was she upset when you told her you weren't coming to Ben's party?"

He closed his eyes, feeling like fifty pounds of shit. "I didn't tell her."

"You ghosted?"

Adam nodded.

"Well, that probably did it then," Max said, standing and gathering up his empties.

"Did what?"

"Ended things. It was a dick move, but it's still better than keeping her on the hook forever."

"Ended." He wanted to cry and puke.

Max grabbed all the empty bottles easily in his two hands, popped them into the box they'd come out of, then grabbed Adam by the arm, hauling him up.

"She'll forgive you eventually, and you guys can be frie— No, you're not capable of being friends with her. You can be acquaintances. Right now, I need you to pull yourself together."

"I can't be her acquaintance," he said, letting Max drag him up to standing. "She's perfection. God queen of the first tier."

Max blew out a breath. "It's just the beer talking. The building inspector is meeting us at the pub in thirty minutes to sign off on the work so far. I need you to charm her."

He threw Adam's arm around his shoulders, started walking.

"It's not the beer," he said, letting Max lead him off the boat and down the dock. "My dad called. Roger got the all-clear from his surgeon, so I won't be at Ethan's build anymore."

"That's good news. You'll have more time for the pub. As soon as we pass this inspection, we can finish the kitchen and the brewery."

Adam nodded. "Maybe you're right. I heard from the brewer in Churchill. We have an interview set up in two weeks."

Max nodded, still walking. "Great news."

Adam walked in silence to Max's car. Max wrenched open the passenger side, started shoving Adam in cop-style, with his hand on Adam's head.

Adam stopped. "I really love her."

Max's sharp features softened as the hardened mask he constantly wore slipped. "I know. But if you have no intentions of being with her for real, you need to let her go. It isn't right to fuck around with single moms."

Adam nodded. "You're right."

"Unless," Max said, waiting. Adam looked at him. "Unless you've changed your mind about relationships?"

Adam shook his head. "How could I?'

Max nodded blankly. "Just talk to her once you're fully sober, and set it right. Then keep some distance until she moves on."

Adam stared off into the distance. "She's going to move on."

"Yup," Max said, slamming the door. Two seconds later, he was behind the steering wheel, turning over the engine. "And so will you."

Adam buckled his seat belt, shaking his head as he watched a couple with a picnic basket walking hand in hand to their boat.

He seriously doubted that he'd move on. But he could definitely pretend he had, for her sake.

"I'll go talk to her this week and end things for good."

TWENTY-FIVE

Chelsea was making her way down the to-do list the first AD had given her, prepping for the all-important scene they were going to shoot in thirty minutes. She could feel the tension in the air. Everyone was rushing to get their jobs done so they could shoot the scene before the thunderstorm set in.

Chelsea had been slammed all morning. She hadn't been sure she'd get to the set that day. When Ben had woken up, he'd still been complaining about his stomach ache, and Jae was out of town for a meeting. She was going to keep him home and call in sick, but Ben had insisted on going to school since it was Bring Your Stuffy Day.

She was looking down at her phone to check the time when a loud sound rang out from across the lawn at Ethan and Natalie's house, grabbing her attention. The construction crew had been there since the break of dawn and were supposed to wrap up as soon as they were going to film. God, she hoped that was the case.

Actually, she'd been looking for an excuse to go over there and talk to Adam. She was desperate to feel out the situation after he ghosted Ben's birthday party, but he was nowhere in sight.

There was an older gentleman with a long beard and a limp now wearing the white hardhat that had set Adam apart and holding the clipboard that Adam had always held.

She assumed that was the guy who was supposed to be on site from the beginning.

She looked away with a sigh, eyes landing on Jasper. He was standing with Winter, going through the scene, probably giving her an overview of what he needed from her. When he saw her looking at him, his face broke into a smile, and he waved.

She returned an awkward smile and looked back down, confused. Best not to think about Jasper.

She finished her to-do list just as the construction crew wrapped up, so they were all set to film. The first AD and Jasper were with Vincent with the shot all set up. Jasper had just yelled action when her phone started vibrating in her pocket. She slipped it out and saw that it was Mapleton Elementary calling.

Shaking off the initial motherly panic, she stepped away from the set and answered in a hushed tone. "Hello?"

"Hi, this is Mapleton Elementary. Is this Chelsea, Ben's mom?"

"Yes," Chelsea said. "Is everything okay?"

"No, I'm afraid not. I have Ben in the office here. He seems to be in a lot of pain."

Chelsea's stomach plummeted to her toes as the clawing heat of panic wrapped around her neck. She could barely get words to surface. "A lot of pain?"

"Yes. We're all quite worried about him."

Oh no.

Words evaded. She started walking toward her house to get her keys.

"Can you come down to the school, Chelsea?"

She was nodding, hadn't realized she hadn't spoken.

"Chelsea?"

"Yes," she squeaked out. "I'll be right there."

She hung up the phone in a daze and had broken into a jog when she heard Jasper's voice calling her. She whipped around and realized she had said nothing.

Fuck.

She ran back toward Jasper. "Sorry, I have to go get Ben from school. He's sick."

She was about to turn and run to the house when Jasper's voice came, hard and mean. "You can't leave. We're shooting."

It was enough to cause her to pause. She stopped and stared at him, shocked. "He's sick. It seems bad. I'm going to get him."

"Get Jae to do it. You can't leave."

She wanted to slap him. Wanted to run. But she ended up just staring at him in disbelief. Why wasn't he worried? Didn't he care?

Of course he didn't care. Because he was the same selfish prick he'd always been.

He only cared about himself.

She hated him.

She stared, seething, trying to remind herself that he was now her boss, and this was her first job, and she probably shouldn't tell him all the things she was thinking.

"Chelsea," Vincent said, his calm, deep voice breaking through her thoughts, "go."

She shook off her anger and nodded. She'd just taken off when Jasper turned on Vincent. Their arguing voices fading in the distance with each stride.

She grabbed her keys and purse from the house in record time and floored it to the school, haphazardly parking in the front and running into the office. The moment she saw Ben, she knew her instincts had been right.

There was something seriously wrong.

He was slumped in the corner of the room on a blue plastic chair. The vice principal had her arm around his shoulders. His skin was greenish grey, and his eyes were barely open.

"Ben," she said, dropping to squat in front of him. She touched his clammy cheek. "You don't look good."

Ben said nothing.

"He threw up just now," the vice principal said.

Chelsea nodded. She hoped he just had a stomach bug, but a nagging voice in the back of her mind told her it was more. She tried to rationalize it away. Maybe he was having a bad reaction to something? Maybe food poisoning?

But the voice in her mind only grew.

Something's seriously wrong.

"Can you help me get him to my car?" she asked the vice principal. "I'm taking him to the hospital."

TWENTY-SIX

Adam exhaled a deep breath as he hopped out of his truck at Chelsea's house and walked around the path to the backyard. She was probably at the film set, and he hoped to steal her for a couple of minutes so he could talk to her about their situation.

He'd tell her the truth, that no relationship with him would ever go long term, no matter how much he liked her. He'd try to smooth things over so they could be acquaintances, without the awkwardness. But awkwardness was better than stringing her along without ever making any kind of commitment to her.

He couldn't do that.

He'd just turned the corner when he nearly collided with Vincent, Chelsea's idol, storming across the lawn with a vein bulging out of his forehead.

"Everything good?" Adam asked, carefully side-stepping out of way.

Vincent fisted his hands as his head shook. "I want to kill that little fuck."

He looked across the lawn at Jasper, who was now throwing something that looked like a croissant at the ground in a tantrum.

He *was* a little fuck.

Adam nodded, searching the area but not finding Chelsea. "Is Chelsea okay?"

Vincent's head shook more, and Adam's heart stopped.

"Where is she?"

Vincent took a steadying breath. "She left to get Ben. The school called. She looked scared."

"Scared?" he nearly shouted. "What's wrong with him?"

"I don't know," Vincent said. "All I know is that bastard was trying to stop her from leaving."

"He wouldn't let her leave?"

"No," Vincent said. "I think she felt something was seriously wrong with the boy. I remember when my kids were young, my wife always seemed to know when something wasn't right. I told her to go, and she just left," Vincent said, gesturing up the drive-way.

Adam nodded and walked to his truck, breathing deep as he fought back hyperventilation. He got in, sat for a moment, convincing himself that she'd be back soon, since the school was only down the road.

Should he wait in her driveway for her to come back? Probably not. She'd want to look after Ben, not have a shitty conversation with him about how he was emotionally unavailable.

But he'd feel better if he stuck around to make sure the little guy was okay. He could arrange to come back later, when Ben was feeling better and Chelsea was ready to talk.

He sat in the driveway, the minutes ticking by, wondering why she wasn't back yet. He waited a total of fifteen minutes before the feeling that something was seriously wrong settled into his gut, and he pulled out his phone to call her.

Maybe she needed his help. Maybe she'd tell him to go fuck himself. It was hard to tell.

The phone rang and rang, but there was no answer. He texted, waited. Tried calling again. Finally, he decided it couldn't hurt to drive to the school and see whether she was there.

He arrived in under a minute, but he didn't see her red car anywhere.

He knew he was overreacting by going there. Knew he was way, way, way overstepping his boundaries with her, but he decided Vincent was worried enough that he would just pop inside and check in. His cousin was the vice principal, and his close friend. She wouldn't tell anyone he'd come looking for Chelsea. Besides, they would often meet up for lunch or to hang out. He could pass it off as if he were there to see her.

It was shitty, but he had to know whether Ben was okay.

He pulled up out front, rang the buzzer, and the door unlocked. His cousin came around the corner from her office.

"Adam?" she said.

"Hey, Mia, how's it going?" he asked, glancing through the glass doors to the office. He knew the space well. It hadn't changed at all since he used to sit there as a kid whenever he'd get in trouble.

But Ben was nowhere to be seen.

Mia blew a breath up her face that made her bangs puff out. "It's okay. There was just a boy in here, and I'm worried about him . . . but I can't really talk about it. Did you want to grab lunch?"

Adam's shoulders started tensing up. She looked as worried as Vincent had, and he knew something was seriously wrong.

"Was it Ben?" he asked, ignoring the fear in his voice. "Ben Davenport?"

Mia's head jerked back. "You know him?"

Adam nodded. "Yeah, his mom . . . she and I . . . Is he okay?"

Mia's face slipped into a professional mask. "I can't talk about children except to their parents or guardians. And I *know* you and his mom can't be serious. You're never serious with anyone."

"Did they go to the hospital?" he asked.

"Wait, did you come here for lunch or because of Ben?"

He had no time to explain their friendship-non-friendship-situationship mess. He took this as a confirmation that Chelsea had taken Ben to the hospital and gave Mia a kiss on the cheek.

"Let's have lunch next week. I'll text you," he called as he headed for the door.

He got into his truck and peeled out of the parking lot toward the hospital. He'd just swing by the emergency room and check up on them, make sure they didn't need him. If she told him to get the fuck out, he'd leave. But he couldn't *not* be there for her.

It was probably nothing.

But what if it wasn't nothing?

What if it was something?

He pressed a button on the steering wheel until his phone dinged.

"Call Antonio's cell," he said to his phone, then waited as the phone rang. He was already in this deep. What's one more person he'd have to explain his overreaction to?

TWENTY-SEVEN

Chelsea sat in the cracked green vinyl chair with Ben's head on her lap, fighting back heart palpitations. To the right of her was a teen in a gym uniform who looked like he'd broken several fingers. To the left of Ben was a frail old lady who was coughing so badly Chelsea thought she might crack a rib.

The emergency room was filled with sick and injured people growing more and more desperate to hear their name called.

She pushed Ben's sweaty hair back from his forehead as he clutched his stomach and moaned.

She wanted to cry. Wanted to scream. Wanted to go back to the window for the fifth time since they'd got there twenty minutes ago and ask how much longer. Her leg bounced. She looked around wildly, wondering who in the room they might prioritize over her, and hoping no one worse off showed up at that moment.

She heard the sliding door open behind her, braced herself in case it was an ambulance coming in with a heart attack patient, and turned.

And saw Adam.

He jogged in through the doors past her, looking around frantically. It happened so fast, she barely registered that it was him when he whipped around, and his eyes landed on hers. Then flitted down to Ben in her lap.

He came over, loomed over them with his hands on his hips. "Something *is* wrong."

Chelsea stared at him in shock. "How did you know we were here?"

Adam looked sheepish for a second, then shook it off. "I . . . people told me."

"People?" she asked.

What the hell?

"I know people. They tell me things. What's wrong with Ben?"

She was too tired to discuss why he'd refused to come to Ben's birthday yet found them at the hospital. Honestly, she was just happy he was there. She'd been on the cusp of a nervous breakdown for the last hour and would gladly take all the support she could get.

She reminded herself to take deep breaths and calm down. But when Ben shifted and whimpered in her lap, she felt the tears prick and her eyes fill.

"I don't know," she said, the last word coming out more like a cry. She took a deep, shaky breath.

Adam went pale. "You should have called me," he said, his voice a mixture of anger, annoyance, and fear, "right away."

Chelsea shook her head. "Why would I call you? He needs a doctor."

Just then, the sliding doors opened again, and in came Antonio wearing black gym shorts and a muscle shirt. He looked as if he'd just stepped off a treadmill.

Adam gestured with his hand at Antonio, as if to say "This is why you call me."

"Ant!" he said with a wave.

Antonio jogged over to them, sinking down on his haunches in front of Ben and taking his little hand in his.

"Hi, Chelsea," he said.

"Hi," was all she could get out.

"You must be Ben," he said, looking at Ben's scrunched little face.

Ben didn't respond.

Antonio put a hand on his forehead, down his pale cheek. "What are his symptoms?"

Chelsea swallowed. "He's had a stomach ache since last night, barely ate, and he threw up about thirty minutes ago."

Antonio gave a nod. "I'm just going to feel your tummy, Ben. Is that okay?" he asked.

Still no response. He looked up at Chelsea, and she nodded.

As soon as he gently pressed his fingers into Ben's lower abdomen, Ben flinched and gasped, then let out a whimper.

Antonio stood with a nod. "It's probably appendicitis. We need an ultrasound to be certain."

Chelsea sat motionless, unblinking.

Appendicitis? People died from that. It required surgery.

The thought of a scalpel slicing into Ben's skin made her tears tumble down her cheeks.

"No," she said, shaking her head. "It can't be. It's a stomach bug or something. I can't do this."

Antonio looked at her with his calm brown eyes. "Everything is going to be okay, Chelsea. Ben is going to be okay."

Chelsea started blinking out the tears that were blurring her vision. She couldn't think. The terror and panic mixed up her brain.

Antonio stood, looked at Adam.

"You, take him. Everyone, follow me." He turned and walked toward a set of doors past the triage desk.

Adam bent down and picked Ben up in his arms, causing Ben to whimper again. "Shh, it's okay. I got you," he said, resting him gently against his chest and following Antonio through the doors.

Chelsea finally made her body move, stood up, and followed Adam.

Thirty minutes later, Ben was on a hospital bed in a blue-striped gown, being wheeled to surgery, while Chelsea fought back full-body tremors.

"I'm scared," Ben said, giant tears rolling down his blotchy cheeks.

"You're going to be fine," Chelsea said, annoyed with herself that her breath caught on the last word. She took the green stuffed dinosaur he'd brought to school that day and tucked it into Ben's chest. His little arms came around it and squeezed.

"Don't be scared, Ben," Adam said, walking along the other side of the bed. "I've had tons of surgeries, and I'm okay."

"What's gonna happen?" Ben asked.

"Well, they put a little mask over your face, and you fall asleep. And when you wake up, they give you popsicles."

Ben tipped his head toward Adam, resting his cheek on the pillow, tears pooling in a wet spot on the white fabric.

Adam glanced down at him and smiled, then looked away. "Then everyone you know comes and visits and brings you gifts."

"Really?"

"Yup. It's pretty awesome."

"We're here," the nurse said, stopping Chelsea and Adam from going through the swinging doors into the operating rooms. "You can wait in the cafeteria. We'll let you know when you can see him."

"He's going to be okay, right?" Chelsea asked, searching the nurse's eyes.

The nurse smiled and took Chelsea's hand, patting the back of it gently. "Yes. This is our sixth appendectomy this week. Very routine. He'll be out in less than an hour."

Chelsea nodded. She felt better for a moment, but then heard Ben call for her through his tears, and all her emotions overflowed.

The last thing she remembered was Adam's arms coming around her, pulling her face into his chest while the floodgates opened and she fell apart.

TWENTY-EIGHT

Adam grabbed Chelsea some snacks from the cafeteria—water, tissues, a turkey sandwich, chips, and chocolate. When he returned to where he'd left her a few moments later, she was still staring at the screen with Ben's patient number, waiting for the status to change.

"Here," he said, putting all the food in front of her. "Eat."

She just shook her head, soft hair fluttering around her face, red-rimmed eyes glued to the screen.

"He's going to be fine. When he comes out, he'll need you. Eat something."

She finally peeled her eyes off the screen and pierced him with them. They'd filled again with more tears threatening to drop.

He cleared his throat, looked down at the sandwich, and started unwrapping the cellophane. "I had three surgeries here," he said, trying to distract them both.

"On what?" she asked, taking a tiny piece of turkey from the side of the sandwich and bringing it to her lips.

"My eyes," he said.

He opened the water bottle and slid it across the table. She was going to get dehydrated with all the tears.

"I almost lost my vision after my accident. My retina was detached, my orbital bone was crushed, and I had glass in my eye from the windshield. It took a few tries to get me back together."

Chelsea's posture stiffened. "Your family must have been a wreck."

Memories of the days following his accident came back too fast for Adam to stop them. His dad in the corner of the hospital room, folded in on himself and crying, which was a terrifying sight. His uncle throwing things and raging, which was just as out of character and equally terrifying.

Adam blew out a breath. "Yeah. Actually," he paused, not sure whether he really wanted to talk about his mom, but ultimately, the words tumbled out without him being able to stop them. "My mom had surgeries here, too. I remember waiting in this room with my dad as he tried to make himself look okay as his whole world fell down around him. She only had two operations. Then she spent two months here doing chemo, but . . ." Too much emotion bubbled up. He swallowed it back. "Ultimately, it didn't work, and she moved back home."

Chelsea's warm hand came across the table, took his, and squeezed. "How long did you have after that?"

"Thirty-four days."

Chelsea nodded once before more tears slid down her cheeks, and she brushed them away with the back of her free hand. "I'm so sorry you went through that."

Adam swallowed hard, trying to tamp down the emotions rising. He hated bringing it up, preferred to keep it buried. But maybe it would help for her to hear it. Maybe she would understand why he couldn't keep being with her.

"I found her," he said.

The three words hung in the air for an eternity between them. She stared at him, waiting, so he went on.

"Every morning, I'd run to her room as soon as I woke up. Each day, she looked worse and worse. The last morning, I went in, she didn't . . . She wasn't . . ."

"She was gone."

The heaviness in Adam's chest was suffocating him. He swallowed, trying to clear it. "That's going to happen to me."

Chelsea shook her head. "Life is unpredictable."

He wasn't sure whether she was saying it to be nice or whether she didn't really get it, but he had to make her understand. "No. It *will* happen to me. And I can't let someone find me like I found my mom."

Chelsea squeezed his hand. "There just aren't guarantees in life like that."

"This *is* a guarantee, Chelsea," he said, feeling the pain of her pulling her hand away. "I'm on borrowed time."

Chelsea held his eyes, staring for a long while before her eyes softened and her head tilted off to the side. She sucked in a deep breath, then said, "I love you."

Adam violently shook his head. "No, you don't."

"I know everything about you, your health, your past, your fears, and I still love you."

His stomach rolled. "I shouldn't have done this," he muttered.

A long silence spanned the distance between them.

"You won't change your mind," Chelsea said, looking down and speaking more to herself than him.

"And I'm naive enough to think that if I show you how much I care about you, you'll stay with me."

Adam squeezed his eyes shut against the self-hatred.

"Why did you come here?" she asked.

Adam took a deep breath. "I went to your place to talk, and Vincent told me you got a call about Ben," he said, running his hand through his hair.

What the fuck was he doing?

"I sort of . . . tracked you here. I thought maybe you'd need me."

Chelsea calmly nodded. "What did you come to my house to talk about?"

He couldn't look away from her eyes. There was pain there. And it wasn't just because she was dealing with her son in surgery. It was from him, too.

"We can't keep this going," he said. He hated what he was doing. The timing couldn't be worse. But he couldn't go through something like this and let her think they would be together.

Chelsea laughed a humourless laugh, looked away. Her eyes landed on the screen, then came back to his. "You came to tell me you're walking away. I could puke over this déjà vu."

All the air in Adam's lungs disappeared as if she'd punched him in the gut. "What?"

She slumped over slightly in her chair. "Same old story. I fall in love. He walks away. Is it me? Is there something wrong with me? Or just my horrible taste in men?"

"If you're implying that I'm like Jasper . . ."

Her eyes jerked up to meet his. "You're *exactly* like Jasper. Hit a speed bump, and you bail. And no matter what I say or do, or how deeply I feel, I can't convince you to try with me."

Adam stared at her, disbelieving she could draw a similarity between him and that little fuckwad. "You're completely wrong. I refuse to abandon you. That's why I won't be with you."

Chelsea shook her head. She opened her mouth to say something, then snapped it closed. Finally, she said, "I won't beg you to change your mind like I did with him. And I shouldn't have to." She glanced at the screen and stood.

He couldn't understand how she wasn't seeing that this was best for her and Ben. She could move on and find someone to actually build a life with. They weren't even together, really. They were just friends.

When he looked up, she was gone. He glanced at the screen and saw Ben was out of surgery, so he hopped up and followed Chelsea to the doors. He'd almost caught up to her when the surgeon came through the doors.

"How is he?" Chelsea asked.

"Perfect. Everything went great. They're just waking him up now."

Chelsea pressed her palm to her heart. "Can I see him?"

"Yes, right this way," she said, turning.

Adam followed until they made it to the door, and Chelsea finally realized he was there. She stopped up short and turned, staring silently at him.

"What are you doing?"

"I'm still your friend, Chelsea. I'm here if you need me."

"Adam, we're *not* friends. We never were friends. We're awkward acquaintances. And Ben and I don't *need* you. We wanted you. But that's over now."

Adam's head dropped as she disappeared through the doors.

He wanted to see Ben. Wanted to make sure Chelsea was going to be fine. She needed someone there to listen to the instructions from the surgeon so she didn't miss any information. Maybe she'd need someone to pick up medicine, or groceries, or something.

He knew she had Jae, and Natalie, and Ethan. Hell, Vincent would probably pick up groceries for her if she asked him to. But he couldn't stop himself from wanting to be the one she turned to. There was no reason he couldn't be there for her, too.

He started to follow her when the surgeon stepped into his path.

"Family only past this point," she said in a harsh tone. Her features softened in sympathy when she met his eyes. "Can I call someone for you?"

Adam shook his head, took a few steps back. Did he look like *he* needed someone?

Probably.

He thanked her, then turned, and walked out to his truck like a zombie, wondering how he'd let himself get so totally fucked up like this.

He just hoped Chelsea and Ben were going to be okay on their own.

TWENTY-NINE

"I don't want it, Mama," Ben said, puckering his little mouth and turning his face away from the syringe of antibiotics.

"I know, buddy, but you have to. I mixed it with some apple juice. It's not too bad."

Ben turned to her with sad eyes and opened his mouth. She shot the medicine in, and as he shuddered from the taste, a fresh wave of guilt hit her.

She was feeling incredibly guilty these days.

"Don't," Jae said from the rocking chair in the corner.

Chelsea met her eyes for a second, then looked away. Jae had been lecturing her since they'd got home from the hospital that it wasn't Chelsea's fault this had happened. It was nice to hear, but it made little difference. She still felt like the worst mother on earth.

She set the syringe down and pulled Ben into a hug, angry with herself for the millionth time that she had sent him to school when he had a stomach ache. She should have made him stay home, but she didn't put her foot down because he wanted to go, and, if she was being honest, because she was relieved she wouldn't miss work.

"I'm sorry, Benny. We only have a few more days of medicine."

"Can I play outside today?"

"The doctor said you need a week of rest," she said, adjusting his pillow and pulling his blanket up around his shoulders. She'd brought his blankets and pillows from his bed upstairs to the couch in the living room, where they had been hanging out together watching movies all day. Jae had worked from the living room on a lap desk so she could be close to Ben, too.

"Let's watch another movie. I'm worried about you falling off your bike when you're still recovering."

Ben shook his head and folded his arms. "I don't want to ride my bike."

"What? All you ever want to do is ride your bike."

"I can't do it," he said, dropping his head down. "I just fall and fall and fall . . ." He trailed off.

She and Jae stared at each other, speechless. She never expected Ben to give up. He'd been bound and determined to ride his bike.

"That's just the way bikes are, Ben," she said. "It takes a while before you get the hang of it."

Ben shook his blond head. "I'll just ride my scooter. I never fall off it."

It was like a slap to the face to hear him giving up. A little too reflective of how she had been feeling inside about her relationship with Adam.

Actually, not Adam in particular. She was completely done with his mind fuckery. He told her he loved her one minute, ghosted her the next, showed up at the hospital, and then broke up with her. She would be quite happy if she never had to deal with him again.

In a way, she was actually grateful to him. She'd spent years after Jasper left refusing to have a relationship with anyone, and Adam helped her realize what she'd been missing out on. She loved the idea of having a partner. Someone to move through life with, build a family with.

But it was hard, and you'd have to fall a lot.

She fell flat on her face with Adam in that hospital when she told him she loved him and he rejected her. She'd imagined he would tell her he loved her, too, and it would be like that scene at the end of

Dirty Dancing when Patrick Swayze and Jennifer Grey finally nailed the lift.

But it ended up more like the shower scene from *Psycho*.

She ignored her failure and pulled Ben into a tight hug. "I know you fall, but it's worth it in the end. You can't just settle for less. You'll never be happy. Believe me, I tried."

Suddenly, Jae cleared her throat and stood. "Can I talk to you? In the kitchen? Now?"

Chelsea nodded. She hit Play on the remote, and the next movie started up. Then she followed Jae into the kitchen.

"Yes?"

"His bike is just like our movie."

Chelsea raised an eyebrow.

"He's settling. You're settling. Everyone's settling."

Chelsea stared at Jae, trying to get her mind to shift from her personal problems to her work ones. She'd only thought about her work problems sparingly since the surgery. She'd pushed them to the back of her mind, not sure how to deal with Jasper. She was so incredibly angry at how he treated her when she got that call, but did she really want to quit the first and only job she'd ever had on a set?

That didn't seem like a smart career move.

"What do you really want, Chelsea?" Jae asked, eyes imploring. "Be honest."

Chelsea stared down at her hands. She knew the answer; she just didn't want to admit it. It was too hard. "I want what I've always wanted."

"To be second AD on Jasper's set?"

Chelsea shuddered. "No."

"Exactly," Jae said. "You always wanted to be an indie filmmaker. You always wanted to write and direct our films, our way. And you've let life, and fucking Jasper, beat you down to where you're settling for a scooter."

Chelsea stared at Jae as she did a mental inventory of her life.

Career? Disaster.

Relationship? Extreme disaster.

Example she was setting for Ben?

Her shoulders slumped.

Maybe Jae had a point. But at some point, you had to set aside your pie-in-the-sky dreams and steep yourself in reality.

"I just delayed my dreams," Chelsea said. "One day, I'll—"

"No," Jae cut her off. "You scootered."

Chelsea stared at her for a moment, wondering whether she was right. She glanced over at Ben on the couch and knew she would never let him give up on riding a bike. She would encourage him to keep trying for what he really wanted. It was probably a little hypocritical to encourage him to do what he wanted when she put off doing what she wanted. What would she say to him if he were her age and trying to decide on a career?

She'd tell him that the harder things are, the more worth it they are in the end.

Easy isn't necessarily better.

"I scootered," she said, plopping onto a chair.

Jae nodded and left the room, returning a second later with a pad of paper and a pen.

Come to think of it, she'd been scootering like a motherfucker. The only things she hadn't scootered were things she really loved about her life. Like her house and Ben's school.

"I scootered with the film set. I should have told them to beat it the moment I saw Jasper. He is such a turd."

Jae nodded, started writing something down. "Turd's gonna turd."

Chelsea smiled. "And I scootered with trying to sell our script. We wrote it for *us*. Not for someone else. What if someone hired Jasper to direct it? I would rage."

Jae kept nodding and writing. "Same."

Chelsea was on a roll now. All the light bulbs were going off in her head. "We're better off making it cheap, but ours, than selling it to someone else who will put millions into it and screw it all up."

"Exactly!" Jae shouted, hitting the pen off the table. "Our cheap crap would *still* be better than anyone else's big budget."

Chelsea laughed at Jae's outrageous ego. But she had a point. They'd poured their heart and soul into that script, and a lot of the magic of it would be lost if someone else put their spin on it.

And being Jasper's second assistant was demoralizing. If she'd had no history with him and wanted to be a studio director, it would make sense to take that job and sacrifice a little now to get what she wanted later.

But there was nothing she wanted that being Jasper's second AD would get her. It was just taking her off the path she always *knew* she wanted to be on.

"I need to quit that job," she said.

Jae smiled, kept writing.

"Maybe I can still keep in touch with Vincent. I literally love that man."

Jae nodded.

Which reminded her of another man she loved. Adam. What a disaster that turned out to be.

She paced the floor, her mind turning a mile a minute. She'd scootered with him right from the get-go. She'd accepted a situation when she wanted a relationship. She'd accepted bits of his time when Ben wasn't around because he wasn't comfortable dating a mom.

She didn't want that at all.

She wanted someone who would blend into her life. Someone who wanted a family.

"I want to get married," she said.

Jae stopped writing, her pen hovering above the paper. Her face was soft, full of pity. "I know, babe."

"I don't want to split up my life into time spent with Ben and time spent with a guy. I want a family. And I want to go on a date."

Jae smiled, snapped her fingers, and pointed. "What about that hot dad at Ben's school?"

Chelsea brought up the image of the guy patting his daughter's head and telling her he loved her, and she smiled. "Maybe I should ask him out."

"You're definitely asking him out," Jae said, pulling the paper she'd been writing from the pad and passing it to Chelsea. "It's already on the list."

Chelsea took the paper, flipped it over, and found a bullet point list.

Chelsea Gets Back on Her Bike

1. Tell Jasper he's a stinky turd

2. *Quit demoralizing job*

3. *Tell the agent the script isn't for sale*

4. *Get some committed dad dick*

5. *Avoid future scooters*

Chelsea read through the list, smiling and nodding, tears pricking at the backs of her eyeballs. She closed the distance between her and Jae, pulled her into a hug.

"You're the best, Jae."

Jae squeezed her tight. "I know."

Chelsea laughed. "Ben and I are lucky to have you."

Jae went silent for a moment. "You're my family."

Chelsea squeezed even tighter, both of them crying now. The past hadn't been very kind to Jae. They were lucky they had found each other.

"Come on," Chelsea said through tears. "Let's go hang out with Ben. Jasper will be here tomorrow. I'll tell him he's a turd then."

Jae nodded. "Sounds good."

Thirty

Adam sliced open the plastic from a stack of tiles in Max's new kitchen, then pulled the first one out, measured and cut it on the saw next to him. He was blaring the music from a speaker to drown out his thoughts. It wasn't working. All he could hear was Chelsea's voice telling him they weren't friends.

It had been nearly a week, and he still heard it.

All the time.

He should have been happy. He got what he wanted. Distance between them so she and Ben wouldn't get hurt. But now that he had created that distance, it was hurting him.

He'd spent every waking hour for the past two weeks at the pub, mostly working on the kitchen before the chef they hired relocated and got to work. He'd installed the walls, doors, flooring, cupboards, countertops, and appliances. All that was left to do was tile the walls. He'd mostly worked alone, avoiding conversations with Max and his crew, who were busy in the dining area and brewery. He was pretty sure they were avoiding him, too.

Just as well. He wasn't really fit for conversation.

He'd carefully placed the tile when her voice came through, clear as a bell once again.

You're exactly *like Jasper.*

Adam shook his head and pressed the tile onto the wall.

"There you are."

He glanced over his shoulder as Max and Antonio breezed through the doors. Without acknowledging them, he turned back to the wall, pulled some spacers from his tool belt, and fitted them between the tiles.

"You okay?"

Adam shook his head at Antonio's voice, reached for another tile.

A few moments of silence stretched before Max broke it. "I ran into your dad and Denise at the gas station. They're back in town and on their way here."

"Great," Adam said, void of any emotion. He couldn't summon it. It was like all the energy in his body had disappeared with Chelsea's words and he was now just moving lifelessly through the world.

He'd just pulled the next tile from the box when his dad and Denise came through the doors. "Adam!" his father boomed.

He raised a hand in a half wave and carried on with the measuring and cutting, hoping everyone would just go the fuck away. If only they were still in the demolition phase of the reno so he could hit something. Release the rage.

Intricately tiling the wall while his mind raced all over the goddamn place was not doing it for him. But it had to be done.

He felt a hand land on his shoulder and turned slightly to come face to face with Denise. "Adam, what's wrong?"

Adam shook his head, summoned all his energy, and said, "Nothing."

Max did a double take, then raised an eyebrow at Adam's lie. "Adam fell in love."

Denise's face lit up. "Really?"

Adam rolled his eyes.

"She left him," Max added.

"Why?" his dad asked.

No one answered.

Adam reached his trowel into the mortar again and spread it over the next tile.

"What did you do?"

Ignoring his dad, he pressed it onto the wall. He knew it was just a matter of time before his dad started demanding answers. Fortunately, someone opened the door again, breaking the tension.

They all turned to find Uncle David decked out in designer golf pants and a polo shirt strolling into the kitchen.

"Well, hello," he said with his signature smile. He took in their faces, and his smile dropped. "What's wrong?"

"What are you doing here?" Adam asked.

His uncle's brows rose. "Jill said I'd find you here. She said you've been here all week. I was going to steal you away for a round of golf."

There was no way he was going to spend two hours walking around in the sunshine, joking with his uncle and pretending everything was perfect.

"Sorry, rain check," he said, and turned back to the wall.

"Did I miss something?" David asked, looking around and settling on the only face he didn't recognize. "Who are you?"

"This is Antonio," Max said, introducing them. "Adam is in love."

"With Chelsea?"

Adam groaned.

"The Monroe girl?" his dad asked his uncle and received a nod.

Silence. He wanted to scream. Wanted to smash the tiles in his hands to the ground, watch them shatter into a million pieces and scatter all over the floor.

And once again, the door swung open. "Fucking hell, what now?" he said.

He turned to find Ethan walking in, confident at first, but his stride faltered at Adam's outburst. "What did I just walk into?"

"A total fucking shit show," Adam muttered.

"Did you know Adam is in love with Chelsea?" his dad asked.

Ethan nodded. "Actually, I just came from her place."

Adam's heart leaped, and he spun on Ethan. "Is she okay? How's Ben?"

"Who's Ben?" Denise asked at the same time his uncle asked, "What's *wrong* with Ben?"

Antonio and Max filled them all in.

"Ben's perfect," Ethan said. "He's recovering well. Natalie and I brought him some games and snacks to keep him busy while he rests. He started riding his bike again," Ethan said with a smile. "Well, not riding, but he's trying."

Adam's shoulders relaxed. "How's Chelsea?"

Ethan tipped his head from side to side. "She's . . ."

"What?"

"Determined," Ethan landed on.

Huh?

"What the fuck does that mean?"

Ethan blew out a breath. "She's moving on."

Adam's chin dropped to his chest.

Silence fell over the group for a few seconds before his dad broke it.

"Why the hell is the girl you love moving on, Adam?"

Adam dropped his trowel into the bucket and wiped his hands down the front of his thighs, transferring the grey dust onto his worn-out jeans. "Just because I love her doesn't mean we are going to be together. She *should* move on. Everything is exactly as it should be."

He reached for his bottle of water and drained it, then looked around at his family and friends, each with varying degrees of confusion.

"Why?" Denise asked.

Adam took in the worried looks of his friends and family and rolled his eyes. "What are you all doing here? Can't I just be alone for a while?"

Every eyebrow in the place shot up. Adam wondered whether he should commandeer his dad's new RV and drive away from this whole mess. He'd never been to the East Coast; maybe he'd go there. Or maybe he'd just get in his truck, drive straight to the airport, and catch the next flight to Ibiza. He'd spend a month drunk on the beach, sleeping with as many random women as he could.

It had never helped before, but maybe this time would be different.

"You want to be alone? *You?*" Denise asked.

"I'd rather be alone than part of this goddamn intervention," he muttered.

Max let out an annoyed grunt. "Adam won't commit to Chelsea, so she told him to fuck off."

"But why won't you commit, Adam? You love her."

A knock on the door caught everyone's attention.

"Who could that possibly fucking be?" Adam asked, unable to contain his anger.

Max turned to look out the window and gave an annoyed shake of his head. "I don't know. I'll get rid of them."

Max disappeared through the door, and Adam tried to get back to his work but caught everyone still staring at him, so he steeled himself to come clean. He might as well let it all out so everyone could just leave him the fuck alone.

"I refuse to drag someone I love, and her son, into my fucked-up life, only to die in a few years and leave them all alone."

It worked.

Silence fell across the room.

No one spoke.

Then everyone spoke at once.

"That's ridiculous," Denise said.

"You can't be serious," his dad said.

"That's not how this works," his uncle said.

Adam rolled his eyes. "Max agrees with me," he said, pointing across the room as Max stepped back into the doors.

His dad slowly tipped his head toward Max, who'd crossed his arms in front of his barrel chest. "What?" he said in an icy voice.

Max stared back, unintimidated. "What?"

"You don't think my son should be with the person he loves?"

Max glanced at Adam, his brows drawn, then shrugged. "Adam has a good point. Is it really responsible to start a family when you know you don't have that long to live?"

"That is the most ridiculous—"

"It's his life and this is how he feels," Max said in a cold, inflexible voice. "I grew up without my dad, so I can see where he's coming from. I support his decision not to get involved with someone who has a kid."

"Ohhhhh," said Antonio, making all eyes turn to him. "Sorry, I just realized that your tier ranking actually *is* right. Your tier one *is* a tier one. You just won't let yourself have them."

"Ranking?" Denise said, dripping disappointment and shaking her head. "Oh, Adam."

His dad ignored all this, seemingly stuck on the "not marrying someone" business.

"You can't seriously think that marrying someone is wrong, Adam. When I married your mother, she was in perfect health. We lost her too soon, but I wouldn't trade those years with her for anything."

Adam shook his head and laughed without humour. "Oh, really?"

"Yes, really."

"Bullshit."

His father's face hardened. "Excuse me?"

"You are still totally fucked up about losing mom. You won't even come to the house."

Another silence stretched, with his eyes locked on his father's, until Denise broke the silence. "I'm going to let you guys talk alone," Denise said.

Adam immediately regretted everything he'd just said. "Sorry, Denise. I didn't mean to—"

She pulled him into a hug, cutting him off. "I married your father because I love you both, and I'm incredibly happy with my life. Remember that," she said. She patted his dad's shoulder, then walked out of the room.

His dad rubbed his hands down his face. "You stopped going to therapy, didn't you?"

Adam rolled his eyes. "Lots of people don't get married. I don't need that."

"But it's what you've always wanted."

"Not anymore. I can have a great life without getting wifed up."

His dad shook his head. "You know, for someone who's always going on about how life is meant to be lived, you're sure leaving a lot on the table. Starting a family *is* living."

Adam shook his head. "I'm happy."

"Oh, yeah. You sure look it, too. What about you?" he said, directing his attention to Ethan. "You agree with this?"

Ethan gazed at Adam for a few beats before calmly answering. "No. I don't agree. But . . ."

"But what?"

"Well, Chelsea is technically my sister-in-law now, and I'm Ben's uncle. I want what's best for them, too. She wants a partner, and she deserves that. If Adam refuses to be that for her, then he should let her be."

They all fell silent, introspective.

"Have you all lost your fucking minds?"

They all looked up to find Uncle David staring at them all with a shocked look on his face.

"This is *not* how this works."

"Uncle David—"

"If Gracie were here right now, she'd slap you."

Adam reared back.

"Love doesn't just disappear when someone dies. It stays with you, coats you, like another layer of skin."

Adam was already formulating a counter-argument, but his brain snagged on his uncle's words, and eventually, they permeated through him.

Maybe he was right. Adam knew his mother loved him. And the love felt present, as if she were standing right there in the room with him, always.

He fell silent, wondering whether he'd got it all wrong. But still not convinced.

"Grace knew that giving her love away was the best thing to do, even when she got very sick. You're doing what she didn't do—leaving, hiding, and pushing people away. She gave *more* of her love, drowned you in it, so you'd always have it. If you love Chelsea and Ben, you should be spending your time giving as much love as you can to them."

Adam shook his head but with less conviction now. "It's different. My mom was healthy when she married my dad and had me."

"That's my point!" his uncle yelled. "You can't predict what will happen in life."

"I don't think you understand what I mean," Adam said.

"I understand what you mean, Adam. But you're wrong. Look," he said, coming closer. "Chelsea could move on from you and marry a perfectly healthy guy who could get hit by a car and die tomorrow. It's not a question of how long, but how much."

How much.

"Do you think anyone else could love her as much as you do?"

Adam looked down at his boots. He'd been miserable without getting to see her or talk to her or know how they were doing. He'd wanted to be there for them so badly. He'd thought he was sad because everything ended, but maybe it was just a whole ton of love that was bogging him down because he refused to give it away.

But still.

"It feels selfish," he said.

"It's sad that you feel that way, but I understand why. You're extremely altruistic, just like Gracie was. You'd take a bullet for anyone in this room. We all know it. The problem is that you haven't healed from seeing your mother die, and you're trying to save Chelsea from feeling that pain."

Adam's eyebrows rose.

"You need to go back to therapy, Adam, and work all of this out properly."

"I think he's right," Max said.

Adam turned to his friend, in shock that those words were coming out of Max's mouth. "What?"

Max blew out a breath. "Well, it makes sense, doesn't it?"

Adam looked around the room at all the heads nodding. He knew he was fucked up. He'd admitted it. Maybe talking to someone again would help. Having a relationship with Chelsea was so appealing that he would do almost anything. But he'd walked away from her, and she'd moved on.

"She told me I was like Jasper," he said.

"You're not," Ethan said immediately. "You were maybe just acting a little like him. From her point of view."

"She told me she loved me and wanted to be with me, and I told her no. In the hospital. When her son was in surgery," he said, shaking his head. "How am I possibly going to come back from that?"

"I don't know," his dad said, finally speaking after long moments of introspection. "But you can't just give up. You're clearly completely in love with her. This is probably going to be the best thing that's ever happened to you."

"Yeah," his uncle David said. "I'm seeing nothing but green flags. You gotta go for it."

Adam nodded. Even if Chelsea stuck to her guns, he clearly had a lot of issues he needed to work through. His perspective was already shifting. Maybe he'd wasted a ton of time already by fighting off feelings. He knew he had a lot of love to give. Maybe it was time to coat people with it.

"Okay," he said. "I'll call Dr. Sheffield's office."

His uncle pulled him into a hug. "Your mother would be very proud of you."

He pulled his phone from his pocket as everyone began leaving one-by-one. Only Max hung back for a moment.

"Do you need help finishing off?"

Adam shook his head, then glanced at the clock on the wall. "I'll finish up by the end of the day. But you should probably stay. The brewmaster is coming for an interview today. She should be here anytime."

Max's eyebrows scrunched, then he paled. His eyes shifted toward the door.

"She?"

Adam nodded. "Willow Spencer."

"Willow? I thought it was a guy. You said the brewmaster was Will something."

"Exactly. Will—ow. Don't be sexist."

Max swore under his breath as he scratched his jaw. "I think she was at the door earlier."

Adam stopped, his shoulders dropping. He was exhausted. "Fucking hell, Max. What did you do?"

Max shifted his weight between his feet. "I got rid of her."

"By 'got rid of her,' you mean what, exactly?"

Max winced.

Adam shook his head. "I'll deal with that later," he said, pulling his phone from his pocket and scrolling through his contacts for Dr. Sheffield's office. "Damage control with our brewmaster will have to wait."

THIRTY-ONE

Chelsea pulled her phone from her pocket and looked at the notification that had just pinged. It was from hot daddy. She did a little dance as she opened the conversation with him, mentally crossing her fingers that he'd said yes to her last message.

He had.

She squealed.

"What's that squealing all about?" Jae asked from the porch where she was working on her laptop.

Chelsea typed out a quick "Can't wait!" to his offer to pick her up on Saturday, then slipped her phone back into her pocket. For a split second, regret washed over her as she wished it were Adam instead. But then she reminded herself that he was a flaky deserter and shook it off. "I have a date on Saturday."

"Ooh, with hot daddy?"

Chelsea looked behind her where Ben was a hundred feet away, practising on his bike, then turned back to Jae. "Yup. He's picking me up at seven. I'm finally going on a date. Can you believe it?"

Jae smiled. "I absolutely can believe he wants to take you out. What I can't believe is how fast you're ticking off the items on your list."

Chelsea smiled, mentally checking off "Get some committed dad dick." "I *love* that list. I have taken care of my agent, too, and I am on high alert for any scooters."

"Mm-hmm. All that's left is to deal with the turd."

Chelsea nodded. She looked across the lawn at the film set where she found Jasper and Vincent together, filming a scene. She hadn't been back to work since the surgery, refusing to leave Ben's side. She'd called Jasper the day after the surgery to let him know what had happened and that she'd be taking time off to be with their son, and wasn't surprised at all when he showed almost no concern. In fact, all he said was, "When will you be back?"

"Mama!"

Chelsea looked away from Jasper and put her attention on Ben. She knew she'd have to go over there soon, but she was feeling uneasy about quitting.

"Yes?"

"Are you recording?"

Chelsea picked her DSLR camera that was around her neck up and pointed it at him. "Yup. You ready?"

"I'm gonna do it," he said, swinging a leg over the bike.

He'd said that a million times, but maybe this would be the one. "I have a good feeling about this time, Ben."

She'd also said that a million times now.

Chelsea hit Record and yelled, "Action!"

He got the pedals lined up, put one foot on, and furrowed his little brow in concentration. He pedalled down, then lifted his other foot, and placed it on the pedal as the bike began tipping dramatically to one side.

She stepped forward to steady him, but he pulled back and balanced himself out . . . and kept pedalling.

"Oh my God," she said, nearly dropping the camera.

"Holy shit!" Jae yelled from the porch. "He's doing it!"

Chelsea held the camera steady, following behind him. He was actually doing it. She focused on Ben's legs going around and around as he created more and more distance between them.

"You're doing it, Benny!" she yelled, jumping up and down and jogging toward him. "You're biking!"

He went through a few more rotations, moving about twenty feet in total before falling. But when she got to him, he was ecstatic. He was jumping up and down, punching the air, and chanting, "Oh yeah," over and over.

"Did you get it?"

She kissed his cheek, pulling him in tight. "I got the whole thing, buddy. You did so great! You should be so proud of yourself."

When she pulled back and looked at his round eyes and flushed cheeks, the pride swelled in her chest.

"I'm proud of me," he said, beaming a smile. "I'm never riding a scooter again!"

With that, he let go of her, picked up his bike, and got on again.

Chelsea stood staring for a while as Jae ran past her to Ben and hugged him.

Never riding a scooter again?

Me neither.

She pulled the camera off her neck and handed it to Jae. Jae took it with her brows raised. She opened her mouth to say something, but Chelsea had already turned away and started marching down the path and across the lawn toward Jasper.

She kept walking until she stood behind him, yet she couldn't find words to say.

His back was to her as he focused on the scene he was shooting, until she interrupted him with an impatient tap on his shoulder and a loud throat clear.

He turned around, pulling a set of headphones off. "Chelsea. Wow. Are you *finally* coming back to work?"

Chelsea's eyes went wide, then she smiled. Oh, this was going to be fun.

"You're a turd," she said.

Literal gasps went up. The first AD, gaffers, and talent all gaped at her as if she'd lost her mind.

"Excuse me?"

"You heard me," she said, nodding. "A turd. An asshole. A douchebag. A selfish bastard. You don't care about anyone but your self and your job. You never even came to see Ben after his surgery, and you've been here the whole time! You will never change. And I fucking hate you," she said, screaming the last two words.

Jasper looked around at the people staring at them, then yelled, "Take five," but few people moved.

"In case you weren't sure, I quit. I'm honestly not sure why I ever even agreed to work for someone like you. Even for a few days. It was hell. You're the worst."

Jasper's nostrils flared. "Got it. Leave. Now."

Chelsea nodded. "I want you off my property as soon as you're done here, and not a second later."

Jasper's jaw clenched. "Fine. You done now?"

Chelsea smiled and shook her head. "One more thing. You'll be hearing from my lawyer. I want the child support you've never given your son, since you're just such a selfish asshole."

"He never paid you child support?"

Chelsea's head whipped over to Vincent, who she'd just realized had been listening to the whole thing. She shook her head. "Only a few hundred bucks here and there."

She looked back at Jasper. "Now I'm done." She turned and started walking away when Vincent's voice broke through again.

"Wait, Chelsea," he said. "I'm coming with you."

She stopped in her tracks and spun around. Vincent was already busy packing his equipment up.

"What?" Jasper said in a vicious tone.

"Yeah," Vincent said dismissively. "I hate you, too. I have no respect for someone who abandons their child, and I'm way too damn old to be spending time with someone I have no respect for. I'm going with her."

Chelsea looked around at the rest of the crew, all in shock. She'd never seen so many unhinged jaws.

"You can't be serious," Jasper said. "You signed a contract—"

"Sue me," Vincent said, flipping his camera case closed and hoisting it up, then looking Chelsea dead in the eye. "Ready?"

Chelsea smiled and nodded, then they walked off the set together to her house.

"I can't believe you just did that," she said once they were out of earshot.

"Your words were very inspiring," he said, then stopped and looked her in the eyes. "I want to make your movie."

Chelsea stared at him, hardly able to believe what was happening. She couldn't form words.

"Look, I know this is scary, but I can help you through it and shoot it for you. I have about a million contacts in the industry. I can get us in front of some investors, or we can just do it on the cheap. Your call. But I want in."

How could this be happening right now?

"You're not saying anything," Vincent said with a laugh. "Maybe you want to do it alone, and I respect that. But I'd love if you'd take me on board. Your script really stuck with me. I can see entire scenes. I have ideas for lighting, sounds, locations . . . I know the perfect place to film the office scenes."

Was her idol really asking her if he could help make her movie?

Vincent laughed. "Do you want to see my resumé? I'll need to update it. It's been a while since anyone's asked for it."

"Oh my God," she said, her face splitting in two. "Of course not. You really want to make this with us?"

Vincent nodded. "Yes. And I'd love to meet Jae."

Chelsea glanced at her house, anticipating Jae's excitement. "Okay."

"Okay?"

Chelsea laughed. "Yes!"

Vincent smiled. "I can't wait. God, it feels good to do something I want for a change. Let's go meet Jae."

They walked toward her house, Chelsea still in a state of shock.

"Hey," Vincent said after a few strides. "Can I tour the inside of your house, too? I wondered if you had an attic or a basement that might work for the murder scene."

Chelsea nodded. "I have the perfect barn."

THIRTY-TWO

Adam walked up and down the toy store aisles, filling his cart with anything and everything he thought Ben might like. It was half full, but he was going to keep adding toys until the cart was overflowing and gifts were literally falling onto the floor. He'd just left his therapist's office, and his words still rang in Adam's ears.

He knew exactly what he had to do.

He'd tried to call Chelsea two days before to see how they were doing, but his call had gone directly to voice mail, so he figured she'd probably blocked his number. Less than ideal, but he was determined to come back from it.

And as his uncle had told him, if she was smart enough to tell him to fuck off, she was worth the effort to win back. Even if it took a lifetime.

He rounded the corner, pulling a few boxes of building sets from a display and tossing them into the cart, and looked up to find the superhero aisle.

Perfect.

He walked down the aisle with his arm out, sweeping every Spider-Man toy into the cart. Ben was going to love this.

He paused for a moment, wondering whether Chelsea would accuse him of trying to buy his way into their lives, then shrugged and kept walking.

Ben had invited him to his birthday party, and Adam was just making up for the fact that he'd missed it. If he hadn't been so stubborn back then and had accepted the fact that he was completely in love with them, he would have brought gifts for the kid. So this wasn't an inappropriate gesture.

He looked down at the cart and could hear his father's voice in his head about spoiling kids. Shit, maybe this was a bad idea.

Another shrug. He'd worry about raising kids the right way if—when—Chelsea forgave him and let him into their lives. For now, he was going to spoil.

"Hi, do you need some help?"

Adam blinked at the salesgirl, looking at his cart as if he'd lost his mind, and smiled. "Nope. I'm done."

"If you're shopping for a toy drive, we have complimentary wrapping and delivery."

Toy drive? Shit. He *definitely* took it too far.

"Uh, no. No, this is just for me. But I do need wrapping paper. Where is that?"

She led him down the aisle, and he searched for Spider-Man wrapping paper, but there was none, so he bought the toys and went to a different store for the wrapping paper.

Three hours and four stores later, he was on the floor of his living room, surrounded by toys and empty rolls of wrapping paper and tape, with scraps of paper everywhere. But there was a towering stack of red and blue presents ready to go.

He loaded them all in his truck, then realized he'd lost almost all day and evening. It was 6:48.

What time did kids go to bed? He had no clue.

He sent a quick text to Mia asking what Ben's bedtime might be. She texted back "prbly 8," so he figured it was safe to go over. Ben might not have time to unwrap all the presents, but he could work on the rest in the morning.

Grabbing his keys, he left the house and hopped into the truck. He tried her cell again but got no response, so he suppressed his anxiety and drove on.

It took only four minutes to get there, time he spent thinking about what to say.

I'm sorry. I was stupid. I caused you pain by projecting my own fears onto you, and I will never do that again. I'm dealing with my trauma now. I'm in therapy. I love you. If you still have feelings for me, please let me love you for the rest of my life.

He braced himself, knocked on her door, and ten seconds later, it swung open, revealing Chelsea and her huge dimpled smile, looking as beautiful as ever.

His mind blanked.

He couldn't form words.

Beads of sweat formed at his temples.

Her smile dropped immediately, and a deep scowl emerged.

Shit.

"Hey . . ." he said, his voice full of nerves. He couldn't stop it from shaking, couldn't think of all the things to say. It really wasn't like him to flounder like this around women. But to be fair, charming random women out of their panties was way different than asking the best person in the whole world to be his . . . his.

She stared at him, waiting, annoyed. A pretty eyebrow cocked up at him.

Say something!

"What's up?" he said, immediately regretting it. What the fuck was he doing? He was way, way out of his depth here.

He glanced at his feet, shook his head a little, then looked up to start over. But she was already rolling her eyes. "Ch—"

"What's up?" she asked, cutting him off with a humourless laugh. "My standards. *That's* what's up."

Smack!

The door slammed in his face so hard the windows rattled. This was going badly. He took a deep breath, started rehearsing his lines again while making ten trips to his truck to unload all Ben's presents onto the porch. It took him a few minutes, then he braced himself and knocked again.

He was actually a little surprised when the door opened.

"You again?" she said, her pretty hand on her squishy hip. God, he fucking loved her hips.

"Me again."

She looked down at the porch covered in presents. "What the hell is all this?"

"Presents. Birthday presents. For Ben."

Her scowl deepened. "He doesn't want presents. He wants people that will show up and sing 'Happy Birthday' to him. Go away."

The door started closing in his face again. "Wait! Please!" he said, relieved when she paused. "I'm sorry I missed his birthday. I will *never* miss another one for the rest of my life."

"You won't have the chance to disappoint us again, Adam. Goodbye."

"I'm so sorry, Chelsea, for the way I acted. I was stupid and I hurt you and it's the last thing on earth I want to do."

Chelsea's face softened slightly, and she rolled her beautiful eyes. "Fine. Now leave."

"Actually, I was hoping—"

"Stop," she said, cutting him off. "Don't hope. I've moved on, and you should do the same. We are awkward acquaintances, at best. Let's just leave it at that."

Adam started shaking his head. "I can't leave it at that. I'm in love with you."

Chelsea squeezed her eyes shut. "Why are you mindfucking me like this?"

Adam's attention snagged on a pair of sparkly gold earrings dangling from her ears. He looked more carefully at her and saw that she'd dressed up more so than usual. She'd styled her blond hair beautifully around her face and had makeup on her eyes.

"Are you going somewhere?"

"I told you, I've moved on."

As if on cue, car tires began crunching in the gravel behind him. He spun around to see a grey SUV coming up the driveway and stopping next to his truck.

He turned back to Chelsea. "Are you going out with someone?"

Chelsea nodded.

"Who?"

Just then, the car door opened and Scott Tanner stepped out, holding a fucking bouquet, his step faltering as they made eye contact.

"Adam?"

Fucking hell.

"Hey, Scott," he said with an awkward wave. What the fuck did you say to the guy bringing your dream girl flowers? Especially when you knew he was a good guy. He had a daughter, too, if Adam remembered correctly. Probably around Ben's age.

Chelsea was better off with Scott.

Adam stopped his self-loathing train of thought and shook it off, hearing his therapist in his ear. He *knew* no one could love Chelsea as much as him. There wasn't anyone who would treat her better.

"What's going on?" Scott asked.

"Adam's just leaving," Chelsea said, stepping onto the porch and pulling the door closed behind her. "I'm ready to go."

"Actually," Adam said, turning to Scott and bracing himself for the awkward bomb he was about to detonate. "I'm here to shoot my shot with Chelsea. I'm in love with her."

Scott's thick brows rose. "You?"

Adam gave a half laugh. "I know, right?" he said, trying to ease the tension. His reputation was known far and wide.

"I love her, more than anything. I respect you, Scott. I like you a lot. But I'm not going to back down."

Chelsea brushed past Adam, walked down the stairs. "Not gonna happen, Adam. If you thought you were going to come here, say some nice things, and I was going to forget everything that happened, you were mistaken."

Adam shook his head. "I know it's going to take time. I just came by to bring Ben his birthday presents and let you know that I'm going to be trying to get you back."

"There is no *back*, Adam. We never were . . . anywhere. Just go."

Adam nodded, trying not to let the heartbreak show on his face. It probably was, though. He knew he was shit at hiding emotion. And the sadness and regret was bubbling up in his throat. If he could feel it this much, then it was definitely showing.

"We were *somewhere*, Chelsea. And I loved it. And I want it back." He blinked hard, cleared his throat, worried he'd end up crying as he had when Max's dog died. "I'm gonna go. But I'm *not* giving up on this."

He walked to her, and when she stared at him, paralyzed, and he felt sure she wasn't going to slap him or recoil, he leaned in and kissed her cheek. "I love you, good night."

He turned to Scott, shrugged, and said, "Sorry," then climbed into his truck, and drove off, leaving them standing in the driveway together.

He felt like an asshole. A horribly depressed asshole. He desperately wanted to take her on a date. He couldn't help thinking about the irony of the situation compared to the baseball diamonds when he'd first asked her out. If he hadn't run away, what would've happened? If he had known then what he knew now, how much different would things be?

What a fucking mess.

He tried to ignore the dread that imagining Chelsea sitting across from Scott brought up. She'd smile with her dimples and laugh at his jokes. Her face was irresistible when she was happy. Scott would try to make her smile the entire night.

There was a really good chance he'd succeed.

Which meant there was an equally good chance that Adam was totally fucked.

But he meant what he'd said. He wouldn't give up. He just needed to think of a way to show her how much he loved her and make her understand he would love her until the end of time, even long after he was gone.

Thirty-Three

"Sorry about that," Chelsea said, taking another step toward Scott's car and trying desperately to shake off the image of Adam's face. She knew he regretted what had happened. And she had no doubt he loved her. But she wouldn't take a chance on a flighty guy like that again.

Scott was the right choice.

"Ready?" she asked when she realized she was the only one moving.

Scott glanced between her and the presents on the porch in silence. Back and forth. Back and forth. Until finally, he dropped the bouquet he was holding to his hip, slumped his shoulders forward, and sighed.

"Chelsea, I'm sorry. I don't think I can do this."

Chelsea shook her head. "It's all over between Adam and me. Really. You don't have to worry about him."

Scott winced. "It really doesn't seem that way. Besides, I've known Adam since I was a kid, and he's never, and I mean *never*, been serious about someone. I can't be the one to . . . try to steal his girl."

"I'm not his girl," she said, ready to grab her date by the arm and drag him to the car while he protested. "We weren't even really together."

"He looked heartbroken, Chelsea."

Chelsea felt her own heartbreak at the thought of Adam being heartbroken, but only for a moment. She shook it off and stared at her date, unable to believe this was happening. He'd been happy when she called, eager to make plans for them to go out for dinner, and now he was bailing on her.

How was it *this* impossible to find a dude that would follow through?

"So you're standing me up, then?" she asked.

Scott lifted a hand through his hair, looked her up and down, then blew out an almost astonished laugh. "I can't believe it, but yes. I'm so sorry. If things really end with Adam, please call me."

Chelsea sighed, resisting the urge to yell at him that things *were* over, but she wouldn't stoop to begging, no matter how much she wanted to finally go out on a date.

"Why do you care so much about what Adam thinks? Did he save your puppy from getting hit by a car or something?"

Scott laughed. "No. But he helped me build a wheelchair ramp on my grandmother's house. She's ninety-three. He refused to take her money, too."

Chelsea hummed and nodded. "Saint Adam strikes again."

Scott laughed. "You're funny," he said, his gaze sliding down her body. "I must be out of my mind," he muttered as he passed her the bouquet and walked to the driver's door. "I'll see you around, Chelsea."

She waved him goodbye as he went down the driveway, standing in the gravel, wondering whether he'd come to his senses and come back, but he didn't. She let out a sigh, walked past the mountain of presents on the porch and back inside, then kicked off her shoes, which flew across the floor until they hit the wall.

"Chels?" Jae said, coming around the corner with Vincent close behind.

She'd planned to leave Jae and Vincent brainstorming in the kitchen for a few hours while she went out with hot daddy. The bright side was that she wouldn't miss out on any of the planning. She'd much rather be on that date, though.

"Why are you back?" Vincent asked.

"I got stood up."

Vincent and Jae both looked shocked, which made Chelsea's ego pick herself up off the floor a little. She filled them in before calling to Ben to go out to the porch and bring all the presents inside before it started raining.

"Oh my God," Jae said, walking to the kitchen table and slumping in a chair.

Vincent stood staring at the front door as Ben brought in armload after armload full of presents.

"Are these all for me?" Ben asked, looking at her with wide eyes.

She wanted to scream. "Yes."

"Can I open them?"

Chelsea sighed and nodded. What was she going to do? Load them back in her car and throw them onto Adam's porch? That seemed kinda low.

"The Hartley kid isn't one for subtlety, eh?" Vincent asked, closing the door behind Ben after he'd brought in the last of them.

Chelsea reached to her ears and pulled her fancy earrings out. Her sadness was turning into anger. She'd spent an hour and a half getting ready for that date. Then Adam showed up on her doorstep and cock-blocked her. Subtle? No. He was anything but. He'd blown his chance, and now he was just fucking with her.

"He's a nuisance."

Jae finally got over her shock enough to speak. "So, Adam said he loves you and wants to get back together? And he said you were perfect, and he was heartbroken, and he looked like he was going to cry?"

Chelsea nodded.

"And you didn't run into his arms and forgive him?"

"Of course not." Chelsea turned, making her way to the stairs. "I'm not scootering anymore. Remember number five?"

Jae guffawed, too shocked to speak.

Vincent spoke up for her. "I don't think *anyone* would consider Adam a scooter, including those who don't know he's a billionaire."

Chelsea paused, considering his words. "Walking out on me is something a scooter would do."

Vincent narrowed his eyes. "Are you sure about that? He *did* have reasons. And no matter how misplaced, those reasons came from a place of love."

Chelsea glanced over at Jae, who was now shaking her head violently, then looked over at Ben tearing into the zillions of presents. The Spider-Man wrapping paper was all but swallowing him up on the floor.

She'd convinced herself that Adam, and her situationship with him, was a broken-down, rusty old scooter.

And she was right.

Right?

Maybe he *had* changed. Had he somehow morphed from a scooter into a bike? God, if that were true, she wanted to hop on and ride him forever.

She shook her head at how that sounded, happy she hadn't said it out loud.

She had no reason not to believe him. He was a great many things, but a liar was *not* one of them. But could she really trust him to be there for her after everything that had happened?

"I need some time to think," she said, lumbering toward the stairs.

"Careful," Vincent said, giving her a pointed look. "Don't spend too much time on the wrong path. The clock is always ticking."

THIRTY-FOUR

Adam took a utility knife from the workbench in his garage and opened a box that had just been delivered. He'd gone a little wild that week, ordering all manner of things, hoping one of the many plans he'd concocted to get Chelsea back would actually work.

He'd sent her chocolates, and flowers, and even a note telling her he'd reserved tickets to TIFF for next year and hoped they would be a couple by then. If they weren't a couple by then, and it took years and years to get her back, he was determined to convince her that he was in it for the long haul.

He pulled a huge vintage stereo from the box and laughed to himself. He was going to look ridiculous holding it over his head in front of her house, like the scene from *Say Anything*. At least she would laugh.

Probably.

She was always quoting movies, and would probably find it funny.

Unless she hated that movie.

Was that a movie that film nerds liked? Probably
not. It was just a silly romcom, right? He had no clue.

Adam shook his head and set the stereo down on
the bench. She'd still laugh at him. And he'd get the
dimples. Maybe even an eye roll if he was lucky.

He knew she loved *Jaws* from the framed poster
he'd seen in her house. And *Pulp Fiction* and *Good-
fellas*. Maybe there was something in one of those
movies that he could do for her. He'd have to think
about it. He was surveying his options when his
phone rang.

"Uncle David!"

"Nephew Adam! How's it going?"

Adam eyed the stereo. "I'm not sure yet," he said.

"Well, that's better than bad. Have you been going
to your therapist?" he asked.

Adam smiled. "Yes, I have. Everything is going well
on that front."

"And things with Chelsea?"

Adam scratched the stubble on his jaw as he took
in the stereo and wondered for the millionth time
how her date with Scott had gone. Hopefully, they
hated each other, though he couldn't see how that
would be possible. Best-case scenario, they were

just casually dating and not officially together. He really didn't want to steal Scott's girlfriend.

But he would.

"It's going so-so," he settled on. "How are you?"

"I'm great. I have some news."

Adam sat down on the stool, looked at the buttons on the stereo. "What is it?" he asked.

"Well, I offered to fund Chelsea's feature, and she turned me down."

Adam's hand froze as he tried to process the words. "Chelsea's feature?"

"Yeah, you didn't know? She quit Lilian's project, told Jasper to go to hell, and poached Vincent off the set."

"She did?" he asked, his face breaking into a grin.

"She sure did. It's all anyone is talking about. She's made quite a splash."

"She has?" he asked again.

"Yeah. Jasper's become something of a pariah—Lilian's shitting herself. And everyone in town is trying to get in on Chelsea's project."

He hopped up from his seat. "They are?"

Uncle David laughed. "Yeah, the premise sounds brilliant, and once Vincent backed it, it caught everyone's attention. Where the hell have you been?" he asked, as if everyone had access to this information.

Adam rolled his eyes at himself. He'd been racking his brain, thinking of ways to get her back, and hadn't even deployed all his resources. "I've been trying to figure out how to win her back."

"She shot you down pretty hard, eh?"

"Like a highly trained sniper."

Uncle David laughed. "Good girl. I could tell she was smart," he said, then fell silent for a moment. "I was calling you to see if you could convince her to let me invest, but I'm guessing she told me no *because* of you."

Adam nodded. "I wouldn't doubt it," he said. He looked around his workbench until his eyes landed on his mitre saw, and a brilliant thought popped into his mind. He let it roll around for a moment, then smiled. If she was hesitant to take his money, maybe he could help her with her film in a different way.

"Adam—"

"Sorry," he said, cutting his uncle off. "I just had a thought. Can you get me a copy of the script?"

"Of course."

"Like, right away?"

"I'll have it couriered to you within an hour," he said.

"Thanks, that would be great. I think I know what to do."

"To help me invest?"

"No," Adam said, shaking his head. He grabbed his keys from his bench, jogged to his truck. "To get her to see that I'm with her until the end. I gotta go."

"Okay. Good luck."

"Thanks," he said, getting into his truck and turning it on. "I'll talk to you later."

He hung up the phone and headed straight for the hardware store, feeling way better about his new plan than the stereo.

THIRTY-FIVE

Chelsea pulled up in Adam's driveway, killed the engine of her car. She saw him even before getting out. He was standing in his garage with his back to her, surrounded by a cloud of sawdust. When she opened the car door, she was struck with blaring music and whirring saws.

He set aside a long piece of wood, pulled a measuring tape from his belt and a pencil from behind his ear.

She could stare at him all day. But for now, she needed to sort out this . . . thing between them.

She had sworn off him for good, but then he'd declared his intentions, and given presents to Ben, and insisted he loved her.

And then she heard a rumour from Vincent that he'd asked for a copy of her screenplay. She had to know what his game was.

"Adam," she said, but her voice didn't even reach her own ears over the sound of the music and saw, let alone his.

"Adam!" she yelled.

Still nothing.

She walked closer to him, tapped his muscular shoulder blade through his thin white T-shirt.

He stopped sawing and spun around, surprised, but his face immediately melted into a smile. He set down the wood, pulled off his safety glasses.

"Chelsea," he said, looking so happy it melted her heart. Slightly. He broke eye contact for a moment, looking around at whatever project he was working on, and when he looked back, he was a little less confident.

"Hi," she said.

He leaned in, the smell of wood and cologne messing with her brain, and placed a sweet kiss on her cheek. It was the same kiss he'd given her that night after he'd professed his love in front of her date and left.

She fought the emotion that it brought up, the exasperation, and yes, the love. But she also felt apprehension. She wasn't interested in going back to the way things were.

She wanted a whole entire committed relationship with someone, and she refused to settle for less.

"Sorry to drop in on you," she said, suddenly feeling shy.

Adam shook his head. "You're always welcome here."

Her gaze went to her fingers intertwined at her stomach. She was incredibly conflicted. She wanted to hug him. Wanted to kick him in the shin. Wanted to call him an ass. Wanted to run.

Mostly, though, she wanted answers.

"Congratulations," Adam said, "on going for it with your film. And for telling Jasper to go fuck himself. I tried to call, but . . ."

Chelsea met his eyes. He looked sad. He probably knew she'd blocked him. But he deserved it.

Didn't he?

"That's why I came here, actually."

Adam's eyebrows lifted. "I know you're mad, but I really think you should reconsider blocking—"

"Not the blocking, Adam."

Adam looked down. "Oh."

Chelsea sighed. "Did you ask your uncle to offer me money? Because if you think that will make me forget about you walking away from me—"

"No," Adam said, shaking his head. His eyes linked to hers, and she knew he was telling the truth. "I didn't know about that at all. He likes you, and he trusts Vincent, so he wants to invest in your film. It was a business decision."

Chelsea narrowed her eyes at him, but she wasn't really sure why. She believed every word that came out of his mouth.

"I swear, Chelsea."

A smile slipped on her lips, and she turned to look at his workbench to hide it. And that's when her eyes landed on the familiar stack of bound papers. She walked over and picked up her script.

"Why do you have this?"

Adam huffed out a breath, stuck his hands in his pockets. "Uncle David called and told me about you walking off the set and taking Vincent with you. I just asked for a copy."

"Why?"

Adam's shoulders stiffened. "I want to help you."

"Help me how?"

He shuffled his feet, looking more nervous than she thought possible for him.

"Well, I can build almost anything, and I know a lot goes into the sets . . ."

He trailed off as Chelsea flipped to the dogeared pages of the script, read Adam's notes in the margins, then stopped.

"Are you building my sets?" She looked up at his eyes. He looked worried.

"I don't have to. I can think of something else. There's always the stereo."

Chelsea shook her head. "Stereo?"

Adam nodded. "'Fraid so. See?" He pointed at a ridiculous eighties-style boom box on the floor by the sawhorses. "I was going to hold it up outside your window if the set building thing didn't work out."

Chelsea laughed. "That is so . . ."

Adam.

She couldn't think of anything more Adam. Except maybe offering to build her sets. He would do anything for the people he cared about.

"The boom box thing doesn't work for John Cusack," she said. "Ione Skye's character ignores him."

His posture sagged. "I fucked up so bad," he said, out of the blue, but also not. "I hurt you when I walked away, and it's my biggest regret. Actually, I regret not showing up for Ben's birthday. And the baseball diamonds when I ran off . . ." He let out a long, low sigh. "I have a lot of regrets when it comes to you. Literally everything I did was wrong."

Chelsea hugged the script to her chest, completely overwhelmed that he was in his garage building something for her. Something that meant the world to her.

"I wish I could turn back time, Chelsea. All the way back to that baseball tournament when I asked you out. I've replayed it repeatedly and can't believe that I let my fears keep me from you for so long."

Chelsea's heart was filling up, as if it were a bucket and he was holding the hose.

"I made mistake after mistake. I experienced a lot of traumas when I was young, and it's shaped my fears, and then I projected those fears onto you."

Chelsea stared at him, shocked.

"I'm back in therapy," he said with a shrug. "I can see everything that I did was to protect myself from feeling too much. But I'm working on that. I just . . . I can't . . ."

He huffed out a breath, looked down at the ground to steady himself, then back up at her. "Do you still have any feelings for me at all?" he asked, his eyes full of emotion.

Did she? Of course she did. It was impossible not to. But she was terrified this would end again and totally wreck her. It all came down to whether or not she trusted him.

She should.

But did she?

She set the script back down on the bench and took a deep breath. "What do you want, Adam?"

"I just want to see you. And talk to you. And touch you. And coat you with my love for as long as I can," he said.

Chelsea's eyes went wide. "Coat me with your love?"

Adam smiled. "Metaphorically, but I mean, if you want me to coat you in something—"

"Adam . . ."

He laughed. God, she loved that laugh.

He closed the distance between them, reached his hand to her chin. "It's my intention to prove to you how much I love you, date you for an appropriate amount of time, and as soon as you seem open to the idea, I want to marry you. I want to see you every day. I want to make you smile every day. I want to be a family. I want to teach Ben how to do everything. I want to take him to Disney World. I want all of it."

Chelsea stepped even closer to him, melted as his arms came around her, engulfing her and pressing her into his chest. He was warm and smelled like fresh-cut wood.

She adored him.

"But for now," he said, resting his chin on the top of her head, "I'd kill to take you on a date."

She'd buried her face in his chest, but her smile took over. "A date?"

Adam hummed in his throat, causing a rumble deep in his chest. "I never should have walked away from you at that baseball diamond. Never."

Chelsea tamped down the emotion filling her throat. "Okay."

Adam pulled back, looked into her eyes. "Okay?"

Chelsea nodded, tears pricking her eyes.

"Thank God," he said, then pulled her in and kissed her.

Thirty-Six

Adam wiped his sweaty palms on the front of his pants as he stepped out of his truck and walked to the front door of Monroe Manor. Inside was Chelsea. God, he loved her so fucking much. It was weird to be going out on a first date with a girl you already knew you'd spend the rest of your life with, but it was also incredibly exciting.

He'd just have to control his adoration for her a little. He didn't want to be too intense and scare her off.

He rolled his eyes at himself. He probably should have thought about that before he went to the jewellery store and bought her a ring that would make a queen drool. Oh well. He'd just have to wait for the right time.

And the right time was *not* when she opened the door for their first date. He had to remind himself of that again when she opened the door and his heart nearly jumped out of his chest. He wanted to drop to one knee and beg.

Maybe he'd give it fifteen dates?

Ten was probably plenty.

Five, at least.

"Hi," she said with a little laugh.

"Hi. You're so beautiful. Here," he said, handing her a gigantic bouquet of peach-coloured roses. He'd bought every single one the florist had.

Once she'd taken them, he pulled a jewellery box from his pocket and handed it to her as well.

"What's this?" she asked, staring at the box in her hand.

"Open it."

She flipped open the lid and smiled.

Then laughed.

"Did you get me macaroni earrings?" she asked, sliding them from the velvet.

"To go with your bracelet," he said, happy that she seemed to like them. They were custom made, with a diamond stud and a 24K gold macaroni dropping from each lobe. She quickly replaced her earrings with the new ones.

"How do they look?" she asked, giving her head a little shake so they'd dance around.

"Not as beautiful as your eyes, but nothing is."

He looked at the earrings and the bouquet, but it didn't feel like enough. Maybe he should have got her a cheesecake, too.

And a new car.

And the PIN to his credit card.

And a key to his house.

Her smile grew, and so did his heart. He couldn't believe he was getting a second chance. This time, he wouldn't mess it up.

"Ready?" she asked, stepping onto the porch and closing the door behind her.

Adam leaned down, kissed her lips. When he pulled back, her beautiful eyes had gone all dreamy, and her dimples were flashing.

"I'm ready," he said.

They walked to his truck hand in hand, finally on their way to their first date.

Twenty Dates Later

Chelsea sat in the front seat of Adam's truck as he pulled to a stop on the street in front of Keller's Pub.

"Wow," she said, looking up at the brand new sign above the door with sconce lights illuminating it from above. "This looks amazing, Adam."

Adam nodded. "It really came together."

"I can't believe you guys are going to be opening soon."

She hopped out of the truck, and he and Ben followed, meeting on the sidewalk. Adam took their hands in his and they made their way to the front door.

She looked down at their linked hands, wondering why his skin was so hot even though the temperature had dropped the night before and the cold wind whipped through the town at them.

He was downright sweaty.

They reached the door, and before even entering, he'd begun unzipping his coat and unbuttoning the top button of his shirt.

"You okay?" she asked.

Adam jerked his head up and down in a nod without uttering a word, then opened the door. Ben darted past them into the restaurant before Adam pressed a hand into the small of her back, gently nudging her through the door.

She shook her head and stepped inside, excited that they had decided to have a "soft opening" for their friends and family so she could finally see what Adam and Max had been working tirelessly on for months.

She hadn't been inside for more than thirty seconds when she knew, without a doubt, that Keller's Pub would be a hit. They'd nailed the warm and cozy atmosphere they were trying to achieve.

The entryway had a massive fireplace, which warmed the heavenly scented air. Inside the dining room, the back wall was a gorgeous exposed brick, with the others painted a rich coffee colour that complimented the leather upholstery on the deep booths.

Chelsea caught sight of Ben, who had already sat down with Lawrence and Denise. They smiled indulgently at him as a waiter dropped off a glass of orange juice, and Chelsea's heart swelled. She couldn't believe how lucky they were to have Adam in their lives. His family had accepted her son as if he were their own.

She bit back the emotion flooding in as the hostess greeted them and ushered them through the dining room. They waved and smiled to friends and family they passed along the way, then sank down into the plush seats.

"So comfy," Chelsea said, squishing deeper into the cushion. "I could sit here eating and drinking all night."

"That's the idea," Adam said, taking her hand back into his sweaty palm across the table.

Chelsea ignored it, assuming he was just nervous for the first full house. She knew things were coming down to the wire with the grand opening looming and that everyone was a little on edge hoping it would be ready in time. They had hoped this would be a good trial run so they could test all the systems and make sure things would go smoothly.

Her gaze swept around the room until it landed on Max by the bar with Willow, his head bent down quite close to hers as they looked over some papers. When she turned to leave, Max's gaze lingered on her butt, and a smile came to his lips.

A real, actual smile.

Chelsea reared back, unable to believe it.

"I just saw Max *smile*. At Willow."

"Huh?"

"Max smiled. I didn't know his face could do that. Is something going on between the two of them?"

Adam quickly glanced at his friend, then did a double take before shaking it off.

Chelsea's heart rate pick up. "Are you sure you're okay?"

"Yeah," he said. He reached for the back of his neck, then quickly changed course, bringing his hand down and nearly knocking over a glass of water on the table.

"Sorry," he said, pushing it aside, then rubbing his face.

Chelsea narrowed her eyes. "Something's wrong."

Adam shook his head. "No."

"Yes," she said. "You look . . . nervous. And you're all sweaty."

He pulled his hand from hers and wiped it on a napkin. "I was just thinking this is our twentieth date."

"It is?" Chelsea said as she glanced around the room, wondering whether she should call for help. Natalie's smile and wave from the booth in the corner caught her attention. Chelsea waved back, thankful Natalie had been appeased by Adam's blood oath that he would never hurt Chelsea or Ben again and started supporting their relationship.

"Yeah, well," Adam stumbled. "I guess it depends on how you define a date. Some are easy to count, like the Leafs game or the Halloween party."

Chelsea smiled, her eyes dropping down his body as she remembered how he'd looked in that Spider-Man costume.

And the Leafs jersey.

Honestly, he always looked good.

"But others are harder to decipher," he said, drawing her eyes back up to his. "Like there was that time I dropped off lunch for you and Jae and Vincent, which doesn't seem like a date, but I did stay and eat with you. I counted that. Does that count?"

Her mind spun as his knee bounced violently under the table and beads of sweat formed on his brow.

"I don't know," she said.

"Or that day we met up for coffee at Brin's. Or when we went to the rink to teach Ben to skate. Do those count?"

Chelsea shook her head a little, trying to make it all make sense. "Why are you counting our dates, Adam?"

He let out a deep exhale. "I figured twenty dates was a good amount of time to wait before proposing."

Propo—

Chelsea's heart literally stopped, and the room started spinning. It was as if someone had changed her life to slo-mo. She stared at him as her jaw slowly dropped toward the table.

Did he say proposing?

"Good evening!"

She slowly blinked as an overbright voice accompanied by a dark shadow moved into her peripheral vision. Adam's mouth moved, presumably ordering drinks, but Chelsea couldn't hear anything. Finally, the waiter retreated, and she was left with Adam staring at her with a blank expression.

Her mouth opened to fill the silence, but nothing came out.

All she could think was how long it had taken them just to go on the first date. She'd figured she had at least a year before he'd wrap his mind around proposing.

She was certain there was no one, and never would be anyone, except Adam. Marrying him was a done deal. But they'd only been officially dating for a couple months.

Not even.

"If those dates don't count," he said, taking her silence as a rejection, "I can wait a few more. Maybe we could take Ben to the movies again. Or the arcade. Or that indoor water park we were thinking about going to."

Her eyes slowly filled, and her love for him overflowed as he suggested dates that included her son. She had never felt more loved and cared for. In the time since their first date, he'd always put her and Ben first. It was more than she'd even hoped for.

She'd marry him this instant, if she could.

"They count," she said, finally making her mouth and brain work in tandem. "Twenty sounds right."

Adam's smile took over his handsome face. He stood, took a step toward her, then dropped to his knee.

"I love you, Chelsea. And I love being a family with you and Ben. I don't know how long I'll be on this earth, but I can guarantee not a day will go by without you being loved."

He pulled a box out of his pocket and opened it as the tears in her eyes broke through and started streaming down her face.

"Will you marry me?"

"Yes," Chelsea said without hesitation, nodding frantically. "Yes, I will marry you. Of course."

"Thank God." He pulled the enormous ring from the box and slipped it onto her ring finger. She looked down at the huge diamond resting there, taking up almost all the space between her two knuckles.

"Holy crap."

"Do you like it?"

"I love it. I love you."

He smiled wide, stood, and pulled her into a hug as the room erupted in applause. Suddenly, they were engulfed in the arms of their friends and family, everyone happily celebrating before Lawrence called out for a round of drinks on him.

When the crowd finally calmed down, Ethan spoke, grabbing everyone's attention.

"So," he said, "you guys gonna elope?"

Chelsea burst into laughter as Adam shook his head dramatically from side to side. "Not a chance."

"No?" Chelsea asked, looking into his eyes.

Adam's face fell. "Please don't tell me that's what you want."

"Well, I kinda like the idea of marrying you immediately. I don't really want to waste any time."

His face softened as he pulled her close. "This deserves to be celebrated."

"Big wedding, short engagement?" Chelsea asked.

Adam kissed the top of her head and let out a relieved sigh.

"Perfect."

· · · ● · ● · ● · · ·

Bonus Scene

Author's Note: This is a rewrite of Chapter 14 in Max's point of view when he 'gets rid of' the person at the door. I hope you enjoy!

How soon was too soon to say *I told you so?*

It was a question Max was struggling with as he watched one of his oldest friends amid a breakdown. He'd warned Adam not to get in too deep with Chelsea, but did he listen?

No.

He pulled in a deep breath as he crossed his arms and leaned against the framed wall in his torn-apart pub, the smell of sawdust filling his nose. He tried to get over the fact that their renovation crew was supposed to be there getting the kitchen ready for their chef, who would arrive in a few days to build their menu before opening.

Instead, Adam had told his entire crew to take the day off so he could be alone, not knowing every member of his family would show up to give him a damn intervention.

It wasn't that Max didn't care about Adam's feelings. He hated seeing his friend like that. But if he'd just listened to Max and pushed aside the feelings he had for Chelsea before they got too big, he could have saved himself all of this pain.

But no.

Adam ignored him, and now he was suffering because of it.

Max listened to Adam's uncle and father debate back and forth about Adam's situation, until a knock came at the door, and Adam's shoulders slumped. He'd clearly reached the end of his rope with people showing up at the pub that day.

"Who could that possibly fucking be?" he asked, his tone cold and angry.

Everyone's eyebrows shot up. Max wasn't sure he'd ever heard Adam so pissed. He looked around the room and thought Adam had raised a pretty good question. Practically everyone they knew was already there.

He leaned over to look out the kitchen window, through the dining room, and out the glass of the front door. When he saw a flash of bright-red hair, he shook his head, searching his mind for whom that might be and coming up blank.

"I don't know," Max said, already moving toward the door. "I'll get rid of them."

He marched out the kitchen door, relieved that he was no longer part of the deep, emotional discussion. He'd rather have something else to focus on, a useful job to do where he could actually be helpful. Getting rid of whoever was on the other side of that door was just what he needed.

He walked through the dining room, ignoring all the work that screamed at him to get done. Adam really needed to pull his shit together. If he just shifted his focus to things that were within his control, he'd get over Chelsea and they'd actually be able to open on time.

And they *had* to open on time. They'd taken on a much bigger renovation than Max had wanted, and now his margin for error was thinner than his patience.

Well, almost.

He reached the door, unlocked it, and swung it open to find a beautiful woman staring in the middle of his chest. She tipped her head all the way back until her pretty pale-green eyes finally met his. Then she smiled.

Who the hell was this? And why the hell was she here?

He scanned the area, but didn't see anyone else, then checked her out more closely. Bright-red hair was the first thing he noticed. It stood out against the backdrop of the world like a spotlight. Her face was dainty and pale, and she had pretty freckles across her nose. He'd blinked away from her face, eyes trailing down her body on instinct, when it finally dawned on him.

She was on Adam's crew.

A plumber or electrician or something, judging by the flannel jacket, thick jeans, and worn brown boots.

"Hi," she said with a happy little wave, then tipped to the side, trying to look past his frame through the door, even though he took up most of the space.

"Hey," he said. Honestly, he was a little sorry that he was about to get rid of her, and not just because he wanted his renovation to continue. She'd piqued his curiosity. He'd thought he knew everyone in the crew. Maybe she was a specialist for something that Adam had brought in? He didn't know, but his curiosity would have to go unsatisfied, because they were in crisis mode, and she had to go.

"You must have missed the memo," he said.

"Memo?"

"Yeah, you're not needed."

Her eyes rounded as they snapped back to his, and her pretty little bronze eyebrows shot up. "I'm not?"

"No."

She stared at him in silence, her lips parting and closing as if she was speechless, and Max fought the urge to roll his eyes. It was just a minor scheduling conflict, and she was reacting as if he'd delivered a cancer diagnosis rather than the news that she'd be missing a day of work.

With pay.

"Okay, then," he said, tamping down his annoyance at her dramatic reaction. He pushed the door closed when she finally found her voice.

"Wait," she said. "I came all this way."

He let go of the eye roll he'd been holding back. He couldn't help it. If she'd just checked her email, she wouldn't have this problem. He had very little patience for irresponsible people who wanted to blame everyone else for their own mistakes.

No matter how pretty they were.

"These things happen," he said, trying to put on his most patient tone. "Just go home, and Adam will let you know when he needs you."

Her jaw unhinged as if he'd said something horribly despicable, and he shook his head. The worst thing about it was that he wanted her in there working more than anything. But Adam was leading the crew, and he'd called it off today. There was nothing Max could do.

He once again tried to close the door, when her chin tipped up and her voice rose with indignation.

"You're not even going to say sorry?"

Max stared at her, unable to believe the audacity. It was bad enough that she was wasting his time. Asking him to apologize for something that he had nothing to do with was too far.

He gripped the door in his fist and felt his eyebrows drop into a scowl. "You expect me to apologize to you because you can't read your email like an adult?"

She leaned back, but instead of looking scared or contrite or any of the other reactions he usually got, she looked indignant.

"You are unbeli—"

"Okay."

Max swung the door and closed it in her face, then punctuated the gesture by loudly locking the deadbolt.

What the fuck was that?

You'd think he'd just run over her dog with the way she reacted. He shook it off, forgetting about her snotty attitude, and returned to the kitchen where Adam's intervention had reached a fever pitch and he finally told them all what the real problem was; he didn't have long to live so refused to get involved with a single mom and her kid.

Max had been busy mentally pushing aside his interaction with the redhead when Adam dragged him headlong into the fray.

"Max agrees with me," he said, and all the eyes in the room fell on Max in an instant.

"What?" Adam's father said.

Max could almost feel the icy anger rolling off him.

"What?" Max asked back, crossing his arms. He was sick of dealing with everyone, but unlike Adam, this was his usual demeanour.

Impatient and annoyed.

"You don't think my son should be with the person he loves?"

Max stared at Lawrence for a long while before he felt a shift in his perspective as he realized he could actually relate to the guy. Lawrence was just a protective father, and although Max wasn't a dad himself, he'd had to step in and take care of his little sister when she was four and their dad took off.

Max would rip the face off of anyone who said Cara shouldn't have what she wanted. But this wasn't his little sister. This was Adam. A thirty-year-old man who'd decided for himself. Who was he, or anyone else, to tell him he was wrong?

And although Max knew Adam would be a great dad, he'd felt the sting of growing up fatherless and knew that was a hard thing to live with.

"Adam has a good point," Max said. "Is it really responsible to start a family when you know you don't have that long to live?"

"That is the most ridiculous—"

"It's his life," Max said, cutting Lawrence off. Lawrence's eyes flared as if he'd never had someone cut him off before. Max carried on. "This is how he feels. I grew up without my dad, so I can see where he's coming from. I support his decision not to get involved with someone who has a kid."

There. Done.

Adam's choice was perfectly logical. Honestly, Adam's problem wasn't his decision to get involved with Chelsea. The problem was in his execution. He should have kept a lid on his emotions and treated her like a friend, because if you don't control your feelings, they will control you.

That was a lesson Max had learned the hard way decades before. He tried to save his friend from learning it the hard way, too, but Adam refused to listen. Or more accurately, Adam wasn't capable of it.

Max and Adam were just built differently. Adam wore his heart on his sleeve, felt every emotion, and Max seemed like someone without a heart entirely.

At least, that's what his sister told him.

It was almost like icing people out was his default, and he had to fight against that to let his close friends and family in. But life was much easier that way.

As Max listened to Adam's uncle talk about losing his little sister, Adam's mom, and how loving she was, something in Max shifted, and he wondered whether he was wrong.

Just because it made sense to Max to control his feelings didn't mean it was right for Adam. In fact, if it made sense to Max, it was probably guaranteed to be wrong for Adam. Maybe this whole time he had been wrong. He'd been blindly supporting his friend before asking himself whether he should do that.

Part of it felt hypocritical. The whole "Do as I say, not as I do" bullshit. But in this case, there was probably a good reason for it.

"I think he's right," Max said after Uncle David ran through all the reasons Adam should pursue a relationship with Chelsea and told him to go to therapy.

"What?" Adam asked, looking at him as if he'd lost his fucking mind.

Max winced. He hated that he might have been part of the reason Adam was miserable. Adam wasn't cut out for being miserable.

"Well, it makes sense, doesn't it?"

Adam took the advice of everyone else in the room before finally agreeing to call his therapist and figure out his shit. One by one, everyone left until Max was alone with Adam, feeling like a ten-pound bag of crap. He shoved it aside, moving on.

"Do you need help finishing off?" he asked.

Adam shook his head. "I'll have this done by the end of the day. But you should probably stay. The brewmaster is coming for an interview today. She should be here anytime."

Max nodded. That sounded good to him. He'd help Adam with the tiling—

Wait.

Did he say *she*?

Max glanced at the door, then back at Adam. "She?"

"Willow Spencer."

"Willow? I thought it was a guy. You said the brewmaster was Will something."

"Exactly. Will-ow. Don't be sexist."

Oh shit.

He looked back at the door, then down at his feet. Was the girl at the door the brewmaster they'd flown in from Churchill to interview? It hadn't even crossed his mind that she might be the brewmaster.

"I think she was at the door earlier."

Adam stopped, his shoulders dropping. "Fucking hell, Max. What did you do?"

Max winced. He'd been such an asshole to her. He'd told her to go home and wait for a call, not realizing her home was a twenty-hour flight away.

And he'd told her she couldn't read her email like an adult.

And he'd made it clear he thought she was a dramatic bitch.

He rubbed his hands down his face.

"I got rid of her."

"By 'Got rid of her,' you mean what, exactly?"

Fuck.

She'd never come back after that. He'd have to find someone else to head up their brewery. But they'd already scouted around other breweries, and no one else was as good at brewing as her.

Adam shook his head. "I'll deal with that later," he said, scrolling through his phone. "Damage control with our brewmaster will have to wait."

Max thanked his lucky stars that Adam was so good at dealing with people. If anyone could fix this mess, it would be Adam. In the meantime, Max would do more work scouring the country, looking for alternatives. His mind brought up her pretty, fuming little pixie face as he closed the door on her.

Yeah, she was never coming back there for an interview. And even if she did, there was no way she'd actually agree to work for him. Will-ow was a lost cause.

He retreated to his makeshift office and got to work searching for another brewer.

. . . . ● . ● . . . .

Up Next in the Mapleton Series: All or Nothing Get ready for **grumpy/sunshine sparks** and irresistible **workplace tension** in Max and Willow's story! **All or Nothing** brings you slow-burn chemistry, emotional stakes, and a love story that proves opposites really do attract.

Grab your copy here: https://mybook.to/2aYHv4